MOONLIGHT CLIFF

AND OTHER STORIES

Ivan Efremov

Paperback ISBN: 978-1-947228-56-6
ePub ISBN: 978-1-947228-65-8

Written by Ivan Efremov
Published by Royal Hawaiian Press
Cover art by Tyrone Roshantha
Translated by Rafal Stachowki
Localized/Edited by Glenys Dreyer
Publishing Assistance by Cheeky Kea Printworks

Originally published in Russian.
Translated and published in English with permission.

First Edition

MOONLIGHT CLIFF AND OTHER STORIES

Moonlight Cliff

"Let me tell you something," said Georgy Balabin, who, until now, had been silent the whole evening. He was a stocky, dense, bear-like man, overweight, and with a short bristly beard. However, behind this rustic exterior, there was hidden knowledge, and the respect that a researcher of Siberia with such vast experience deservedly earned in the scientific world.

"In all of your stories," continued Balabin, "I noticed one peculiarity: the extraordinary has met almost every one of you, as it corresponds to the inner searchings of everyone... Are these meetings not the result of long-term, maybe unconscious, searches? Patient aspiration trains our sensitivity gives the ability to separate the present from the accidental one. It is a kind of internal compass, which at the right moment always tells you that you are on the right path... And who knows, maybe that's why we meet in this life with interesting and wonderful events that constantly followed this compass.

"In Eastern Siberia, there is the Vitimo-Olekminsky National District. The north-eastern part of this vast mountainous country, adjoining the southern border of Yakutia, is a continuous knot of mountain ranges, perhaps the highest in all of Siberia. The inaccessibility and solitude of these places are exceptional. Until very recently, travelers never visited them. Fifteen years ago, I had to cross the first 'white spot,' on the map. I say 'first,' implying, of course, scientists-researchers. The indigenous inhabitants of the country – the Tungus and the Yakuts – during their hunting migrations, proceeded along and across this wild region. The Tunguska hunters informed me more than once of precious information about sites not yet crossed by routes, and confidently drew detailed maps of rivers, keys, and mountain ranges. Even the smallest rivers, which served as the main routes for nomadic activities, had their own names.

"This was not the case with the char however; and just as an aside for those of you who don't know what char is, it's the residue material that is left after gases and tar have been burnt out. Anyway, I digress. The practical mind of the taiga hunter avoided unnecessarily filling their memory with names that were not important for the movement or habitat of places, and therefore, I had to come up with names myself for mountain peaks."

And so, Georgy Balabin began to tell his story…

… At the end of December 1935, I was on the Tokko River, preparing to leave the Yakutia region in the heart of Siberia and go to the upper reaches of the river, to the Vitimo-Olekminsky National District. I kept only a small detachment from my original great expedition; the rest of the staff I sent to Aldan and Lena, effectively expanding the area of my research.

I, despite the ferocious frosts and inadequate supplies of food, strove to cross the mountain knot which is accessible most easily in winter, when the stormy rivers raging in impassable ravines are frozen, and the movement along the bottom of the gorges on reindeer sleds does not encounter special difficulties.

Three of my companions were irreplaceable each in their own way. Yakut Gabyshev was the guide; a leader and the owner of a deer caravan. Then there was my geologist, Anatoly Alexandrovich, and our worker Alexei, who acted as a cook, gold digger, and hunter. All were experienced taiga men who had often visited me in remote places of Siberia.

The eighth month of my journey was nearing its end, but there was still a very difficult part ahead.

Our caravan of seven sleds, with four spare deer, moved quickly along the frozen river, and more and more places of the Tokko valley were first put on a geographical map. The river changed its meandering current, justifying its name, 'Tokokorikan,' which in Tunguska means 'tortuous,' and flowed now strikingly straight. Day after day, the plates of our shooting were attached to a large map – the result of many months of hard work, showing a wide, straight valley, heading to the sources of the river – to the south. Day after day, there was a faint rapping of deer hoofs and the squeaking of swaying sleds breaking the silence, as we made our way farther and farther to where the jagged line of gloomy mountains rose above the rounded waves of low hills.

We moved across a monotonous terrain, along the southern edge of the Lena platform. This low plateau dissected into endless rows of hills of almost equal height. We tried, despite the short days, to pass through this region as soon as possible.

Finally, on the twenty-first of December, the rounded hills covered with dark bristles of spruce forest were replaced by long, pointed ridges, overgrown with larch, whose rusty gray color stood out sharply against the dark green of the forests of spruce and cedar. This meant that we'd left the platform with its monotonous relief and limestones and approached the advanced bastions of the mountainous country from granites and gneisses – the hard rocks of the ancient plinth of the continent, raised here by recent movements of the earth's crust to a greater height. The revival of the geologist, who up until this time had been gloomily sitting on his sled with a photography tablet on his chest, showed the change in the surrounding area as well as possible.

The sky cleared to blue overhead, while low clouds covered the south with a dense veil, skewing obliquely over the threshold of the mountainous country. The frost grew stronger, the creak of the sled grew louder and higher in tone, and a cloud of steam from the short and frequent breathing of deer, twisted over the caravan.

I'd conveniently settled on wide cargo sleds, on top of things tucked under my left leg and dangling the right, playing the role of the brake and steering wheel. From time to time, I shifted the reins from one hand to the other or moved my toes anxiously, trying to catch the terrible signs of freezing that required an immediate run. We'd long finished our stock of oil – and this lowered our resistance to cold.

Gray clouds ahead turned red, and in the deepening of the snow shroud, lay long blue shadows. The steep convex side of a massive char protruded at the turn of the river. Having rounded it, we saw that the valley formed a wide fork, separated by a massive hill with a jagged crest. This was the large fork of the Tokko peak at the site of the confluence of the large left tributary of the Chiroda. From here, the Tokko valley turned into a narrow gorge, cluttered with rapids, that flowed to the south-west, as it approached the headwaters of the Chara.

There, in a vast hollow, between two high ridges was a small town with a trading station and a radio station and it was there we sought to replenish our food supplies. Turning into the valley of Tokko at dusk, we quickly chose a place for our tent. Our long-traveled detachment set about and completed with speed, all the necessary evening work, and, I would say, with the grace of a well-played troupe of artists. In the gathering darkness, we tied the poles, raked the snow, set up the tent, and sawed wood. Alexei installed the stove and started cooking dinner. A pale flame burst out from the side that protruded from the entrance of the tent to the chimney.

Giving the snow sled one last look over in the fading light, we went into the tent and, carefully passing the hot stove, plunged into heat. What could be more pleasant than the first minutes in a heated tent after a hard day out in a severe frost? You fiercely tear off your icy wet scarf that had been covering your face all day and remove your hat. With a little more patience, reindeer skins are laid out on larch branches, stretched out to warm above the frozen ground, and sleeping bags are deployed. Having freed yourself from your heavy clothes, you enjoy a thick cigarette, inhaling and absorbing it into one's body with great pleasure, enjoying its wonderful warmth.

And so, it was the same on this particular evening, when we were seated in our tent with our legs tucked together, and had begun to absorb an incredible amount of hot tea while waiting for the meat to cook. Big frosts can dry one out no differently than heat, and when there is nothing to drink all day, by evening an unquenchable thirst arises. In the blessed warmth, with the reddish flicker of a cozy crackling stove, our gloomy, weather-beaten faces soften, and our severe wrinkles smooth out.

Finally, once we stopped putting more firewood into the stove, the icy air would begin to climb into the tent inexorably. It then became necessary again to put on our quilted jackets, spare fur socks, and get into our sleeping bags, carefully damping the lingering fire. In the stillness and sharp coolness of the cooled tent, the already faint flame of the fading furnace fluttered for some time, before the oven went out. Hanging on sticks above our heads to dry were our mittens, hats, and scarves, as well as dry wood for the morning, and in the corner, a packed suitcase.

Filtering into our consciousness as we slumbered, came the rare sounds of the outside world: the distant rumble of the settling ice, the cracking of a crashing tree, the running of the reindeer warming...

The next day, the day of the winter solstice, brought good weather, and even more severe frost. The pale sky was above us was clear and blue. In the motionless air of a frosty morning, the burst of steam from our breath immediately turned into tiny ice crystals. The friction of the ice floes moving against each other produced a characteristic quiet rustle. This quiet rustling, called the 'whisper of the stars,' by the Yakuts, meant that the frost was more than forty-five degrees. When the geologist reached with his naked hand for the mercury thermometer he'd left outside for the night, he involuntarily uttered a cry of surprise: the glass rod of the thermometer shattered into long, sharp splinters, and a frozen mercury ball stuck to his fingers. I had to remove an alcohol thermometer from the bottom of my suitcase, which soon showed a respectable figure of fifty-seven degrees.

Having renewed the stock of firewood and warmed ourselves with hot tea, we wandered about our business. The geologist went on the sleds up Chiroda, the guide went to check the deer, and Alexei washed the gold. I decided to climb the char and look around and take photos from the height of the surrounding area. Otherwise, it was difficult to understand the fence of mountain peaks.

The camp was empty. Our tent, half hidden by small larches, seemed quite small – lost among the huge rocks. Having chosen a gentle spur, I began to slowly climb through the creaking, unthinkably clear, snow. The smooth soles of my boots glided, so I had to cling to the trunks of trees, and the frosty air made it impossible to breathe deeply. It was very tiring, so it wasn't long before large drops of frozen sweat surrounded my face along the edge of my fur cap. But still, I reached a small area on the top of the char, where there were two large blocks of granite, wind-blown and covered with lichen. I scrambled to the top of one of the blocks and looked around.

Behind the slope of the char, it was steeply cut off into a wide valley, densely overgrown with cedarwood, and appeared on top of a fluffy carpet with a pattern of dark green and white spots. To the left, behind a ribbed hill, there was a white strip of the frozen Chiroda, to the right the same strip designated the Tokko. From the south of the blue, sunny dale, the wall of the Udokan Ridge covered with a silvery haze approached. This wall, about a distance of fifty kilometers from me, broke the corner and turned east towards Olekma. In the place of the break of the ridge, there was a mass of huge char hills, much higher in height than all that I saw here.

One char, in particular, caught my attention. It stood in front of all the others, closer to me, rising lonely, like a giant, slightly tapering upward tower, the top of which was crowned with three huge teeth. It was with some difficulty coping with a pencil in my stiffening hands, I sketched what I saw and took a compass reading. It was time to go down.

The same still silence surrounded me — there wasn't even the slightest air fluctuation. As before, the clear blue of the sky, as deep as the surrounding silence, stood high above me. The stone, frozen, frost-bound world was hostile to me. And I felt a sharp yearning for warm countries move in my soul...

Ever since my early childhood, I had been unconsciously in love with Africa. Children's impressions of books about adventure travel were replaced in my youth by a more mature dream of a little-explored black continent full of mysteries. I dreamed of sunlit savannahs with wide crowns of solitary trees, of huge lakes, of the mysterious forests of Kenya, of the dry plateaus of South Africa. Later, as a geographer and archaeologist, I saw in Africa the cradle of humanity — the place from where the first people entered the northern countries, along with the flow of animals moving to the north. The interest of the scientist further strengthened my youthful dreams about the soul of Africa – about the mighty, all-conquering ancient life, spilled over the expanse of high plateaus, the waters of mighty rivers, windswept coasts open to the two oceans...

However, I didn't have to fulfill my dream and become a researcher of the Black continent because I realized my northern homeland, in immensity, was not inferior to Africa, and there were no less unexplored places in it. And so, I became a Siberian traveler and fell under the charm of the boundless uninhabited expanses of the North. Only occasionally, when my body and soul was tired of the cold, and the gloomy and harsh nature, did I become gripped with a longing for Africa, so interesting, inviting, and inaccessible...

A ruthless chill brought me back to reality. I went down the slope and back to the camp. The sun had already gone behind the char, but none of my comrades had returned. I stoked the stove, put on the cauldron with the frozen tea, and dropped down on the deerskin, waiting for the tent to warm up enough to undress.

The twenty-third and twenty-fourth of December were difficult days. The Tokko valley had turned into a narrow gorge, squeezed by the sides of tall loaches. All the snow from the ice was completely swept away by the winds that raged in the gorge. The river had frozen with uneven knolls, that rose up the whole stream, repeating the contours of the waves on the banks and rapids. There was often a distant rumble in the ravine or a low moan of cracking and settling ice. In places, sharp teeth of stones protruded from the ice.

It was strange and eerie to walk with a mix of gliding and balancing and to see right under your feet, through a greenish transparent ice slab of half a meter in thickness, the raging waves of a river that flashed in a greenish flicker with great rapidity. It was especially eerie as it seemed that this chaos of water and foam ran under our feet completely silently as if enchanted by the heavy, frosty haze, that hung in the gorge. The advance of the caravan along the smooth ice was conducted with great difficulty; even the reindeer were completely helpless on the slippery, hard surface – their hooves parted in different directions, and the animals would struggle and fall.

There was a growing, deafening noise from the depths of the ravine, and soon it turned into a low, continuous roar, as we approached one of the biggest rivers – the powerful force of which could not even be cured by fifty-degree frosts. A white mist filled the gorge to almost half the height of its steep walls from the dark gray, metamorphic slates. Dark water in a white frame of ice and snow smoothly rounded off the shaft and swelled to a height of three meters. It rolled down, broke into foam, splashed against sharp stones, and roared violently onto a rock on the right bank, where, above the blackening hollowed out water, nestled huge blocks. The left bank was also steep. From the rock, there was a smooth slope of a huge ice floe, that fell right into the threshold. The passage was dangerous and narrow, but there was no other way.

The geologist, who arrived first, frowned, then took hold of the bunch – a belt that connected the halos of each pair of deer – and slowly led his team forward.

I was next in line. I stood anxiously between the heads of my bulls and unhurriedly forged forward, silently following the geologist. I couldn't help my comrade: you can't let go of your own harness, since every centimeter won at the beginning of the passage, to the right, to the wall of the gorge, was decisive. The geologist's team advanced forward, steadily slipping towards the edge of the ice, towards the steaming waves of the roaring river. The deer fell and again jumped. One meter... half a meter... If the left bull fell again, everything would be lost.

Fortunately, the bull did not fall. Another minute passed, and I welcomed the success of the geologist with a cry, lost in the noise of the water. My deer pushed me with noses and horns as if telling me it was my turn. Having come on the left side of the team, I squeezed the deer's shoulder with the shoulder of the deer against the stone wall of the gorge and led the sleds over the very top of the ice ramp. In my wake, the guide and the worker followed; then we moved the cargo sleds. One more unfrozen threshold had to be overcome before the end of the day – and its roar lulled us throughout the night.

The next morning, as soon as we had traversed three or four kilometers, a strong and continuous wind hit us directly head-on, right after the turn of the gorge. On the ice, on steep rocks, among the rare bare trees – there was not a single place in which we could hide from the relentless flight of blowing frost. We walked, bent forward, our faces wrapped so tight that only a narrow line of our eyelashes was left. The deer lowered their heads low, almost touching the snow with their black noses. Strong wind at sixty degrees of frost is almost intolerable. It only took a few minutes in these conditions before I felt the entire front half of my body freeze until it was completely numb. I had to turn my back and walk backward until I'd get warm again. The noise and whistling of the wind drowned out all other sounds...

Towards evening we emerged from the terrible gorge into a huge valley – a hollow with a flat bottom, surrounded by stepped mountains. A smooth snowy field stretched before us, shining in the twilight, bordered by a black strip of forest. After the noise of the wind in the gorge, silence and peace hit us. We named this first-time discovered valley, the Upper-Tokkinskaya Depression. We crossed it through deep snow and reached the edge of the forest in the dark.

Another unremarkable day of monotonous progress passed.

The guide picked us up very early the next day. In the incredible blue twilight, foreshadowing a clear day, like all the previous ones, we began to climb a pass in the saddle of a two-vertex char, covered with abundant snow.

We alternated taking turns leading the caravan – as we trampled forward on our skis, pulling our narts that containing our lighter provisions and supplies behind us. We would change leaders whenever the one in front became exhausted – with steam pouring off us and our backs covered with hoarfrost. Slowly, we crawled to the top of the pass between two gentle snow slopes. When we'd stop for a rest, our deer, snapping at the snow, would immediately lay down, while we'd sit down on the sleds and have a smoke.

With slow progress, we began to descend from the saddle along a wide slope that overlooked a huge flat slope several kilometers wide, falling to the Tarynnakh River, the tributary of the Chara.

Two dark spots appeared on the precipice to our right. Our guide, who was driving the caravan, cleverly stopped the deer running away. I quickly snatched my rifle out from under the canvas. The brown spots soon turned into two magnificent kabarga – adult musk deer. I pulled back the bolt, taking care not to be jolted while I rode in the back of the sled. The musk deer trembled, with their attentive black eyes watching us vigilantly. Their thin legs strained, ready to sweep their owners up the slope. Unfortunately, the bolt of the rifle didn't slam shut, but slowly crept forward and, reaching the edge of the cartridge, it stopped open. No matter how carefully it had been oiled, the severe frost had done its job. I moved, trying to release the cartridge; this started the musk deer, who rose up the slope and disappeared into the thick of the Listvyanka.

The caravan started off again, looping between the trees on the slope.

"Stop!"

A sudden scream made me flinch. Without thinking, I rolled off my sled into the snow and caught it behind the back of the handlebar, to act as a brake with my body. The sled of the guide had already gone behind the turn and had disappeared. Unfortunately, the speed of my sled was too great; the deer jerked, jumped in a leap, and I dropped, clinging to the claw brake. Before I had time to figure out anything, I was already lying next to our guide, and the braking deer of a cargo sled came to my rescue.

Then a new scream: "Stop!"

Looking back, I saw the two sleds of the geologists, form a pile of deer, men, and sleds, roll down a second slope. Nothing much really happened – just the steepness of the descent suddenly exceeded the permissible limit for the passage of the narts being pulled. We hit the bottom of the fall. I hit my back on the ice so hard that I lost my breath for a minute. Alexei appeared on the crest of the cliff behind us. Seeing a pile of bodies and sleds, he was confused and clung convulsively to the sleds, instead of jumping off. There were the bodies of the deer splayed out, the geologist had landed under a slope, and his sleds had flown over top of him, hit the ice, and had strewn their contents everywhere. Alexei remained sitting on his things blinking in surprise and fear, and his deer, tearing off their reins, made several jumps and stopped.

After checking out that all the deer were unharmed, and things weren't damaged, we laughed at our adventure and decided, given the broken state of the narts, to reach the nearest feed and spend the night.

After driving a little before the beginning of the vast hill in Tarynn, we stopped in a rare forest. Here, we found evidence that a long time ago, a wildfire had passed through the area. Now the area was full of the regeneration of young birches and larch undergrowth. The old larches were devoid of branches and bark – the best fuel, and we stocked up on them in abundance, and also, ignited a huge fire, to warm ourselves while we did some repairs to Kopylov's harness. The geologist and Alexei went to the nearest key to do a washing for gold, while the guide and I prepared all the material for repair.

It was getting dark. We had dinner and drank tea, but our comrades did not return. I decided to go out to meet them. The daytime frosty blackness had disappeared, and the moon rose high above the mountains in the clear air. I soon saw two dark figures, hurrying toward me.

"There must be some gold," said the geologist.

"Really, Anatoly?"

"Yes," the worker replied.

We lit our cigarettes and stood silently, enchanted by the frosty lunar night, which covered the world around us with a layer of sparkling matte silver.

"Are they not your terrible char, Georgy Balabin?" I asked the geologist and pointed up the Tarynnakh valley.

To the left of the valley, there was a group of bluish-silver serrate peaks with very sharply defined contours. A deep black shadow hid the foot of the char, and the cold light of the high moon traced the non-existent abysses and deepened the distant plains. It seemed that a giant silver ball saw hung in the air, resting on nothing. Separately from the others stood a tall tower, which I'd noticed before, under which rays shone on the rocky ribs and the icy tails of its southern side.

"Here's a good name for your peak, Georgy Balabin," the geologist broke the silence again. "Moonlight Cliff. You see, you rested your teeth on the moon..."

"Very good," I agreed, directing my compass to the char, and taking a second reading. Now the distance to the char was known, and I could place it exactly on the map...

The work on repairing the sleds was completed by noon, and, lounging in the tent, we rested, discussing the journey ahead. In three days, we expected to get to the Chara basin and a couple of days later, across the hollow to the village. So, in five days, we could sleep in the trading posts house, afford the luxury of undressing, eat well... and even listen to the Moscow news, if there is a receiver!

We decided to take a wash before rolling the tent and laying down to sleep, sharing dreams of the imminent arrival in the village and a little rest.

However, our dreams were interrupted by unexpected sounds – the crunching of deer running, the squeaking of our narts, and a human voice. Everyone except for me, donned their caps and ran out of the tent, and quickly restrained a man who'd appeared out of the taiga frost like a miracle. I stayed in place, as befits a boss who has experienced all kinds of taiga frost troubles and joys. Soon a man unknown to me entered, bending down as he passed through the flap of the tent, followed by my companions. The newcomer sat down, cross-legged, near the stove, proudly raised his head, beat his chest, and said loudly:

"Great boss."

I calmly and attentively looked at him, and he, embarrassed, looked down. He was a tall, old man, unusually thin, of the Yakut people. He had large hawkish round eyes, a hunchbacked nose, sunken cheeks, a narrow face and a pointed beard reminded me of Don Quixote.

I offered the old man a pouch, and winked at Anatoly so that he put fresh tea and meat on the stove: if 'uhlahn toyon' is taken, we would take it with proper honor. After a pause of the proper time, I said the usual convention:

"Tell, friend."

"No, there is nothing to tell, you tell," stretched the old man.

We exchanged a few more conventional phrases of the Yakut people; then the old man suddenly began to speak in Russian – apparently, he decided that his use of the Russian language was better than my Yakut.

With great interest, the Yakut asked me about our trip, nodding his head approvingly at the mention of the names of especially difficult places on the road. Several times the old man tried to pick me up on the knowledge of the peculiarities of the local nature, but thanks to my great experience of exploring, I found myself on top of the situation. He was brought a glass of alcohol, and he ate a hearty meal, softening a little and losing his arrogance. He said that he would show me, 'such a thing,' which I have, perhaps, never seen before. Then the old man quickly left the tent and went to his two sleds.

"Do you know this old man?"- I asked Gabysheva.

"I know," answered the guide. "His name is Kilchegasov. The hunter is good, he knows every place."

The old man returned to the tent, and I stopped inquiring.

"Did you see this on Tokko?" the old man asked, slyly grinning as he handed me a heavy stump of a mammoth's tusk.

I explained to the old man, it was a mammoth's tusk, and described it, drawing an arc through the air with my hand showing it as a whole form.

Kilchegasov was sad seeing my awareness, and when I say that I mean that perhaps he'd found the tusk while scouring the river banks. He really became sad.

"You know a lot, chief," he shook his head.

Flattered by the recognition of the old man, I told him about the islands in the mouth of Lena, where tusks of mammoths lay right on the ground mixed with the bones of whales and the debris brought by the sea of woods. The Yakut listened attentively to me, spat, and moved closer to me as if he was going to tell me something daring.

"Your clever man, chief, but your hunters also know what you do not know. I know the char, where such a mammoth horn is, as the forest lies. There, on the contrary, is not a curve that I found, but a straight to slightly-little curve."

"That is interesting!" I was surprised.

Kilchegasov reached out his hand for the tobacco pouch. He lit a pipe and lifted up his face as if recalling something.

"My father used to drive my brother, he went very far, there." Kilchegasov waved his hand to the east. "I saw it, then I told it. Did you hear about that, Onako?" he said as he turned to the guide.

"I've heard. I thought they lied," Gabbyshev responded indifferently.

"Onako, I did not lie, his piece of horn, the end, brought, I myself watched."

"Where is this char?" I asked the old man.

"And if close, will you go and look?"

"Of course, I will," I nodded.

After a momentary pause, the hesitation on the old man's face disappeared.

I unfolded my large map on which only yesterday I marked the place of the char of the Podlunny.

"Here, between the top of Chiroda and the peak of Tokko, there is a lot of big char, just a pile."

"Right!" I responded.

But the old man did not pay any attention to my response.

"The top of Chiroda and Chirodakan is about the biggest char, like a tall stump."

We exchanged glances with the geologist, having learned from the old man their word for yesterday's discovery – the char pile Podlunny.

"This char is standing alone, here is Tokko near the top. The right of the char is a high, level, clean place – it is still a plateau. This is the place of the horn, Onako, and lie. There's still a big hole, and there's also horns."

"And how far from here will it be?" I asked, catching my curiosity.

"This place is near," the old Yakut said. Tarynnakh go, the peak Tarynnakh will go right, the left will go to Ichonchokit. Ichonchokit peak will go to the middle pass, there is an even flat place below, on the contrary, a small key. This key converges at Talumakit. From Tokko peak to the left there will be a small river... Kivety cliff cuts – it's still a knife. Onnako, Kivety will go that flat place..." Kilchegasov thought some more. "A verst is just over one kilometer so it will be hundred..." he added.

The old man fell silent. We were silent too. Only the wood in the stove crackled faintly. I thought about the possibility of making the route as a side trip, along with the difficult terrain, with almost exhausted food supplies. The geologist looked at me expectantly, not betraying his feelings. Gabyshev turned to the old man, and they both spoke softly in Yakut.

I caught only a few familiar words: "a large threshold... a lot of food... sleds can not be passed... a lot of things..."

"Where is that much trait, Gabyshev?" I interfered in their conversation.

I knew that 'under the devil,' meant 'unexplained,' to the Yakuts and the Tungus; from their point of view, a phenomenon of nature.

"I've heard of that place, it's very expansive," the guide confirmed. "Onako, there's still a big threshold to cross; there's a lot of death there."

"What threshold? The rivers are all small."

"Not a small river: the big threshold is the whole road."

We realized that we were talking about a crossbar – a steep ledge, sometimes blocking across glacial valleys. I hesitated, not sharing my thoughts. In the end, a hundred kilometers one way on the Siberian scale was considered nothing. The question was in extra days, which had to be added to the five that separated us from the rest in the village. It was unlikely for us to get to this inaccessible area.

I looked at Kilchegasov.

"Will you go with us to that place?"

Seeing the animation of my companions, I saw that they understood my decision. The old man deliberated, sucking on his pipe. Without hurrying him, I asked the geologist:

"What do you think, Anatoly Alexandrovich?"

"Well, of course, we're keen, we'll see," he said approvingly.

"And you, Alexei? Is there enough food for ten days?"

"There's enough for you: there's a bag of flat cakes, there are five teas and five cans of beans."

After negotiating with the old man, he agreed to accompany us. Now it was the turn was for Gabyshev.

"What about you, Gabyshev, will you go?" I asked. "We'll leave the cargo, we'll leave the sleds, and we'll drive the deer with us."

The guide unperturbedly slouched at the question bent his head and looked at the ground. Everything very much depended on consent from him, as the owner of the deer.

"Let's go, chief," the Yakut answered calmly and added as calmly: "Onako, will get lost, I'm thinking..."

I firmly shook hands with this glorious Yakut who considered our enterprise to be dangerous and who nevertheless, calmly agreed to walk towards this danger.

Before the evening ended, there was a discussion of the way ahead; and that night a fifth tenant was added to the tent. In the morning, we quickly moved to the valley of Tarynnakh, arranged a spare tent, and sorted out our gear and sleds between that which was essential and that which was unnecessary. Then we turned our backs on the coveted Chara and headed for the terrible headwaters of Tarynnakh.

A white mist streamed down the wide valley of the river from numerous ice floes. In Yakut, 'Taryn' means 'naled,' which is the ice body that is formed by the layering of freezing of river water that splashes onto the surface of the ice. Sometimes the waters were a little under the snow, and sometimes the sleds, like boats, cut the immobile gray water or fell into the icy emptiness.

In some places, we rushed giggling, chasing deer at full speed over thin, sagging ice. Being in a hurry, we covered a sizeable distance of the journey in a day and rested against the steep wall that blocked the valley – a famous ledge a quarter of a mile high. To the right, the bed of the river carved a narrow cut into the edge of the ledge. Through it, frozen ice, like a huge ribbed ice column fell down, over which here and there water trickled and hardly noticeable steam. Bare, yellow rocks formed an impregnable wall to the left, collapsed in one place. It was only possible to begin the ascent from here.

The next morning three pairs of our strongest bulls dragged the light sleds. Each pair was led upwards along the path by one of us, while the others picked up and pushed the sleds. The reserve deer followed, despite the fear inspired by the steepness of the ascent. Slowly, slowly, we climbed up this crevice, at the sight of which even a seasoned man would have refused to bring the sleds onto it. Already at the very top of the precipice, where the ascent was especially steep, the geologist slipped and rolled down onto the deer. A large, black buck caught him on his horns and, in wild fear, reached the edge of the cliff with two strong jerks. There, on a spacious site, we collapsed all without exception – deer and people, hardly alive from exhaustion.

"There's a passage!" exclaimed Alexei. "We better not look down, however... And if someone goes over?

"It'll be very tight, just a hairs width to maneuver the sleds. It's going to take guts," the guide answered calmly.

To go any further, we had to cross the river and the right side of the valley. What would seem simpler, but even here the sudden danger showed that we needed to be on full alert constantly. A fresh crust on the ice of the river formed a smooth and flat mound, slightly powdered with dry snow. As soon as we entered the hillock, the deer slid. Even as we jumped off our sleds, we too slipped and fell and could not hold the teams. I realized that we were all climbing uncontrollably to the edge of the ice cliff, from which a frozen waterfall plunged to a depth of 300 meters... A loud, ringing voice of the guide was heard:

"Hold on, death is close!"

Fearing for the fate of my comrades, I rushed forward, clinging to the back of the most distant fallen sled, slipped again and fell. Ninety kilograms of my live weight fell on the young ice and pierced a large hole in it before I finally got some solid support. Despite my water-soaked cotton pants, I kept the damned sleds stable until the others had coped with the deer and led them back up the steep incline, back from the abyss. Getting to the right side of the wilderness, in steady snow, we drove the deer away from that dangerous place.

That night we slept on Ichonchokite. In the morning, bright light clouds tightened the whole sky with a continuous cover. The invisible sun radiated a strong light, only occasionally piercing through the clouds, reflecting its glare off the snow. This light smoothed out all the irregularities, distorted the perspective, and changed the outlines of objects, extremely hindering movement. Kilchegasov and the guide just frowned, spat, and scolded, seeing this wrong light as one of the features of the devil's place.

Finally, the descent from the pass ended. The basin into which we descended wasn't large. It was surrounded by loaches on all sides, the tops of which were lost in a milky white coverlet, which blended into the sky. Straight before us towered the almost sheer walls of the ridge, which enclosed our goal – the very place that Kilchegasov had talked about.

When we put up the tent and stocked up the firewood, our Yakuts engaged in an incomprehensible business; cutting off some high poles, onto which they hooked up some rags, sharpened plaques, and placed them around the camp, fortifying in the frozen earth with stones and ice floes. I later found out, it was as a protection from the devil, and he really didn't hesitate to appear soon.

As the twilight began to thicken in the basin, there came a terrible squeal, gnashing, and laughter, followed by a primordial yell. These sounds, picked up and multiplied by an unusually strong echo, made me feel that I was more afraid I think, than the Yakuts waiting for the devil. The geologist jumped out of the tent with a gun but saw nothing in the fading light. Alexei joined him.

"Here they are!" Alexei suddenly yelled out and pointed to some spots moving over the low branches of the birch-barked trees and almost completely merged with the bluish-gray flickering of the air.

The geologist aimed his gun. Then a long flash flew from the barrel, accompanied by such a terrific thunder that we were all dumbfounded. The thunder intensified; Then it went on farther and farther down the mountains, like the news of a man's bold intrusion. Something fell at a distance on the snow and began to thrash about. The geologist rushed to the spot and brought back a huge bird. It was more like an owl, only with a different, milky-white colored plumage, with black spots and stripes on the wings, back, and top of the head. Alexei triumphantly carried the owl to the guides who had not left the tents, as if to say, 'here, these are your devils, look!' But he seemed to have had little effect convincing the Yakuts, who declared that there will still be a lot of devils.

We climbed into the tent and began to discuss the plan for tomorrow's campaign on the char with mammoth tusks. Kilchegasov assured us that during summer, we would be able to walk fifteen kilometers to the 'clean place,' even through the inaccessible valley of the Kivet River, and from there to the plateau with the tusks.

Our guide Kilchegasov, did not dare to come with us: his aching legs did not give him this opportunity. So, we decided to leave Alexei with the Yakuts as well. Everything was arranged so that the geologist and I could go to via the pedestrian route.

Just as we were ready to fall asleep, everything around us rattled again. Deafening booms and an ominous rumbling ended in a hellish, long-deadening rumble. I looked at the geologist, thinking about avalanches. The geologist calmly said:

"A rock collapsed, George Petrovich. There are unusually steep slopes due to large young faults, so it is likely to crumble often... And also, there is still an unusual echo here – it's that which they call the devil."

We laughed and quickly settled into our sleeping bags.

Over the last two days, the frost had begun to intensify and a very unpleasant hiuz – that's what we call drifting snow blown around in a very cold wind – rose. The unpleasant wind blew right against my tent wall, made its way around my sleeping bag, and froze the side I had turned to the wall. I woke up from the cold, but I lay for a long time struggling with drowsiness and laziness to get out and to heat the stove. Nevertheless, I finally jumped out of my sleeping bag, and shivering from the cold, lit some prepared kindling, and crouched down by the stove in anticipation of life-giving heat. The firewood crackled slowly. As I sat thinking about tomorrow's expedition, I suddenly I heard distinctly heavy steps – the heavy trampling of a huge animal.

The steps approached our tent, then walked around the tent.

Alexei, who always slept extremely sensitively, woke up and woke the geologist. The tramping resumed, close and formidable. I grabbed my rifle, which, contrary to my usual practice I'd taken to the tent to thaw. I tried the line of action and loaded a 351-caliber lead bullet. The geologist and I quickly ran out of the tent, jumping over the guides on the way, who themselves stubbornly remained wrapped up with heads in their blankets and unwilling to get up.

The sky was clear. The illuminating moon did not look well over the battlements of the peaks. We couldn't find any traces of footprints, no matter how much we strained our eyes, on the flat snow. The frost squeaked under our own feet, and we soon returned to the tent. At my appearance, our guide raised himself, while I sat down.

"Well, what did you see?" Gabyshev asked anxiously.

"Nothing."

"So... And tomorrow you will not find a trace."

"And what was it? What do you think?"

"The local master is here."

"What kind of host is that?"

"What don't you understand?" The Yakut was angry. "'Master,' I said!"

I shrugged and didn't ask him anything else, although I couldn't understand what kind of 'master' was wandering around the tent.

The pre-dawn haze still filled the valley when the geologist and I began to prepare for the journey, and all our activities were only illuminated by candlelight. We decided to leave the gun – the way was far, and it was necessary to go quite lightly to be able to bring back any collected samples. So, a revolver and the bearish knife replaced our rifle and ax. And yet our equipment with an aneroid barometer, camera, shooting board, and supplies, turned out to be noticeably weighty. By the time we all gathered to have a snack, it was daylight. The guide walked around the tent with Kilchegasov and said that there were no traces of anything from last night, other than the tracks of our deer...

We set off and quickly crossed the valley. The blue snow crunched loudly under our boots.

"Again, under sixty degrees!" said the geologist discontentedly, before pulling his scarf back up over his mouth.

Half an hour later we reached the beginning of the Kiveti Gorge and plunged on in. It was still dark in there, and we walked several kilometers in an ashen-gray dusk-like light before the sun's rays broke through to illuminate the gorge.

The scenery inside the gorge was unusual. We involuntarily spoke in a low voice as if afraid to offend some local 'master.' The gorge was on average no more than four meters wide. Smooth, coal-black walls rose, sometimes converging to form arches and tunnels, in which thick darkness reigned. Huge logs, peeled and worn out, were heavily clogged across the gorge at the height of four to five meters above our heads, showing the level to which spring waters flowed. Within the walls of the gorge, water drilled deep niches and pits; we called them mill boilers, and in them lay round boulders with the diameter of an automobile wheel.

The frozen bed of the river fell off ledges. The ice covered the whole width of the gorge so that soon our fur boots were soaked and turned into lumps of ice, which we would bitterly pummel with sticks from time to time. Even so, our frozen fur boots slid desperately along the ice ledges, and these ledges became steeper. At other times, not in winter, the river would be a roaring waterfall, and no forces could help us pass through there in the summer, spring, or autumn. The silence and narrowness of the gorge, the black color of its walls, all acted somewhat depressingly. We'd walked about nine kilometers up the gorge when it turned to the south, and some of the sun's rays penetrated between the overhanging slopes. Here the steep wall had collapsed, and the rocks forming the gorge protruded in a fresh fault. It turned out to be micaceous schists, from fine golden mica. Like pieces of silver and gold silk, they glistened in the sun over the walls of the gorge, completely transforming it. Gold and silver boulders lay everywhere on the clear emerald ice.

Another four kilometers along the ice ledges – and we came out into a small round glade, overgrown with cedars and littered with large stones. On the left, now clearly visible in the clear sky, towered the char straight as an arrow like a monstrous stone tower, which obscured the entire north-east from us. Ahead was a steep ledge, straight and vertical as if cut off by a knife.

Making haste, we climbed this hundred-meter-high cliff, sweating profusely in our heavy clothes, only to see nothing but a granite shaft that blocked our further path. The shaft was low, however, and we easily overcame this last obstacle. From the crest of the shaft, we could see that the path to our target would be difficult – across a small plateau with a convex surface, surrounded by rare conical hills. The convex surface of the plateau was almost devoid of snow cover. Beyond, behind the cedar shale, there were several sharp blocks of light gneiss rock, located surprisingly correctly – in the shape of the letter 'P.'

After we made our way through the thickets of cedar shale, we found several elephant tusks on a large glade – not mammoth, rounded in a half-circle, but huge, slightly curved tusks, similar to the tusks of the largest African elephant. I counted fourteen pieces. The largest were up to three meters long. The ivory had turned black and disintegrated from the backends, into small pieces. There were no teeth or other bones.

But, as we stood on the hill, we looked toward the center of the plateau and saw another big pile of ivory tusks that laid piled up like firewood, occupying a large area. With joyful exclamations, we ran ahead, overtaking each other. There were several hundred tusks here, and scattered in between them in some places, protruded huge bones, which instantly crumbled as soon as we touched them.

Not far from the top of the hill, between the sharp stones, was a deep gully. We wondered if that was the 'hole in the char,' that Kilchegasov had mentioned?

Over to the left side of the gully, we found a wide cave entrance and crawled inside. First, we had to climb up under low icy arches somewhere upwards, then we quickly rolled down and found ourselves in pitch darkness. Fortunately, there was a piece of candle in the geologist's backpack, which was destined to continue to provide us with another important service. The cave was large, with several high passages. Bones of animals protruded from the frost on the floor. We went deep into the highest passage and at the very same moment, gave out a friendly cry of surprise. On the smooth, sheer walls of the cave, in the candlelight, could be seen bold, huge images of animals, made either by sharp strokes or by perfectly preserved colors – black and red. These drawings were made very accurately and faithfully, and with amazing expressiveness. In the wavering light of the candle, they seemed alive.

Beyond myself with surprise, I looked at how the life of Africa unfolded on the black walls. Here were huge elephants with splayed, bat-like wings, ears, antelopes, lions. There were also the heads of the two-horned African rhinos...

"Damn it, rhinoceroses and elephants are African!" I cried.

We found all the new drawings. There was a spotted hyena with its sloping back, giraffes, and striped zebras. Africa, in the heart of the cold Siberian mountains!

Since it was relatively warm in the cave, I forgot about my wet, iced-up fur boots, and instead, I felt hot, as if the sultry heat of the African sky had touched me.

Going further, we found two niches filled with elephant tusks. Here was a collection of especially large ones, up to four meters in length; folded stack, like firewood, they gleamed under the light of the candle flame, with their smooth black and yellow surfaces.

I got carried away and ran into another large passage branching off inside the cave, but the geologist stopped me, reminding me that it was already three o'clock. No more than one and a half hours remained before it would get dark; so, we had to hurry. It was too dangerous to spend the night in this treeless place, in a sixty-degree frost, in wet clothes. Despite this, we still spent another half an hour hastily continuing to search for at least some remnants of those who'd lived and painted African animals here. We wanted to learn as much as possible about the mysterious inhabitants of the cave, but we found nothing except for two stone spearheads and some other bone instrument unknown to me.

The sun had already descended low over the mountains, when, loaded with samples of teeth and tusks, we ascended to the crest of the granite shaft and, for the last time, gazed at the extraordinary place. A quick stream of thoughts swept through my mind. I remembered the great migrations of African animals to Asia that before the glaciation in Transbaikalia and part of Mongolia there was a hot steppe where ostriches, antelopes, and giraffes lived. Now I realized that I'd found the extreme north-eastern outpost of Africa – a place where a wave of migrations had reached the point at the edge of the glaciation.

What happened was really extraordinary: my yearning for Africa was fulfilled in the frosty gorges of Siberia, where I'd discovered a piece of land from ancient times of former Africa and preserved and intact throughout antiquity. Who were these mysterious ancient people who painted animals? If they lived before the glaciation, it meant they belonged to a very ancient race. At the same time, this race was already relatively highly developed, judging by the drawings on the walls of the cave. No one had ever found such drawings in Siberia and in the USSR at all. In the correct location the stone blocks, I found a great resemblance to the mysterious structures of the huge stones, often found in Central and East Africa. Yes, most likely, these people came here from Africa, following the flow of migrating animals – the ancient tribes of artists and courageous hunters of the giant elephants.

Stunned by the discovery, I, as usual, explored quickly, trying to immediately find the most plausible explanation, and only gradually I began to realize the full significance of our discovery. Now the old dispute of scientists about one or several glaciations could be resolved – in favor of one glaciation. In a completely new way, I realized we would have to revise the geologists' previous views on the history of this region of Siberia during the Quaternary period, and the views of zoologists about the spread of animals and the origin of the modern terrestrial fauna. And, finally, the most interesting was the people, the most ancient inhabitants of Central Siberia, who suddenly turned out to be contemporaries and, possibly, relatives of those who until now were found only in the west and south. Yes, scientists would now have to think in every possible way about the discovery, obtained as the result of the labor and perseverance of a handful of people here, in the icy mountains, under a severe frost...

We silently went back downslope to the river, to the beginning of the gorge, where we'd left the samples of rocks collected in it. The geologist asked me what I thought about our find. I told him about my reflections, and he agreed with my guesses.

"Yes, I also think that these pieces and drawings are older than the local uplifts and glaciations," he said. "The cave is washed in limestones by some kind of water, and where now can you find so much water at such a height? When the entire vast region was subjected to uplifts and glaciations, which was about fifty thousand years ago, the earth's crust was split into separate sections. Some rose to the top and formed mountain ranges, others descended, forming hollows. And this char that we discovered – in short, a small portion of ancient soil – was raised to a lower height than the others, and did not undergo glaciation and erosion. At the same time, it hasn't been lowered so much that it has been flooded with moraines and river pebbles. That's why everything on its surface is preserved intact... well, of course, apart from atmospheric influences...

At this, our scientific reasoning ended. The coming night made us focus all our attention on the road. At the entrance to the gorge, we picked up the stones left and entered into complete darkness. Over the many years of my wandering life, I could say that this night tramp to the Kivet Gorge, was the worst of my experiences. Every now and then we fell into the icy waters, and more and more ice grew on our fur boots. With a heavy load behind us, it was difficult to move on the smooth ice, and we'd fall and roll down the ledges of frozen waterfalls. Soon, our clothes froze, and our entire bodies were beaten. I don't know how many kilometers we walked in this way, but in the end, we stopped, unable to continue in such a way. At the same time, however, we knew, it was necessary to go further – stopping for a long rest without a fire would bring our demise. But it wasn't possible to kindle a fire – there were only rocks and ice around.

Suddenly, I remembered the candle. What a lucky thing, that I hadn't tossed the candle after inspecting the cave! In the still air around us, the candle could burn as easily as if it were in a room. So, with difficulty, we lit the frozen wick and moved on, taking turns to carry the candle held up high.

Now the Kivet ice cascades became less terrible – we could gently slide, and roll down them. That thick, 'railway,' candle lasted us for almost an hour. When we became shrouded in darkness again, there wasn't much more distance to cover to reach the end of the gorge.

The late moon hung over the loaches, illuminating the right wall of the black corridor high above our heads. A long time passed before the black walls parted and released us into freedom, into a silvery snowfield. This point indicated to us that our tent was not more than four kilometers away. But there was no forest cover here, and therefore, it was once more impossible for us to consider stopping for a rest.

I'd walked no more than half a kilometer across the basin before I suddenly felt that my over-strained heart was failing. Everything was just too difficult; almost sixty degrees in cold, wet, heavy clothes, with a load over my shoulders – the stress was inhuman descending the gorge – and compounding this was my inability to breathe deeply because my lungs couldn't take the icy air...

Was it any wonder that even two such hardened people, like the geologist and me, began to fade quickly towards the end of the journey? I suggested that we drop our backpacks with the samples and all the other equipment right here, and not give it a second thought for now – and that's what we did.

We barely trudged through the deep, crunching snow, encouraging each other, our strength declining with each step. Another half a kilometer, a kilometer – and the geologist staggered, fell on all fours into the snow and sat down, breathing heavily. Struggling with my own weakness, I approached him and urged him to get up and continue on his way. He replied that he no longer cared about anything, he could not go on. And yet, I made the geologist get up and keep going. But, after a few hundred meters, it was my turn to feel that I couldn't move any further. So, with a great effort of will, I forced myself to count two hundred steps, then another hundred, then fifty, and then, just like the geologist, I fell into the snow.

A blissful peace embraced me. To sleep, sleep – nothing more! The thought that to sleep was to die meant I'd die... and I got very angry when I heard a very loud footstep. It was the geologist returning, life was returning, and I felt the unbearable need to get up and walk again. I don't remember how much time we walked side by side, afraid to move away from each other, afraid to think about rest...

I stepped on a thin branch or knot hidden under the snow. The extraordinary loudness of the sound of the broken branch reached even my fading consciousness. I remembered everything at once: the monstrous thunder of the collapse, the echoing sound of yesterday's night guest, and the loud steps of the geologist... I stopped, pulled off a glove that was frozen as hard as a bark, and pulled out my revolver. The ordinary Browning exploded like a cannon; as the sound of a rolling wave swept through the valley. I repeated my thundering call until I heard the echoing amplified screams. Then I put the gun back into my pocket and, barely able to move my fingers, knelt down next to the geologist.

We dozed off but were awakened by the sounds of approaching tramping: both Yakuts and Alexei hurried to us. Having heard my shots, they'd guessed at once what was wrong. Holding close to his chest, Alexei had brought a jar of hot tea and a bottle of vodka. Supported by our rescuer's arms, we were led back to the tent and we, without undressing, immediately plunged into a deep sleep. Alexei soon woke us up to eat, take off our wet clothes and ensure we were warmed by our sleeping gear. By morning, we'd completely recovered.

The supplies were running out, and, to the joy of the Yakuts, we decided to hastily leave the basin, without even analyzing the samples brought back to our camp at dawn by the Yakuts. We wanted to meet the New Year in a less dreary place.

Gabyshev approached me and waited until I'd finished tying down the sled's cargo before he quietly spoke.

"I understood what night the master was going... Kilchegazov, too," he said. "This sound is so strong here, it's our deer walk..."

The guide laughed gaily and, with a wink at me, went to his sleds.

Back along the familiar, beaten track, we moved much faster.

The second day of the new year 1936 found us very close to the Chara valley. The deer easily ran along the Kilchegasov trail. Alexei sang a mournful song about how 'a Bodaibin-prospector walked along Vitim through a terrible frost.'

The sleds dived and swayed beneath me, while the sun glistened merrily on the white ribbon of a frozen river...

SHADOWS OF THE PAST

"So, the shepherds just picked them up directly off the ground, in the desert... Vasily Petrovich, these are dinosaurs! What a find! This is the first find of its kind in the Union. We need to do something to thank these shepherds."

"Do you think these are high quality?"

"Yes, they are, my friend. They are worth more than all of us! They asked if we needed anything from their farm collective... They said 'no,' they just have a pure interest in science. They're coming again tomorrow — they want to meet with you, and they'll bring some more good pieces. Well, let's cut the melon and judge it at our leisure."

With a chunk of fragrant melon in his hand, Nikitin squatted down in front of a huge map on the office wall, and peered into the lower left corner, dotted with small dots — a sign of formidable sands.

The old scientist leaned over the chair, following Nikitin's finger.

"There's a huge field of dinosaur bones about here," said the paleontologist. "Three hundred and fifty kilometers from the springs of Taldysai. Nearby — Bisekty wells. We'll have to go by the sands to the Layili hills. Then... across the stony desert, and in some places the steppe..."

***

Bright sunlight reflected off the white walls of low buildings and dazzled their eyes. Nikitin squinted painfully as he walked through the spacious yard of the freight station on a soft carpet of yellow dust.

Three brand-new cars had already left the gate and were parked in a single line at the edge of the road, waiting for the chief. Their white canvas tops were pulled back, and a reddish powder of dust lay on the still shiny, light gray varnish. Running alongside the road in the same direction that the cars faced, were larges stones of a wide irrigation canal, in which pure water flowed as if laughing at the heat and dust. The soft babble of its gentle flow hummed in unison to the sound of the car engines as they started up.

Nikitin sat in the cab of the front car and slammed the door. A gilded column of dust shot up into the air as they moved forward. The cars passed through the city lined with white houses and green avenues, which stretched along the northern slope of the sun-scorched hills.

***

Later, Nikitin walked slowly alongside a quietly whispering aqueduct as he returned from a late meeting. The nearby houses, under the dense foliage of the trees, became dark.

Suddenly, a girl slipped out from the shadows of an alley, easily jumped over the aqueduct, and started to walk along the road ahead of him. Her bare legs were so deeply tanned that they almost merged with the soil, giving the impression that she floated in the air without touching the ground. Her thick, black braids that lay heavily down her back almost to her hips stood out sharply against her white dress.

Nikitin stopped as he watched the rapidly receding figure, and yielded to a moment of thought, before he resumed his walk at a faster pace, soon finding himself at the large pathway to the house being used by the expedition. There, illuminated by the electric lamps, he saw all the participants of his expedition gathered around the cars in the courtyard. The people were cheerfully laughing at something; even the sullen senior chauffeur smirked good-naturedly.

Marusya, the expedition's agent who was chosen the other day to be the party organizer, quickly approached Nikitin.

"Where have you been, Sergey Pavolich? We decided to hold a meeting, but you weren't around. We waited and waited, but somehow it just started without you."

"Seems a happy meeting!" smiled Nikitin.

"It's all because of the names of the cars," replied Marusya.

"What names?"

"You know, we decided to start a competition between the crews of the cars. And then Martyn Martynovich suggested, for convenience, let's give each of the cars a name."

"And what have you decided on?"

Martyn Martynovich, an elderly Latvian with round glasses and an excavation specialist, intervened in the conversation.

"Your car has been named, 'Lightning,' and the other two – 'Fighter,' and 'Dinosaur.'"

A powerful three-tone whistle rang out on the street; the black 'ZIL' headlights flashed on the gates and went out again.

Nikitin went to meet the secretary of the regional committee, with whom he had already met on expedition matters.

The secretary looked around.

"They're not bad," he said. "When do we hit the road?"

"The day after tomorrow."

"Very well, Comrade Nikitin! But I have a request for you..." The secretary paused. "I've just come from the meeting. It just so happens to turn out that there is an asphalt deposit at Biscekta, which will be necessary to investigate. My geologist insists... In short, you need to enlist an employee from the Geological Administration..."

Nikitin frowned worriedly. The secretary took him by the arm, and both went into the depths of the courtyard.

"Like everything?"

"Everything, Sergey Pavlovich. You can start loading."

"Act together with Martyn Martynovich. 'Lightning' can be the lead, fuel, and tools, 'Dinosaur,' fuel, planks, and the camp equipment, and 'Fighter,' water, food, and rubber."

***

A sultry breath of the day burst through the slightly open door. Nikitin gathered up papers scattered on the table into his bag and hurried to the telegraph office.

"Can I help you?" A soft female voice came from the yard. A slender black silhouette surrounded by a burning halo lightening the edge of a white dress appeared in the dazzling bright quadrangle of the door. The visitor bent slightly as she peered into the dimness of the room, and yesterday's black braids flashed before Nikitin.

So, what kind of geologist was the secretary talking about? flashed across his mind. A vague premonition of something good made Nikitin's heart leap. He rose to meet the guest, who held a small suitcase in her hand, and they exchanged greetings.

"Miriam... am I right?" asked the paleontologist.

"Nurgalieva. But you can call me Miriam," the girl smiled.

"So, you're not afraid, Miriam, that our expedition will be difficult and distant?"

Her black eyes glittered mockingly.

"No, I'm not scared. Your expedition is so well equipped... Yesterday the dispatcher told me that this trip could replace a ticket to a resort."

"Oh well." Nikitin held out his hand to her. "Choose a car that you like."

"If possible, I'd like to go in the 'Fighter,' to Marusya," the girl asked.

"How did the women manage to come to an agreement?" laughed the paleontologist, stepping into the courtyard with Miriam. "Yes," he realized, "I actually met you last night, on Engels Street..."

He bowed and went to the gate, and the girl looked after him in bewilderment.

***

The cars traveled in single file, swaying, and bouncing as they drove off-road. The flat grayish steppe, overgrown with wormwood, burned under the high sun. The sky was monotonous and bland without a single menacing, pale cloud heavily hanging over the plain. For four days the engines roared. Despite the slow progress of the vehicles, the expedition managed to cover four hundred kilometers from the white city and the railway.

For four hundred kilometers of unfolding high sand dunes alternating with stony hills, flat wormwood steppe, and yellow-white salt marshes.

The gears gnashed violently, and the motors buzzed. The black circles of the steering wheels slipped in the sweaty, weary hands of the drivers, and a light blue mist of smoke puffed into the air over the vast steppe, indicating the devouring of hundreds of liters of precious gasoline.

Only once on this journey, late in the evening, viewed from the high hills, rose the friendly glow of electric light – a sulfur plant. And only occasionally did they come across round felt yurts – the temporary shelter of a person here – where only the permanent and faceless desert is eternal...

Passing the plant, we drove for a long time, using the bright moon and the last stretch of the passable road. At night, the dry, smooth steppe made up of hard clay and barren of vegetation – known geologically as a takyrs region – glittered in the moonlight like countless little stars, and it seemed mysterious and welcoming. We accelerated our vehicles as we crossed this hard surface.

Nikitin eventually gave the order to stop for the night only when the vehicles began to raise thick dust again from the bumpy surface of the plump clay.

Brightly lit bivouac light bulbs were attached to the backs of the cars. But the place they'd stopped to sleep turned out to be inhospitable. Their feet sank, as in dense snow, into the hummocky sedimentary soil, from which the fragile bare stems of some dried grass stuck up here and there.

Ahead, barely discernible behind the veil of moonlight, were the hillocks of Laili – the beginning of the most waterless rocky desert, hiding in its depths a graveyard of fossil monsters.

Beyond the endless rows of mounds, strewn with gray rubble, the isolation from the world was especially strong. The expedition disappeared as if gone into oblivion, because of the innumerable turns, detours, descents, and ascents. Eventually, the three gray cars passed the hills and emerged out onto a dead, endless plain covered with a thin layer of fine sand. A haze of warm air shimmered over the desert, which concealed and obscured the unsightly landscape.

The participants of the expedition now beheld a view of alluring blue lakes, wonderful groves, and snowy mountains glimmering in the far distance. Sometimes, they could see over their car hoods glimpses of a sea which was getting closer, splashing light misty waves and white foam…

After a few more minutes, rows of white houses appeared in the place of the sea, shaded by thick trees, similar to the city that remained far to the south of them, behind the sands they'd just crossed. It was getting dark, with the last crimson rays of the sunset casting the shadows of the cars themselves, usually so clear and defined, to blur then stretch to incredible sizes, then to grow in height and heave like giant elephants.

For the last time, high blue and green towers of a new ghostly castle appeared in the setting sun's rays and then disappeared.

'Lightning,' raising dust pillars and illuminating the plain ahead with its strong headlights, continued on its way at the head of the column – here, one could also drive at night. 'Dinosaur,' and 'Fighter,' fell behind, so as not to drown in the dust clouds of the car in front, as was always done when driving through a dusty terrain.

The engines roared evenly, lulling the senses. Nikitin fell asleep while sitting in the passenger seat, but was soon awakened by the sharp beeps of the 'Dinosaur' who was traveling behind them. 'Lightning' stopped and waited while the other two cars slowly approached.

"What's happened?" Nikitin asked the driver of the 'Dinosaur.'

"I can't go on, Comrade boss," the driver answered, embarrassed. "There's a lot of nonsense..."

"What?"

"It's true, Sergey Pavlovich," said the driver, Martyn Martynovich. "In the afternoon, the mirages are seen in the distance, but now – horrors take place right under our noses."

"But I'm going!" snapped the lead driver, who drove 'Lightning.'

"You are driving in front, Vladimir," said the 'Fighter's' driver who had approached, "and we are behind, in your dust. The lights shine on the dust, and the devil is what we see. We can't go."

"You're talking nonsense!" the lead driver was angry. "I know, sometimes you see things in the dust, but it's not impossible to keep going..."

"Try it yourself. Let me go first!" shouted the offended driver of the 'Dinosaur.'

"Okay, go on," the elder sullenly agreed.

People went back to their vehicles, and the engines roared back into life. The 'Dinosaur,' with its high load shaking on top of it, slowly passed 'Lightning,' and disappeared in a cloud of dust as it gathered speed. The driver of 'Lightning' waited until the dust, speckled with rare golden particles, settled in its headlights, then followed.

Concerned, Nikitin watched the road, wiping the windshield. They sped along for several kilometers without encountering anything, and the driver began to snort derisively, muttering something to himself. The car went smoothly, and their attention began to weaken. Suddenly, Nikitin felt that the driver had abruptly turned the steering wheel and the car swerved to the side. A huge, round hole was clearly visible ahead, surrounded by white tiles. Nikitin rubbed his eyes in amazement – on both sides of the track, highlighted by the headlights, were rows of tall houses lined up in a whirling cloud of dust particles. The vision was so believable that the paleontologist flinched and immediately heard the evil "ugh," of the driver.

Then the houses disappeared, as quickly as they'd appeared, and the steppe scattered in a pattern of black and yellow stripes, and a black crack gaped on the road. Gritting his teeth, the driver gripped the steering wheel tightly, trying to overcome the optical illusion. A few minutes later, an incredibly steep vaulted bridge appeared in front of them, quite clearly visible and so realistic, that Nikitin anxiously turned to the driver, but he was already slowing down the car. Behind them, the 'Fighter' persistently signaled with their horn.

Having stopped the car, the driver smoked, washed his eyes, and had a drink before he stubbornly moved on. And again, in front of their car appeared new dusty ghosts, frightening, close, and real. The nervous tension grew. 'Lightning' braked and spun in an attempt to avoid non-existent obstacles, and finally, the driver moaned, spat and, stopping the car, began to signal 'Dinosaur' to surrender. When the dust had settled, the 'Fighter,' who had stopped a long time before, slowly came up to join them too.

Once they stopped, the crazy, ghostly world disappeared. The night pushed the horizon into dark infinity. The huge stars glowed quietly, and the usual outlines of the constellations delighted with their immutability.

In the next afternoon, accompanied by the roar of the engines and the rocking of the cars, the fantastic visions again gleamed and shimmered. And everything began to seem non-existent and unreal.

Nikitin was very happy when the gloomy black contours of the Arkarly's mountains suddenly rose before them from behind the iridescent wall of another mirage. At first, their peaks stayed at the level of 'Lightning's' radiator cap and stayed that level for a long time. Then they began to grow quickly, covering the entire horizon in the north-west. The guide pointed to a crevassed mountain, whose steep front slope had the outline of a regular trapezoid. 'Lightning' immediately went straight towards it.

Once more, the soil became uneven and rockier as they ascended higher up the slope.

Finally, on the last slope, 'Lightning' made a turn, it's brakes creaking, and the car slowly descended onto a vast plain – down to the bottom of a huge ancient inter-mountain depression.

To the west, dark cliffs sullenly loomed, while the steep slopes of the eastern hills were composed of bright red sandstone. Two eagles slowly circled above the plain.

At the direction of the guide, the expedition moved along the red cliffs to the north. There, at a junction of dark and red rocks, there was supposed to be the Biscekta spring, with a well dug some time ago in the ancient past.

The flat surface of the valley was riddled with shallow ravines scattered around and richly littered with smooth pebbles covered with desert tan. These brilliantly black crusted pebbles gave the soil an unnaturally dark color against the countless crystals of transparent gypsum scattered amongst them, that shone in the sun with a myriad of lights.

'Lightning' turned, avoiding a low cliff of red rocks.

"Stop, stop!" Nikitin suddenly shouted and quickly jumped out of the car. Behind him rushed his loyal assistants, who also saw fossils.

To the left of the cars lay two large trunks of petrified trees, lying at an angle to each other. In the bright sunlight, their straight-grained wood and traces of branches stood out clearly. Huge bones with a dark shiny surface were scattered around the trunks and further to the west.

With great excitement, the enthusiastic researchers scattered across the plain and looked for more and more treasures.

Superbly preserved bones of giant dinosaurs covered most of the valley. The Paleontologists rushed this way and that, with joyful exclamations. The drivers and workers accompanying them became infected with their enthusiasm and merrily took part in the survey as well, filled with wonder at the extraordinary spectacle.

Only a portion of the bones lay loosely on the surface, while others were still embedded in the dark sandstone and pebbles. The bones protruded everywhere in the ravines and overflowed on the exposed rocks on the hillocks, piled up in clusters.

Those shepherds were absolutely right — they'd discovered an unprecedented cemetery of giant extinct dinosaurs, where the remains of hundreds of thousands of various animals had accumulated.

A strange impression was produced by this red-hot black, lifeless valley, littered with gigantic bones; ancient legends about the battles of dragons, about the graves of giants, and about the destruction of the giants by floods, automatically came to mind. And it immediately became clear that these legends had undoubtedly emerged as a result of such open clusters of huge bones.

"Is something the matter? Does something not add up?"

"No, Sergey Pavlovich. We need to dig even deeper."

"There's nowhere to dig, its solid rock there."

Nikitin threw down his notes, jumped up and rushed to the spring. Having convinced himself of the rightness of the Latvian, the paleontologist felt something inside him had broken off. Hiding his fear, Nikitin walked slowly from camp to the mountains to think in private.

***

A terrible discovery came on the second day of their stay in the valley: the amount of water given by the Biskekta spring was not enough for the expedition. Although there was enough water for two or three travelers with their camels, it was not enough for a big expedition with workers and their cars. Maybe the spring was good a hundred years ago, but now it's was running dry.

Nikitin realized they had to arrange emergency supplies. And the water on the way back? It was necessary, having committed themselves this deeply, to make their way to the east, as soon as possible – in two hundred kilometers from here, there would probably be some good wells.

Could we bring water from there? But then, there won't be enough fuel to return, he thought.

Stunned by the sudden impact of fate, the scientist was acutely aware of all his helplessness in the face of the surrounding merciless nature. What could they do? All of this superbly equipped expedition, and without water?

Where to get it here, in the scorched rocks, animated only by a tiny trickle of an ancient well? he asked himself. *Attempts to clear the source have led nowhere. Will this unexpected misfortune really disrupt the entire carefully organized expedition, deprive us of success, force people to risk for it?*

Immersed in desolate thoughts, Nikitin mechanically plunged deeper into the mountains. He walked quietly up a small gorge, which cut deep into the black side of a saddle-shaped mountain. The glowing black precipices doused scientist a sweltering heat. Nikitin stopped and saw Miriam.

The girl sat cross-legged on a rock, having slipped away from the camp herself. She kept an open notebook in her lap and was so deep in thought that she didn't hear Nikitin approach. Her heavy braids seemed to burden her bowed head, and her face was turned towards the shimmering hot distance. Her whole appearance and posture suddenly struck the paleontologist of her compliance with the surrounding nature. Nikitin felt for the first time that Miriam was the child of this country: there was a calm firmness to her, hidden under the guise of external obedience. Nikitin froze in place, afraid to disturb Miriam.

The scorching dead expanse of the country, where nothing is given at once... Only the hard work of many generations brings victory over the cruel nature. He realized it was impossible to go ahead with passionate impulsiveness – that path won't lead to their goal. It was necessary to move forward slowly, patiently, and steadfastly, always to be ready to fight new difficulties, and to suppress the will of each person's thirst for wonderful, sudden happiness...

Miriam, sensing Nikitin's gaze, looked around, jumped up, and went over to meet him. She looked inquisitively into the eyes of the young scientist.

"What's the matter, Sergey Pavlovich?" as always, she spoke slowly.

The scientist caught genuine concern in her tone. In an unaccountable need to be honest with her, he told Miriam about the disaster awaiting the expedition. The girl was silent, and only when they had returned back to the camp itself, she spoke, as if to herself and embarrassed:

"I heard, that in the past year while working on Dyurt-Kyre, they managed to increase the flow rate..." she paused, "with dynamite. Now if we had..."

"Damn it, we have ammonal!" cried Nikitin. "It's not always helpful to undermine a spring's outlet, but sometimes it works! I'd completely overlooked that possibility... Let's try it now!" The paleontologist brightened, accelerating his steps. "We'll risk the biggest charge."

***

... A thunderbolt of an explosion shook the dead mountains. A high column of dust soared over the spring, and a few seconds later, something fell with a terrible crash in the mountains. All the members of the expedition rushed to the spring and began to silently dismantle the rock, again digging out the key. It became even quieter in the camp when Nikitin and Miriam began to measure the flow of water. The expedition leader suddenly straightened up.

"Thank you, Miriam!" He grabbed her hand and shook it tightly.

"Hurray Miriam!" There was a friendly shout.

The girl rushed to seek salvation behind the back of the senior driver. He straightened his mighty shoulders.

"I won't shelter you!" he threatened.

"How are things with the asphalt, Miriam?" Nikitin asked cheerfully.

"It's a very interesting deposit here, Sergei Pavlovich," she played along. "This is not asphalt, but some very special, very solid resin."

"Show me it tomorrow, okay? And now I advise you to get acquainted with our successes."

***

Everywhere across the plain, one could see the hills of dug-up land. A light smoke rose from a fire on which liquid carpentry glue was boiled, and Martyn Martynovich, wearing some shorts and tanned to black, diligently glued bones together. Several people were closer to the center of the plain. There, a large area of rock had been carefully excavated in deep, marked off grooves. Two workers carefully picked at the loose sandstone with large knives, dividing the dugout into three parts. Marusya finished cleaning a skull by pouring shellac – an Indian resin dissolved in alcohol – on the damaged areas giving the bones a lasting lacquer finish.

Nikitin led Miriam to a boulder, where the surprised girl saw a sprawling skeleton of a huge lizard just on the surface. It lay on its side, with its long tail tucked up, and its heavy hind legs crossed over. Everywhere, on its vertebrae, ribs, and even on its hoofs – clearly written numbers were visible. The skull of the monster, which was about two meters in length, had a huge collarbone on the back of his neck, spiked with blunt thorns. Two long, obliquely directed horns protruded above its eyes, a third horn sat on its nose, and its muzzle ended with a beak.

"This is a triceratops, a three-horned herbivorous dinosaur, well-armed against predators," Nikitin explained. "The skeleton is completely preserved, and we'll divide it into three parts, and put it into these sturdy frames," the paleontologist pointed to the prepared frames, "then we'll cover it with plaster and take it away in the form of heavy slabs, in order to finally free from the rock later in the laboratory."

"What were the predators, if this creature needed such terrible defenses?" asked Miriam.

"Predators!" exclaimed the paleontologist. "Well, for example," and he reached into a box and chose a flat tooth with a curved tip and a serrated slicing along both, about fifteen centimeters in length. "This is from a Tyrannosaurus, Lord of the Lizards, a giant who walked on their hind legs... soon we'll move to the mountains with the most excavations," the scientist continued, "where Martyn Martynovich found three skeletons of armor-clad dinosaurs at one time, with bone armor lined with spines. Real tanks, but without guns, unlike modern tanks, which are weapons of attack. After all, the herbivore can only defend passively: it hides behind the armor or uses its horns, but doesn't actively attack.

***

Before reaching the eastern gorge, Miriam turned left and led Nikitin along the foot of the mountain, between scattered boulders.

A dense wall of reddish-black rocks suddenly stood before the paleontologist and his companion. A narrow passage, similar to a trail slashed by a gigantic sword, was cut through it. On either side of this stone gap were two rocky towers, with protrusions that hung high above the passage.

The narrow passage was straight, like a gun barrel, with smooth, almost polished, walls. After taking a few dozen steps through it, Miriam and Nikitin stepped out into a spacious valley, enclosed on all sides by steep cliffs. The side opposite to the passage was curved in a regular semicircle, in the very middle of which was a huge cube of very hard brown sandstone. The base of the cube was buried in a pile of flat, apparently recently collapsed boulders, and a huge black mirror gleamed on the sloping surface. The paleontologist looked around in bewilderment.

"The asphalt deposit," Miriam spoke quietly, "or rather, the hardened tar here. The pitch lies in even layers in solid iron sandstones, probably laid down by the wind, something like ancient dunes. When we blew the spring, the rocks collapsed here and opened up a fresh stratum of fossil resin. Its smooth surface is not yet damaged by weathering, and it glitters like a mirror.

"When, in your opinion, were the tar and sandstone deposited?" The paleontologist asked quickly.

"At about the same time as dinosaur bones," Miriam replied. "All these deposits accumulated here, in the valleys of these ancient mountains, and have remained almost intact."

Nikitin nodded approvingly and sat down on the coarse sand. She sat opposite him in her favorite position – crossed-legged.

For some reason, it was not very hot in this valley closed on all sides and an amazing silence was all around. Dry grass growing at the bottom of this natural mountain hall, rustled like distant crystal bells, barely heard. Nikitin, for the first time in his life, heard their sad rustling call and looked at Miriam in amazement. The girl tilted her head and put a finger to her lips. Soon, the same immensely distant, rare chords of low tones – the voices of the bushes lining the foot of the ring of rocks – intertwined with this weak, eerily ghostly chime.

Under this barely perceptible music of a silent desert, Nikitin sank into deep thoughtfulness.

Grasses rang and called to look into the depths of nature, talked about the hidden world that usually passes by our consciousness, dulled by ingrained habits, and only in the rare moments of life reveals itself with any clarity.

Nikitin thought that nature is immeasurably richer than all our ideas about it, but knowledge of it is never a gift. In close communication, in a constant struggle with nature, mankind can come closer to its hidden secrets. But even then, it is necessary that the soul be clear and pure, like a finely tuned musical instrument, and it will respond to the sound of nature...

Nikitin slowly raised his eyes and saw Miriam staring straight at him. The paleontologist rose awkwardly to his feet, and in a voice that seemed almost rude to him, extinguished the gentle calls of the grasses:

"It's time to go, Miriam!"

The girl stood silently.

As he was about to leave, Nikitin took another wistful look around the valley.

"Why didn't you mention this good place before?" he reproached the girl.

"You were absorbed in your work," Miriam replied quietly.

"I'll move the camp to the foot of the stone towers tomorrow," Nikitin decided. "By the way, the main excavations will now be very close."

***

With a confident, firm blow, Martyn Martynovich drove the last nail into a long box.

"The end, Sergei Pavlovich!" the Latvian exclaimed cheerfully and wiped his sweaty face.

"The end!" answered Nikitin. "Tomorrow we gather things up and rest. Then in the evening – it's on the road, home! We cannot stay any longer."

"Sergei Pavlovich," Marousia interjected pleadingly, "you promised to tell us about these beasts for a long time now..." and she pointed at the boxes that were lying everywhere, "but there's never been the time. What about today? Just another three hours."

"Alright. After dinner we'll go to that valley, and have a chat there," agreed the head of the expedition.

***

All fourteen staff members listened attentively to their boss. Nikitin spoke well, uplifted, and animated. He told how even in the ancient epochs of the development of terrestrial life, slowly, over millions of generations, the animal's organism was perfected, as bizarre, strangely formed four-legged amphibians and reptiles sometimes appeared. As in the struggle for existence, in an overcoming of the influence of the surrounding conditions, gradually all the less perfect, less vital species died out; an unforgiving comb of natural selection mutated the flow of generations throughout the passage of time, sweeping away everything weak and unsuitable.

"By the beginning of the Mesozoic era," he began, "about one hundred and fifty million years ago, reptiles settled everywhere on the ancient continents, and at the same time the most perfect of all animals emerged from them – mammals that developed under the harsh conditions of the late Paleozoic era. But soon the relatively harsh and dry climate everywhere changed to humid and hot, and abundant, luxuriant vegetation covered the land. These conditions of existence were easier, more favorable, and it was at this time that the huge reptiles spread across the whole earth. They conquered land, sea, and air, and reached unprecedented sizes and strength.

"Giant herbivores developed monstrous horns or armor from bone spines and shields to give them protection from predators. Other, unprotected by armor, hid in the waters of coastal lagoons or lakes. They reached up to twenty-five meters long and sixty tons in weight. Some reptiles evolved to flight and of all flying animals, they had the greatest elongation of their wings and, therefore, were the best flyers.

"Predators walked on their hind legs, leaning on a fat tail. Their front paws turned into weak, almost unnecessary appendages. They used their huge head, large mouth, and giant sharp teeth for their method of attack. These were monstrous tripods up to eight meters in height, brainless fighting machines of terrible strength and merciless ferocity.

"Amongst this environment of gigantic lizards lived the ancient mammals - small animals, similar to a hedgehog or a rat. Reptiles in the favorable conditions of the Mesozoic era suppressed this progressive group of animals, and from this perspective, the Mesozoic was an era of grim responses that lasted about one hundred million years and slowed the progress of the animal world. But, as soon as the climatic conditions began to change again, a change in vegetation began to occur – and the lizards immediately suffered. Herbivorous giants required abundant, easily digestible food, so the change in the food base was catastrophic for the herbivores, and consequently, for the giant predators at the same time. The natural balance of the animal population became severely disrupted. There was a great extinction of reptiles and the rapid flourishing of mammals which in time, became the masters of the Earth and eventually gave brought forth a thinking being – humans. Imagine for an instant an endless chain of generations without a single thought that had passed over those hundreds of millions of years," the paleontologist finished, "all the unimaginable number of victims of natural selection following along the blind path of evolution..."

The scientist fell silent. The cry of an eagle was heard high in the already blue sky. The listeners continued to sit quietly, looking at the paleontologist.

Nikitin smiled thoughtfully and again began to speak:

"Yes, the greatness of my science is in the immense perspective of time. In this respect, paleontology is comparable only with astronomy. But paleontology has one weak side, very weak, painful for those striving for deep knowledge: the incompleteness of the material. Only a very small part of the previously living animals remains in the strata of the earth's crust and is retained only as incomplete remains. Take our excavations - we only extracted bones. True, from these bones we can restore the complete appearance of animals, but only within certain limits. The worst thing is that we can never know in detail, the internal structure of the animal, to fully imagine it alive. Thus, we will never be able to verify the accuracy of our ideas, to establish our mistakes. Physical laws are unshakable. The power of the human mind is to look straight into their faces, not being enticed by fairytales..."

A deep melancholy sounded in Nikitin's voice, which he passed onto the listeners. The paleontologist rose abruptly.

"Nothing. For those not experienced in science, there is the free and powerful imagination of writers. Not constrained by the narrowness of exact facts, they can vividly and convincingly resurrect the vanished animal world. I advise you to read 'The Lost World,' by Conan Doyle and 'The Struggle for Fire,' by Roni Sr. These are my favorite writers who can even act on a paleontologist with the power of their imagination, a beautiful description of an ancient life, successfully capturing the shadow of the past..."

"'Together with the thickened twilight the vague shadow of the past has fallen, and across the steppe, all red, an evil stream is rolling...'" the paleontologist quoted.

A slight scream from Marousi forced the scientist to interrupt the quote and turn around. The next moment his breath stopped, and he froze, shocked.

A gigantic, green-gray ghost emerged from the black depths above the casting pitch of the fossilized resin slab. The huge dinosaur lingered motionless against the skyline, above the upper edge of the rocky cliff, rising ten meters above the heads of stunned people.

The monster held its horned head high; its big eyes looked dimly and gloomily away into the distance; lipless, wide jaws exposed a long row of backward-curving teeth. The back of the animal, slightly bent, flowed abruptly into an incredibly powerful tail that supported the dinosaur from behind. Huge hind legs like two columns bent at the joints, were not inferior in power to the tail, punctuated with three-pronged, widely spread toes, armed with gigantic curved claws. Finally, almost under its neck on the incline of its chest, hanging absurdly and helplessly, were two thin, clawed forelegs, tiny in comparison to its giant body and head.

The black cliffs of the mountains shone through the ghost, while at the same time one could discern the smallest detail of the animal's body. One could see the monster's back covered with small bone plates, its rough skin sagging in places in heavy folds, and a strange growth on its throat. There were bulges of gigantic muscles and even broad purple stripes along its sides. All of this gave the vision an amazing reality. It was no wonder that fifteen people stood numb and enchanted, devouring with their eyes, a gigantic shadow, real and ghostly at the same time.

A few minutes passed. With the subtle turn of the sun's rays, the vision of a motionless dinosaur melted and died away. Nothing but a black mirror remained before the people, which had lost its blue tint and gleamed with copper.

A loud sigh escaped simultaneously from everyone. Nikitin licked his dry lips.

For a long time, no one was able to say a word. The incredible appearance of the ghost of the monster destroyed all the established education and life experience beliefs. Everyone felt that something quite extraordinary had suddenly burst into their life. The most shocked was Nikitin himself – a scientist who was accustomed to analyzing and explaining the mysteries of nature. But now no reasonable explanation for what had happened occurred to him. Everyone was lost in conjecture. The camp was noisy until late at night until finally, Nikitin calmed down the excitement by saying that in this country of mirages, one shouldn't be surprised to see a mirage of a monstrous fossil. This ghost, by Nikitin's definition, could be none other than a Tyrannosaur.

**

The engines were checked before they'd start out on their long journey. The motors hummed, and a bluish smoke spread over the brown pebbles of the plain.

Nikitin glanced at his watch and hurried to the narrow crack in the rocks.

The black mirror looked at him deeply and dispassionately. The former silence wasn't in this place of peace anymore because of the noise of the motors that filtered through from behind the rocky walls. A vague sensation of something broken, lost forever, swept over Nikitin. He'd hoped for the appearance of yesterday's ghost, but this time, it didn't appear. Nikitin must have missed the time of its appearance and was too late.

Regretting the omission and marveling at the strength of his grief, Nikitin stood for a long time in front of a pile of stones that formed the pedestal a mirror. He heard the crunch of sand behind him and saw Miriam quickly approaching him.

"Martyn Martynovich says we can go. I volunteered to run after you... I wanted to take another look..." the breathless girl said abruptly and quickly.

"I'm going now," the paleontologist replied hesitantly, paused, and added: "Wait, Miriam!"

The girl obediently approached and became just like him, peering into the black mirror.

"What will you do when you return, Miriam?" Nikitin suddenly asked.

"Work, study," the girl answered shortly. "And you?"

"Also work... on these dinosaurs, and think..." the scientist faltered and unexpectedly abruptly finished: "about you!"

Miriam lowered her head without answering.

"If I were in your place, I would give all the strength to solve the riddle of the ghost of a dinosaur. After all, this wasn't just a mirage..." she spoke after a minute.

"I do know that it wasn't a mirage!" Nikitin exclaimed angrily. "But I'm only a paleontologist. If I were a physicist..."

Nikitin cut short the conversation with an unclear annoyance at himself and walked closer to the layer of amazing petrified resin. For a long time, he gazed long into its black, unrequited depth, and an almost unbearable, wild desire grew in his soul. For a moment, the impenetrable, inaccessible to man, curtain of time opened. Of all the huge number of people, only him and his companions were given a glimpse into the past. And of them all, only he was sufficiently armed with knowledge and experience in scientific work. Miriam was right... Nikitin was seized with a powerful desire to uncover the mystery of nature.

Suddenly, Nikitin realized that he could see some silvery shadows emerging from the black depths. The paleontologist began to peer deeper, meaningfully, straining his eyes and attention. Scattered pieces parts quickly formed into an obscure but solid image; it was like a poorly developed image of huge dimensions. In the center appeared an inverted figure of yesterday's Tyrannosaurus, but it was greatly reduced, to the left he could see a group of huge trees, and behind and below it all he vaguely guessed were the tops of some rocks.

Taking out a notebook, Nikitin called out to Miriam and began to sketch a new ghostly vision. Both eagerly peered at the silvery-gray shadows, but the image did not become clearer. Soon, light spots swam before their tired eyes, and again the deep blackness of the mirror became blind and pointless.

With effort, Nikitin forced himself to leave the mysterious place, even though he knew instinctively, that he should say for a few more days to observe the mirror.

Thanks to a rare whim of fate, he'd happened to meet with an incredible, extraordinary phenomenon. Very soon, maybe in a few days, the sun and wind will destroy the smooth surface of the resin layer, and the mystery that they couldn't understand would disappear forever. The duty of a scientist – yes, their duty! – the whole meaning of a scientist's existence was to not miss the chance that had been revealed to him, to convey it to all people.

And, in spite of everything, they had to leave a wonderful eye to the past, in distant, remote mountains. He had no more time. Delaying their departure would be too dangerous. And with that knowledge, the full expedition had worked the excavations until the last day. Ahead of them was a difficult return trip with overloaded cars. To risk it all because of a semi-delirious, inexplicable phenomenon, to the human lives entrusted to him? No, he couldn't.

Nikitin quickly, almost running, returned to the cars.

Approaching the 'Lightning,' he once again looked at Miriam. She stood motionless at the 'Fighter,' looking back to the entrance to the gorge. This was the last impression the paleontologist took with him as he left this mysterious place.

"Go!" he shouted loudly slamming the door of the car. As they drove off, he began to watch the sparkle of gypsum in the valley of the bones as it flashed running under the wheels of the car...

***

The cold, overcast light quickly faded into a leaden sky. A black, icy roof with large patches of snow was visible through double-glazed windows. The smoke coming out of the chimney was quickly dispersed by sharp gusts of wind.

Nikitin pushed aside the book he'd been reading and straightened up in his armchair, filled with an unspoken longing.

The scientist's stubborn mind didn't want to surrender, but somewhere inside the bitter consciousness of impotence was ripe.

With sadness, Nikitin recalled that only his impeccable reputation saved him from obvious ridicule, even suspicion of abnormality. The help, for which he'd turned to the physicists, resulted in joking bewilderment – wasn't it enough, in the end, that they thought he'd been deceived by vision, mirages, and hallucinations! And, putting himself in their place, he couldn't condemn the scientists.

Still, back there in the mountains near the cemetery of the dinosaurs, Nikitin had realized that the smooth surface of black tar contained a kind of photographic image that had been projected into the air in some incomprehensible way. But how could a picture without photographic plates, manifest and remained fixed? And, most importantly, ordinary diffused light doesn't create any image – you need a dark camera with a narrow slit or hole, through which the light rays can pass an inverted picture of what was in focus. And the Tyrannosaur in the depths of the black mirror seemed upside down! But...

To solve this mystery, an extraordinary impulse was needed, a passionately focused mind and a will that merged to achieve a single goal. It needed inspiration, but inspiration here, in his measured, habitual existence, did not come. Moreover, everything that happened there, four thousand kilometers away, beyond the steppe and the hills of hot sands, became more and more distant. Was it possible to tell someone, ask them to possibly believe the ghostly vision of the country of mirages, here, in the pale and sober light of a cold winter evening? And Miriam... Had she not also left his life... had she not also become a vanished mirage?

Nikitin closed his eyes. Almost immediately, the darkened window, snow, and cold disappeared, and before his mind's eye, pictures appeared one after another.

Blinding, bright white walls, dark green foliage infused with hot gold, gurgling irrigation ditches, copper clouds of dust... Again, swaying cars accompanied by the roar of motors vibrated with hot air, cutting through the blue chains of bizarre mirages. Through the haze of a fantastic, elusive world that hung over a boundless burned plain, the familiar face of the Miriam stood out brighter and brighter. The paleontologist jumped up, rattling his armchair.

How did I not understand this immediately? Why didn't I tell her then? he thought as he paced the room. *But you can still go and write...*

Nikitin was worried – something powerful had approached his heart and required an immediate solution... He would go to her, tell her everything. Right now.

Nikitin awkwardly waved his hand and touched the vertebra of a dinosaur, which lay near the edge of the table. The heavy bone fell with a crash to the floor and broke into several pieces. This jolted Nikitin back to his senses, and he rushed to pick up the scattered fragments. He felt ashamed as if someone else could see into his intimate dreams. Nikitin hastily looked around, and the environment around him again inexorably filled his soul. This was his world, calm, simple and bright, although at times, perhaps too narrow. A tall cabinet with glass doors kept many more unexplored treasures on its shelves – the remnants of ancient life...

And besides all this, the great mystery of the shadow of the past. 'Is it not all enough for you, a clumsy heavyweight, always late,' as his teacher had said? So, with Miriam – he was late, hopelessly too late to tell her there, in the mountains of Arkarly, in the valley of singing grasses... And now, to conquer Miriam, he needed to focus all his thoughts, all his strength to this – just like when he has to use all his time and energy to solve the shadows of the past. Could he do it? Is he enough for everything? And why was he so sure that Miriam was ready to love him? And if she loves another?

Nikitin suddenly calmed down and sat back down in the chair.

The human mind could not lower its powerful wings before the incomprehensible. The ghost of a dinosaur should have had an explanation! This steadfastness when faced with the most difficult tasks, the protest against blind faith, is the most remarkable feature of the human mind...

And yet Nikitin's thoughts involuntarily returned to the expedition to the desert. He recalled everything to the last detail, especially the last days before returning to Moscow. The naturalist's tenacious memory unexpectedly rendered him a great service.

Nikitin remembered how he'd waited for a car at the hotel on the day of their departure from the white city, stretched out on a wide sofa. The window of the room faced the street drenched in the mighty southern sun. The shutters were closed, and a direct but faint beam of light pierced the room through the gap between the shutters into the semi-darkness.

Some shadows flashed across the wall against the window. Subconsciously tracing their movement, Nikitin suddenly saw a clear reversed image of the opposite side of the street. The naked branches of poplars, a squat house with a new roof, and the lattice of iron gates were clearly visible. A man passed quickly, throwing his scarf around his neck, funny, small, turned upside down...

Like a fresh wind, a quick thought swept through Nikitin's head: *a small, closed depression shaded by overhanging rocks in the Arkarly Mountains... a narrow crevice – a passage to a spacious plain and exactly opposite to it, a pitch mirror made of resin... This was a huge natural camera, a focus that could be calculated!* Now it was clear to him how the image could have turned out, but... *but the main thing is still unclear: how did the picture get captured? How could a fleeting play of light and shadows be preserved for thousands of centuries?* The photo had not given any answer yet.

But stop!...

Nikitin jumped up and began to pace the room.

The image was in color! We need to carefully review the theory of color photography.

***

The next day Nikitin, forgetting everything else, studied a thick book on color photography. He'd already taken the time to get acquainted with the theory of colors and an analysis of human vision and now, looking through the last section, 'Special methods of color photography,' he suddenly came across Niépce's letter to Daguerre, written back in the 30s of last century.

'... moreover, it turned out that the varnishing (asphalt pitch) of the plate changed under the influence of light, which gave something like an image on a slide in the transmitted light, and all the color shades could be seen very clearly,' wrote Niépce.

Nikitin gave a low groan and squeezed his temples as if to restrain his fluttering thoughts, and began to read further:

'When the resulting image was viewed at a certain angle in the incident light, you could see a very beautiful and interesting effect. This phenomenon should be related to the Newtonian phenomenon of colored rings: it is possible that some part of the spectrum acts on the resin, creating the subtlest differences in the thickness of the layers...'

A precious thread explaining the ghost of the Tyrannosaurus stretched across the pages. At first thin and fragile, it gradually became stronger and more reliable.

Nikitin learned that under the influence of standing light waves, the structure of the smooth surface of photographic plate changes; that these standing waves create certain color impressions that are independent of the usual black image obtained as a result of the chemical effect of light on the silver bromide of a photographic plate. These prints of complex reflections of light waves, completely invisible even at strong magnifications, differ only in one ability – to selectively depict light only of a certain color when illuminating an image at one strictly defined angle. The sum of these prints can give a magnificent image in natural colors.

Hence, in nature, there is a direct effect of light on certain materials, sufficient to obtain an image without the help of light-decomposable silver compounds. This was exactly the clue that the scientist had lacked so much.

***

Nikitin hastened his steps. Rare drops fell from the melting roofs. The scientist, worried, hurried to the institute. The last three months of work were not in vain – he knew what and where to look, and now the help of opticians, physicists, and photographers had far advanced the solution to the problem. And today, for the first time, he'd decided to address his findings to the scientific world.

The topic of the report and the name of Nikitin gathered a significant audience. As the paleontologist related the incredible case with the ghost of a Tyrannosaur, he immediately noticed a cheerful revival of the audience. Nikitin frowned but continued unhurriedly and clearly.

"This freshly-exposed layer of fossil resin, it turns out, kept the light prints in it – a snapshot of one moment of the existence of the nature of the Cretaceous period. The sun's rays, reflected from this black mirror at a certain angle, projected like a silhouette, some ghostly image of a living dinosaur, no longer upside down, creating airflows of a mirage. It turned out a kind of fusion of the reflected image with a mirage, which increased the size of the light imprint.

"No doubt, the exposure needed to obtain a light imprint in the resin was great… But perhaps the power of sunlight at that time in areas with a tropical climate was somewhat stronger, and perhaps dinosaurs could have stood motionless for hours. Modern large reptiles – crocodiles, turtles, snakes, large lizards – remain stationary for several hours without changing their position. They can not be compared with the boiling energy of mammals. Therefore, under the condition of a long exposure, it is quite possible to take pictures of live lizards, which is proved by the dinosaur I saw.

"I calculated the place from which the picture was captured," and the scientist pointed to a large map of the area pinned to the board, "it is one hundred and thirty-nine meters from the foot of the stone towers. The image obtained due to strong illumination, or the particular arrangement of clouds, or some other conditions, was apparently immediately trapped in the flow of subsequent layers of asphalt tar, and thus preserved it from destruction. The concussion from the blast we made, separated all the upper layers, revealing the asphalt pictures directly…"

Nikitin paused, trying to overcome the excitement that seized him.

"In the end," he continued, "it is not this miraculous incident that is important, not that several people for the first time in the world saw the living image of a fossil animal. The greatest significance of the observation just reported to you lies in the real existence of the light imprints of the most ancient epochs, imprinted in the rocks and persisting tens, maybe hundreds of millions of years. These are real shadows of the past from such depths of time that we cannot even grasp with our minds. We never suspected this existence. It never occurred to anyone that nature could photograph itself, so we never looked for these light imprints.

"Of course, images of the past require so many coincidences of different conditions to happen, that these are likely only in extremely rare cases. But, given the huge amount of time passed, the number of these cases should be very large! For example, every case of conservation of fossil bones also requires very rare coincidences. Nevertheless, we already know a lot of extinct animals, and their number increases extremely rapidly as paleontological research develops.

"Light prints, images of the past, can be formed and preserved not only on asphalt resins. No doubt, we can search for them in some common substances of rocks – salts of oxide and ferrous oxide, manganese, and other metals. It has long been known to photograph by the method of fading, by destroying some unstable paint to the light and thus obtaining an additional color.

"So, where to look for them – these pictures of the past? In those deposits of rocks where we can assume very rapid stratification in the open air or in very shallow water. Opening without damaging the surface of the strata and catching the light reflections with some instruments that facilitate the perception of light prints is something we must learn to understand, to capture these traces of light waves of bygone times.

"Finally, we have the right to assume that nature photographed its past not only with the help of light. Don't forget to remember those pictures that have not yet been fully explained by science, which are occasionally left by lightning on wooden boards, glass, and on the skin of people affected by it. You can imagine capturing images using electrical discharges, and invisible radiation, such as radium. Give yourself only a clear account of what you are looking for, and you will know where to look, and you will find it!"

Nikitin finished his report.

The subsequent speeches were full of skepticism. One well-known geologist, who eloquently described Nikitin's performance as fascinating, but from a scientific point of view, considered it scientifically penny-worthless, paleo-fantasy, was nevertheless particularly excited.

But all the attacks didn't touch the scientist. He'd already made a firm decision a long time ago.

***

Metallic blows echoed through the huge hall. Nikitin stopped at the entrance. In the two display cases facing each other, were squat lizards gnashing their black teeth. Behind the windows, the floor was littered with beams, iron pipes, bolts, and tools. Two tall vertical stands rose upwards in the middle of crossed beams – the main foundations of a dinosaur's large skeleton. Hard, curved iron bands had already been joined on the rear stand. The two preparators carefully attached to them to the huge bones of the monster's hind legs. Nikitin glanced along the smooth curve of the pipe that supported the frame on top and bristled with copper ties. Here, all eighty-three Tyrannosaurus vertebrae will be attached along the contour of a predatory curved back.

Martyn Martynovich balanced on a rickety stepladder with a large gas key at the front desk. Another preparator, gloomy and thin and in a linen gown, scrambled on the opposite side of the stairs with a long pipe in his hands.

"It won't work!" shouted the paleontologist. "Careful! Don't be lazy, move those forests."

"Oh? So, what's the trick Sergey Pavlovich!" answered the Latvian cheerfully. "We – yes, we can't? Old school!"

Nikitin shrugged his shoulders and smiled. A gloomy preparator inserted a pipe cut into the upper tee that ended the stand. Martyn Martynovich vigorously turned the key. The pipe – to support the massive neck – turned and poked the gloomy assistant. He and the Latvian collided chest to chest on the narrow upper platform of the ladder and collapsed in different directions. The crash of the fallen pipe was drowned out by the shattering of glass and a startled cry. Embarrassed, Martyn Martynovich got back up rubbing a fresh bump on his bald head.

"To fall is also 'old school?'" asked the paleontologist.

"And what about it!" picked up the resourceful Latvian. "Others would be crippled, but we have a trifle – one glass, and it's not a mirror... But you're right, we'll have to move the forests, it's wrong," Martin Martynovich finished as if nothing had happened.

Nikitin put on his lab coat and joined the workers. The slowest part of the work – the pre-assembly of the skeleton and the manufacture of the steel frame stage, was already completed. Now the frame was ready, and all that remained was to assemble it and attach the heavy supports to the already prepared fixtures and screw it to the stops, clamps, and bolts – also the result of many months of labor. The preparators had also freed the skeleton from the rock, glued together all the smallest broken and scattered parts, and replace the missing pieces with plaster and wood.

The skeleton was fitted successfully, with only insignificant corrections made during the skeleton mounting. Scientists and preparators worked with enthusiasm, lingering until late at night. Everyone wanted to restore an extinct monster in a lively and formidable pose.

***

A week later the work was finished. The skeleton of the Tyrannosaurus rose to its full height; it's hind legs, like the legs of a giant bird of prey, frozen in a half-step, with a long-straightened tail stretching far behind. A huge openwork skull was raised to a height of five-and-a-half meters from the floor, and its half-open mouth looked like a sharp-bended saw with sparse teeth.

The skeleton stood on a low oak platform, shining with a black polished surface like a piano lid.

The oblique rays of the evening sun penetrated through the high vaulted windows, playing with red reflections on the mirrored glass windows and drowning in the blackness of polished pedestals.

Nikitin stood leaning on the window, and looked meticulously at the skeleton for the last time, trying to find some error that had not been noticed before against the strict laws of anatomy.

No, perhaps, everything is quite true. A huge dinosaur, extracted from the cemetery of monsters in the desert, now stood accessible to thousands of visitors to the museum. And the bones for other skeletons of horned and armored dinosaurs were already being prepared – an excellent result of the expedition...

The brilliance of the sun on the black pedestal cover vividly reminded the paleontologist of that resin mirror in the mountains of Arkarly... Yes, of course, the skeleton had been put in the same position as the ghost of the living Tyrannosaurus that was indelibly stuck in his memory. And this pose gave the impression of complete naturalness, which couldn't be said about the mounting in other museums.

If my dear colleagues knew what I was guided by! Nikitin grinned to himself. *However, the winners are not judged.*

Again, the thoughts of the scientist, like the needle of a compass, turned to the mysterious shadow of the past. The ghost had ceased to be an enigma, the phenomenon was clear to the scientist. His passionate, focused thoughts, the indignation in his mind before the incomprehensible mystery of nature, had also disappeared. The course of his reflection was now calm, cold, and deep.

The scientist was well aware that until he proved to the world the real existence of light imprints of the past, he would have to work alone. He, in all likelihood, will not have any special means, or extra time – he would have to do everything along the way himself, at the same time as his main work. A huge, overwhelming task! And the geology itself is against it.

In the processes that create sedimentary rocks, that is, those layers that can perceive light imprints, cases of rapid deposition of one layer after another are extremely rare. Especially on the surface, and not in the depths of lakes and seas! It'll be necessary to find strata deposited at a speed sufficient to avoid subsequent exposure to light. And this should coincide with conditions, even remotely similar to the pinhole camera, so that not just diffused light, but a light image would fall onto the surface of the layer. And how many snapshots that have already been taken may die in the future from compaction, recrystallization, or other chemical changes in sedimentary rocks!

What are the chances to find in an infinitely large number of strata that exactly match those conditions, and that one of the millions of that kind has kept the past image?

Will the depths of time, forever remain unanswered and unattainable for us?

No, it is this infinite, bottomless depth of the past that should help us. We need a rare accident, one that may happen once in a thousand years, and there is no chance to stumble upon it. But if millions of these millennia have passed, then a million accidents are already quite a number that is available for observations... And it is many times increased by the fact that the surface of the Earth is huge.

The territory of our homeland is hundreds of millions of square kilometers, composed of different rocks, formed in a variety of conditions, he reasoned. *When dealing with large numbers, we need to abandon the narrow ideas that have been born from everyday experiences... In search of the past, my Motherland is for me. Where else can one discover new images of the past, if not on its vast expanses!*

Confidence and the desire for a new search, a new fight, once more resurrected in Nikitin's soul.

First of all, I'll need an apparatus that catches the light reflected from the rock layer. Maybe a camera with a very high-aperture and at the same time a wide-angle lens. It'll be very important to correctly set the angle of reflection... Maybe make a rotating prism?

Nikitin, not looking at the Tyrannosaurus skeleton anymore, hurried to his office.

***

"No, not here, Comrade Professor." A bearded collective farmer with a stern face stopped Nikitin, who was walking past, deep in thought. "This is a horse path, and we need to go left, into a ravine.

"And far from the red cliffs?" asked one of Nikitin's assistants. "How far to get down to the river through the ravine?"

"About a kilometer down and then four kilometers along the riverbank," replied the guide as he briskly walked forward.

Huge, thick fir-trees hampered the path. In between the greyish-green trunks and drooping, mossy lower branches, the river glistened deep below, like scattered fragments of a broken mirror. The air was saturated with the sweetish smell of spruce resin, softer and sweeter than the smell of pine. The ravine, overgrown with alder, resembled a long corridor covered with a thick layer of brownish old leaves. The leaves grew blacker and wetter, as the water swirled under them. Then the ravine was over, and the researchers found themselves on the banks of a fast and cold river, a narrow channel that ran between high steep banks. Each turn of the river and a quiet splash were indicated from afar by the bright glint of the sun. The hills were dull, and this made everything feel gloomy and cold. Nearby there were steep cliffs of dark purple clay, fringed by overgrown green arches on the upper edge of the slopes.

Soon, the small detachment reached the cliffs, and the workers got down to business. Shovels and pickaxes quickly dug in quick hands. Coarse clay clumps rustled and rolled into the river, like a rain of nuts. Carefully tamping up the wedges, they exposed the shiny, smooth surface of the clay layer, which lay at a slight inclination. Nikitin built a platform and set his device high above the exposed layer. Having finished their tasks, the workers left, the assistants went to the shore with fishing rods, and the paleontologist was left alone.

The watch was on. Nikitin was on duty at the apparatus, occasionally allowing himself to close his tired eyes for two or three minutes. The scientist wasn't worried, in fact, he was almost completely confident of another failure. Repeatedly and in different places, Nikitin had already installed his device, and with agonizing expectation peered at the dead surface of a stone. Each time the excitement and expectation of a new discovery weakened, hope faded, but the scientist stubbornly continued his observations in all the places that he considered appropriate. And now, almost without interest and bound only by a strong sense of duty, Nikitin observed in the apparatus at a freshly-opened layer of hardened purple clay. The sun slowly changed the angles of the illumination. The mighty fir trees weakly swayed their tops, and the water along the riverbank could be heard splashing slightly.

Then suddenly, in a uniform level of illumination, rare dark spots appeared, became sharper and scattered throughout the exposed layer. By selecting the slope of the reflection using a rotating prism, Nikitin finally achieved clear visibility.

A very bright shore of an unusually clear, green sea appeared before him. An almost perfect plane of silver-white sand imperceptibly turned into emerald water. Long, straight crests of small waves froze in their cascade, tracing the crystal-clear surface of the water with bright, bluish-green stripes. In the more distant plane, the stripes were crushed into triangles, and the pointed tips of the waves turned upside down, showing flashes of dazzling white, and also silver foam. In the purest green of the water, the distance seemed blue, the wonderful clarity of the air and the amazing brightness of the light were felt.

Almost with fear, Nikitin looked at this piece of inexpressibly bright and clear world, realizing that the crests of the waves had frozen in the sunlight that had shone more than four hundred million years ago. It was the shore of the Silurian Sea...

The vision disappeared very soon with a minute turn of the sun. Daylight, causing a vision, and himself also extinguished it, not giving the opportunity to use the photographic apparatus.

Nikitin stayed overnight right there, under the platform. Only tomorrow at the very same time could the sun bring ghostly shadows to life again.

But sleep mostly evaded the scientist throughout the night as he shook from dampness and fought off annoying mosquitoes.

The northern summer is changeable, and a cloudy morning ended in rain. In the dank fog, the scientist watched with despair as water flowed over the smooth surface of the clay, as the trickles of rain gradually turned red and how, finally, a snapshot of the wonderful Silurian sea turned into sticky brown mud.

This had been the second time Nikitin had managed to see a shadow of the past if only for a moment admiring the beautiful vision. But still, if his search had succeeded once, he knew he needed to try again and again!

Now Nikitin decided to try to look for pictures of the past on the walls of caves – these natural pinhole cameras. There, the image is protected from the vagaries of the weather, from changes in sunlight. And he, taught by bitter experience, knew now, to prepare the camera in advance, before the observation. Then the past will not slip away. It was necessary to search in shallow caves, where substances that vary from light will appear in the calcareous lime deposits.

***

A rare gray fog slowly crept over the thick, oily water. The banks shone with hoarfrost, and the steeply declining mountain slopes blackened gloomily, melting in the rays of the rising sun. The blunt nose of the bulky scow, enclosed with a strapped down tarpaulin, was aimed at a distant, steep, rocky cliff, which rose across a mighty river.

A wide swirling air flowed through the piercing cold, soundlessly, and quickly. A rumbling, heavy roar could be heard in the distance. Nikitin stood on the bridge of the boat near the pilot, holding tightly to the wooden pegs driven into the beam of the rudder. The rowers holding the paddles of the oars tensed.

The pilot, wearing mittens, rubbed his reddened nose awkwardly.

"Then Bolloktas roars," he said hoarsely, moving closer to Nikitin, "the most dangerous part of the passage!"

"Beyond the bend?" Nikitin asked slowly.

The pilot nodded glumly.

"Is there a cave there?" continued Nikitin. "On the left bank?"

"Do you really want to moor?" the pilot wheezed anxiously.

"Yes, there is no other way out; it's impossible to pass along the steep banks," the scientist replied firmly.

The surface of the water began to swell with long and flat waves. The Carbaz – the heavy, flat-bottomed boat with a triangular nose – began to slowly sway and dive. The water churned under its bow. The roar was approaching, growing, and surrendering to the high rocks. It seemed that the very stones roared menacingly, warning the newcomers of imminent death.

The pilot gave a command, and the rowers shook their heavy oars. The Carbaz turned, tossing around. The river entered a narrow gorge, which squeezed itself into a powerful expanse. Giant cliffs, about four hundred meters high, rose menacingly, drawing ever closer together. The riverbed resembled a wide triangle, the top of which, stretching out, disappeared around the bend of the gorge. At the base of the triangle, a high, foamy shaft singled out a large stone, and behind it a triangle intersected with a series of sharp, black tusked-like stones, surrounded by frantically swirling water. The gorge in the distance was filled with sharp standing waves as if a whole herd of rearing white horses was squeezing between steep dark walls. To the left, a wide semi-circular bay went into a stone wall, curving the left side of the triangle, and there the main flow of the river fiercely frothed, tossing up columns of sparkling splashes.

Nikitin lowered his binoculars and grabbed the rudder, helping the pilot as they rushed toward the middle stone, in the deafening roar of rapids. The Carbaz had to avoid pockets of whirlpool waters, so they had to navigate along the dangerous left side. Otherwise, the irresistible force of the water would pull the ship onto a ridge of stones... and that would mean they'd not make it to the cave this year and have to wait until next year for the next window of opportunity to access it. If they couldn't make it through this challenge, it would mean the work of this expedition would be over, because the timing was tight and there was a hurry to return.

"Hold her steady! Steady!" shouted the pilot.

The Carbaz soared to the crest of a high wave – then the water fell into a deep, dark pit behind the stone, where the Carbaz stalled to the sound of a dull thud as it scraped its bottom against the stone. The jerk of the rudder almost threw Nikitin and the pilot off of the bridge, but both firmly pressed against it and maintained control. The ship turned slightly and then ran at an obtuse angle to the shore, leaning towards the menacing stone fangs. The Carbaz filled with water and foam, desperately jerked, bouncing on high waves.

"Row!" the pilot ordered as he sat back down.

The drenched and sweaty oarsmen – the workers and employees of Nikitin's expedition – struggled to control the unruly oars. The less experienced of them fearfully awaited a crash while glancing at their obstinate boss. His face, overgrown with a dark beard, seemed formidable.

Nikitin stood with his legs wide apart on the shaking bridge, mentally measuring and calculating the distance to the white frothing line – the boundary of the reflected reverse current. The pilot, biting his lip, also looked there. The Carbaz slowed down, then again rushed forward and surged straight into the boiling foam. Nikitin wanted to close his eyes and squeeze into a ball – a second more, and the ship would inevitably break into pieces on the rocks. However, the Carbaz began to slow down again. With a sharp thrust, the ship stopped and, picked up by the reverse current, entered the deep, black water, gently splashing at the foot of sedimentary ledges which fell steeply into the river.

Nikitin did not restrain his sigh of relief. In the end, the risky exploration of the caves of Bolloktas was not part of the mission for his expedition at all, and if misfortune had happened in the pursuit of the shadows of the past... But the Carbaz had already moored, gently poking at the rock. The paleontologist jumped onto the ledge of the rock with a long leap and secured the mooring rope to the stone.

"Happy landings, Comrade Chief!" the pilot jokingly bowed before Nikitin.

"So, I can see!" the scientist said approvingly.

"Oarsmen let's get cracking!" ordered the pilot.

The steep slopes towered over the Carbaz for about a-hundred-and-fifty meters. Above the slope was a natural formation of a wide ledge, with a long natural platform in a semicircle, enveloping the ledge of the shore, and above that platform, the mountainside eased back to a gentle slope. At its base were nine black holes – entrances to the caves. The whole slope was overgrown with low curly pine trees, whitened with dry reindeer moss, and Nikitin and his assistants easily managed to transport up all necessary equipment.

The rest of the day was spent by the paleontologist in the caves until he was convinced that he was right in his assumptions.

On a flat rear wall of the cave, thin, smooth seams were layered successively with the overall wall stained in a dark yellow-green color. Nikitin hoped that the impurities of iron and chromium salts, having changed under the influence of light, could have preserved in any layer a light imprint of that epoch when living creatures were here, and the volcanic activity had not yet completely died out – about sixty thousand years ago.

His assistants cleared the entrance. A round hole cast a light on the back wall, and the cave really looked like the interior of a photographic device.

With infinite patience and thoroughness, Nikitin set to work. Scraping away layer by layer, he illuminated the surface of each layer with a specially designed magnesium lamp. He'd turn a lamp or a prism to change the angles of illumination and reflection, but not even the slightest hint of a vision appeared in the instruments glass.

More than ten thin layers had already been inspected and knocked down from the wall, and there was only a very thin crust remaining. Nikitin imperceptibly worked all night, but, embittered by failure, did not feel tired. Only a few flashes in his eyes from the bright light and the stock of the magnesium mixture would come to an end.

He worried if this would be another summer lost – surely, he was armed enough now to catch a shadow of the past!

The eleventh layer seemed smoother to Nikitin than all the previous ones. The scientist again lit the magnesium lamp. Several turns of the ball head – and a round, vague image appeared in the device. The gray, obscure shadow in the right-hand corner was like a bent human figure with some oblique line behind its shoulder; to the left vague spots delineated something rounded and incomprehensible. Nikitin adjusted the device, but the vision did not become clearer. He understood that he was seeing a new picture of the past, but it was so obscure that it would be difficult even to describe it, not only to take pictures. Nikitin sprinkled a new portion of the magnesium mixture, increasing to the limit the light of the lamp.

Yes, it's without a doubt, a human figure. So... it's all about the power of the lighting, the scientist thought. *Although magnesium light gives a spectrum similar to solar, its strength hasn't been enough. Only the mighty sun can give life to the same generated shadows! And the sensitivity of my device is insufficient – it's too simple, this device copying the camera. We'll have to wait for the technique to create a wonderful illuminator!*

The overheated lamp, having flashed for the last time, went out. In the darkness of the cave, the round opening was clearly distinctive... Dawn! The usual calm left the scientist – and in a rage, he slammed his fist on the innocent device.

Nikitin was furious. He felt himself gasping for air inside the cave, so he rushed out, heavily banging his head on the arch, and fell to his knees. The blow sobered the scientist a little, but the rage that bubbled in him did not fade. With his eyes narrowed, he glanced over the block that hung over the entrance.

So, my lamp is no good! he fumed to himself. *But I will see the shadow of the past in the sunlight!* He always had ammonal with him, so that if it were necessary, he could quickly open the necessary layers, blowing up the rock lying on them.

The paleontologist busily examined the slope above the cave and noticed long vertical cracks that cut through the sedimentary blocks. It would be nothing to bring down this stone wall!

The scientist began to descend to the shore, where his companions had settled for the night, but changed his mind and returned to the cave. There he determined the angle at which the light of his lamp fell on the surface of the limestone layer, and took the direction along the compass. Excellent! The sun will be here between two and three o'clock. He could get a proper sleep because his eyes were so tired that even in the sun, he wouldn't see anything. Well, that morning promised a fine day!

***

As soon as the dust cleared from the explosion, Nikitin began to hastily mount the apparatus, balancing on piles of stone fragments. A smooth greenish wall, undamaged by the explosion, gleamed wetly in the bright daylight.

No, now he will not be naive – this time he firmly clamped the prepared cassette tightly in his hand. As soon as the image created by the sun flashes in the glass of the instrument, and it sets the focus, the cassette will be immediately inserted into the apparatus. As a result of a successful snapshot, existence will be proved, and moreover – the possibility of saving transmitted shadows of the past. A decisive turn in a difficult path – and no longer would he go on alone! What the efforts of a single person mean in comparison with the amicable work of many people is very well known to anyone who has tried to build new roads in science or technology.

Nikitin looked at his watch – two hours and twenty-three minutes – and placed it next to the glass, tightly securing it to the rotary screw of the prism. Time slowly stretched out again, but now the wait was tense – the scientist knew that he would see the past.

Slowly, very slowly, the sun changed its position in the sky. Nikitin forgot everything around him. Eventually, the light touched the plate, giving rise to vague glints.

Here the gray bent shadow to the right gradually emerged with a clear outline of a human figure. A slanting line depicted a spear.

Hunching his head into his broad shoulders and tensing his aching muscles, the scientist sat down, crouched, and focused towards a long spear. A broad, wrinkled face was half turned toward Nikitin, but his eyes were fixed on the rounded, forested mountains, which opened beyond the cliffs. Nikitin managed to notice thick, disheveled hair framing a rather high forehead, prominent cheekbones, and massive jaws. It seemed to the scientist that he could read an anxious and pained meditation on the person's face as if he was really trying to look into the future. All this Nikitin considered in a few moments. Despite his intense interest in other details of the picture, the paleontologist could not allow himself to peer into the device any longer – he needed a picture.

So, Nikitin quickly inserted the cassette and grabbed the slide to open the disc, but then suddenly froze in place, without making the necessary movement. The brilliance of the smooth wall suddenly went out, everything turned dark, and looking back, Nikitin saw a massive long cloud slowly creeping across the sun. And behind it in close rows, settling on the tops of the surrounding hills and creeping from behind the mountains, further heavy leaden clouds of that ominous lilac hue which always portends heavy snow.

Desperately, the scientist examined the sky. If it snows, then he won't see anything more – the finest prints of light will inevitably be erased.

Holding onto a vague hope, Nikitin covered the apparatus with a raincoat, leaving it in place until the next day, before he apathetically trudged back to the tents. An absurd accident, a new failure poisoned his mind and weakened his body.

Nikitin's companions fell silent as they watched their depressed chief silently seat himself; they talked in low voices like one would at the bedside of a seriously ill patient.

The wind howled piteously through the rocks, and large flakes of snow twirled.

Nikitin poured himself alcohol, drank it quickly, and ordered to bring the apparatus from above. Not only did all hope of seeing the image of the ancient man perish again – it was no longer possible to allow a single extra hour of delayed departure.

Nikitin pulled himself together: any more delay could lead to the Carbaz getting stuck in the ice and frozen river below the rapids, amid the deserted taiga.

The next morning, as soon as the peaks of the hills had barely come into sharpness, people began to bustle about packing their things.

The mooring line softly splashed, falling into the water; The Carbaz barely moved out into the foam boundary of the main stream. Suddenly, like a monstrous soft paw had grabbed the ship, the Carbaz surged forward and rushed to the gorge, where it disappeared, jumping like a sliver in the roar and foam of sharp waves.

***

It was dim in the large study, illuminated only by a table lamp with a large shade that cast a circle of light on a table full of books. Nikitin sat motionlessly sitting by the table.

Three years, and still he can't find peace... His previous work now seems to him so calm and clear, so it beckoned once again to surrender to it entirely! But he couldn't, and now he was torn between the old and the new, trying to conscientiously perform his previous tasks, while his whole soul wanted to chase the shadows of the past. Over these past three years, he'd twice had the past in his hands; twice he saw what nobody else could see. And yet still, he was also as far from accomplishing the task now, as he was at that unforgettable moment in the mountains of Arkarly. And the apparatus... it was no good – it was still not refined enough.

He must have made a mistake in the past. A person should not be alone...

Nikitin lit the top light and squinting, began to gather up his scattered papers. He glanced at his device, which stood on a separate table, shabby and scratched from its travels. For a second, he compared himself to him, grinned bitterly and left.

***

The museum was dark. Nikitin's office was located at the end of a huge hall full of showcases and skeletons of extinct animals. Nikitin was briefly blinded as he stepped out of the lighted room and into the darkened passageway. However, he knew the way through the displays, and he also knew that in several places, horns protruded, and bared jaws of skeletons stood on open platforms. In the dark, it was easy to get hurt or, worse still, break fragile bones.

The scientist stopped and waited for his eyes to adjust to the darkness. The glass panes of the displays shone slightly, but the dark bones of the skeletons merged with the dark space of the hall, which seemed empty. For many years, Nikitin has felt the invisible presence of the dead people of the museum. Once again, the paleontologist was struck by the strange impression – as if the hall was filled with ghosts, perceived but invisible.

Nikitin moved forward, grumbling at the imperfections of his own eyes. He knows everything that is here, knows where it stands, and he still sees nothing. No worse than the shadows of the past! Skeletons exist and at the same time disappeared – too little light for the eyes...

Suddenly Nikitin stopped – a comparison with the shadows of the past struck him. How naive he'd been, relying on his own eyes! Why had he lost sight of the fact that the finest prints of light waves can, in most cases, reflect only tiny amounts of light, quantities not perceived by ordinary vision? Therefore, artificial lighting could not cause quite clearly imprinted pictures of the past. And how much, therefore, was missed in the weaker prints!

Nikitin felt ashamed. He, a scientist, had acted as an amateur in the creation of his device! He'd forgotten about the power of modern technology, which has instruments that sense the most insignificant amount of light!

Slowly making his way through the dark hall of the museum, with every step the paleontologist took, a new design of his apparatus strengthened. Once again, he would have to turn to the physicists and technicians. He needs to receive the perception of light reflected from the image not directly, but through a combination of sensitive photocells – to translate the light into an electric current, amplify it and turn it back into a light readily visible to the eye.

He anticipated that the most difficult issue will the in the exact transfer of colors, but here it could be combined. One could give the reinforcement of the contours, and the color would be obtained from the direct reflection.

Nikitin brushed his shoulder against a display and adjusted his direction...

Yes, this is something to think about, but it seems that I've found the key to the solution of the problem. If we can create such a device, the scientist continued to think, *I'm not afraid of anything. Outdoors, I make a canopy and produce artificial light. And underground – the same! Then the shadow of the past... we will see it!* The paleontologist clenched his fingers into a fist. *With several photocells, I can change the setting of the device, increasing or decreasing the sensitivity to different beams of the spectrum.*

***

... A cheerful young graduate moved closer to the chief engineer, who was escorting a group of clearly above-ground people to the mine.

"How are they, Andrei Yakovlevich?" he asked in a whisper as he pointedly winked at the visitors. "A walk in the park, or needing babysitting?"

"What are you insinuating? Don't you know anything!" The engineer was horrified. "This is a famous scientist!" He furtively pointed to Nikitin who had lingered. "And if you're not careful, you'll damage their apparatus... So be careful!" the chief engineer threatened.

Nikitin, well known for his sharp hearing, heard all this short and incomprehensible conversation for the uninitiated and hastened to intervene.

"Let's get moving, and get this behind us!" He turned to the graduate. "Neither I nor the apparatus will do anything," he said loudly. "Ah, I love to remember the old days! And my assistants are useful – so let's use them.

The embarrassed young engineer looked at the scientist in surprise, then smiled broadly and nodded his head.

The cage slowly began to descend and suddenly plummeted, as if the rope had broken. Nikitin's legs separated from the floor, his heart seemed to leap into his throat, and he held his breath. The fall of the cage accelerated, then it suddenly and sharply slowed down. A huge deceleration crushed people to the floor, as if invisible hands pulled everyone with a wide, inexorably tightening belt.

This sensation lasted no more than a second, and again the floor left from under the feet, the body became weightless, and the sinking heart rushed up.

"Oh!" cried Nikitin's assistant.

But the cage had already smoothly slowed down its descent and stopped at one of the deepest seams of the mine.

"To them it was nothing!" the assistant swore, trying to stop his knees from trembling.

Nikitin burst out laughing, much to the indignation of his frightened employees.

The paleontologist descended into the mine with unprecedented confidence for success. The reason for this confidence was the newly redesigned apparatus and the fact that the miners here had discovered a layer of petrified resin, similar to a black mirror that first showed him the ghost of a dinosaur. And... he'd just received a letter.

Nikitin smiled, turning over a few of the lines from memory. Miriam had written to him, letting him know she'd neither forgotten him or the shadow of the past.

She wrote that a year later she'd managed to visit the asphalt field again. The black mirror was destroyed, but nothing could destroy the impression of the ghost of the dinosaur, deeply sunk into her soul... She'd managed to spark the interest of the shadow in a talented researcher called Karzhaev. And now they were searching for layers that have preserved the imprints of light waves.

She hadn't written to him earlier because she'd felt it wasn't necessary yet to bother him — here Nikitin felt a reproach hidden between the lines — but all this time she'd been following his work and believed that he would finish the work right to the end. And now they have found an interesting layering, so she'd decided the time was right to ask him to come to them.

Nikitin had not yet realized the full meaning of Miriam's letter to him. He'd too little time for reflection on the last day of preparation for the study. Only the lightness of the former young days returned to him, and this returned youth surprised the people around him.

... A powerful fan, silently rustling, sucked the dry air out of a long, old tunnel, pinching and burning the throat. Nikitin was in a hurry to begin the trial immediately after the blasts. Here, in the old workings, aside from the busy movement of electric locomotives, the rumbling of trolleys and flashing lanterns, all was empty and quiet. The gloomy underground darkness tightly embraced the people, who merged in with the nameless blackness of the coal walls.

Somewhere in the distance water trickled, barely audible, and the supports cracked, warning the miners about the heavy pressure of the rock.

"Who showed you this wonderful place?" in a low voice Nikitin asked the assistant who was walking beside him. He nodded at the little old man who had taken up the rear of the procession with the engineer.

"He is a rare mountain master, he knows every layer in all the faces. If it were not for him, it would take years of searching in these endless workings..."

The paleontologist looked with silent gratitude at the old miner.

Ahead, a clean colonnade of new anchored pillars gleamed white. Judging by their number, one could guess that the journey ended in an extensive camera. Indeed, the black walls parted, revealing a large empty space with a high ceiling.

Nikitin's assistants hesitated, dragging the bulky apparatus between the pillars. The engineer stepped forward and held up a strong flashlight. Torn by explosions, a thick layer of coal shales surrounded the researchers, threatening them with countless sharp protrusions and flashing steel on smooth chips...

At the very beginning of the chamber, on both sides stood slightly swaying thick, ribbed trunks. Ingrown on one side into the mass of coal, they stood out only by the rhombic pattern of the bark. Mighty stumps with branched roots sprawled like huge spiders across the cleared surface of the floor. The roots spread along ancient soil, which had served as a support for them in the infinitely long past times. All stumps were cut to the same level – the water level in a flooded coal forest. In the large trunks that survived, the great hollows gloomily gaped.

The site of the dead had turned into coal and lime when the forest was suppressed over profound years of antiquity. It was as if not two hundred meters of thick strata hung over the heads of the people, but an almost incomprehensible depth of hundreds of millions of years that had swept over these trunks and stumps.

At the back of the chamber was a pile of collapsed shales that indicated where the explosion had taken place, and a slanting black-brown slab glistened above them – the solidified sludge of bitumen. This was the target for the test, deposited on the steep slope of a small hill in the coal forest.

***

Soon the magnesium lamp it's bright white beam on the slab, and Nikitin set the focus of the reflective camera. The scientist was worried and coughed.

"We will try…" he said hoarsely.

What will this so carefully chosen surface layer have to say now? the paleontologist thought as he switched on the photocells and amplified the current. Turning the prism screw, Nikitin looked again at the apparatus: the vein was no longer black – vague vertical lines appeared on a transparent gray background.

Patiently and cautiously, the scientist adjusted the device until a fourth shadow of the past was revealed to them with unprecedented clarity – a shadow that thousands of people will now see!

Nikitin looked at the glade of a forest regularly flooded: pale-gray tree trunks with diamond-covered bark surrounded by oily black water. The top of each tree was divided into two thick branches diverging at an angle and disappearing in the dense shadow of tightly shackled crowns. A thick scaly trunk lay across the water, falling on a small hillock protruding to the left. The hillock itself was overgrown with strange plants, similar to mushrooms, and tall and willowy purple grasses which dotted the wet red soil. The fleshy lapel cups of each fungus showed an oily, yellow interior. Beyond the hillock, above the sharply curved stems without leaves, was a gap filled with a distant hazy, slightly pink mist. A twisted, naked birch stuck out of the mist, and an incomprehensible living creature crouched on it, pulling its head in.

Peering into the image, Nikitin shuddered – from under the purple mushrooms, hiding the body in their midst, a wide parabolic head protruded, covered with a mucous membrane of purple-brownish skin. Huge bulging eyes looked directly at Nikitin, senselessly, inexorably, and viciously. Large teeth protruded from its lower jaw, exposing themselves in the hollows around the edge of its muzzle. On the right, a dim pearl of light poured in, illuminating the whole picture. The lighted air seemed blackish, as if through a sooty but transparent glass...

Nikitin looked for a long time into this magical window of the past, into the life of the world of the Carboniferous era. Three hundred and fifty million years span between the present and the time when this rare event of light waves captured their picture. Incredibly, the evil eyes of an unknown creature were clearly visible, purple mushrooms, still water, and strange gray air. And in the mine, all that could be heard was the projector hissing weakly and the intermittent breathing of the people...

Nikitin thought that he was going crazy. He recoiled from the apparatus. Real, roughly broken coal walls, ancient stumps – maybe the remains of the same trees that are now alive and slender are visible in his apparatus... The concentrated faces of the surrounding people... Having mastered himself, the scientist hastily prepared the camera and took several color photographs.

***

A stack of prints of Nikitin's article was placed on the table, and each was accompanied by a color reproduction of the captured shadow of the past. Having autographed the last of the prints assigned to his distribution list, the paleontologist sighed.

So much time had passed that it was no longer easy for him to feel joyful.

Now many younger, perhaps more talented people, will follow in his footsteps. The first page of the secret book of nature has been revealed. Loneliness on a long and difficult journey had ended! But loneliness – it was only in knowledge... Many dozens of people had helped him in his work, not to mention his collaborators, many of them strangers, people far from science...

A string of familiar faces passed before the scientist's memory. Here they were – miners, working quarrymen, collective farmers, hunters. All of them trustingly and unselfishly, without even asking about the ultimate goal, respected the famous scientist and helped him find and capture the shadow of the past.

So, he worked and owed them a great debt... Yes, and now that debt was paid – that's where the tremendous relief came from!

Nikitin remembered how in the same office he had more than once, questioned and doubted the correctness of his life's path.

The scientist smiled, quickly sketched the text of the telegram to Miriam, informing her of tomorrow's departure. Confidence in his future path overwhelmed him with joy. No, he had not made a mistake, and it wasn't for nothing that he'd spent years in a difficult struggle with the mystery of nature!

LAKE OF THE MOUNTAIN GHOSTS

A few years ago, I was on a scientific expedition through parts of Central Altai, along the ridge of Listviaga and across the left bank of the Upper Katun's Springs. Back then, my goal was gold, and although I didn't find any valuable deposits, I was nevertheless delighted with the interesting geological landscape, and enchanted by the wonderful nature of the Altai.

There was nothing particularly noteworthy in the places where I worked. Listviaga is a relatively low mountain chain whose peaks are not covered with eternal snow, the so-called 'bielki,' meaning 'white caps.' So, accordingly, there aren't any sparkling variety of glaciers, mountain lakes, formidable peaks, and all that high-mountain charm that amazes and captivates a person in the higher ranges. However, the raw beauty of the massive, naked rocks, rising their stone ridges over the flowing taiga, and the hills crowing at the foot of these rocks like sea waves – all this rewarded me quite a dull existence in the wide swampy valleys of the rivers, where I did most of my research.

I love the nature of the North with its silent gloom, the monotony of unsophisticated colors – I like it just for its primitive isolation and wilderness that is peculiar to it, and I would never exchange it for the pictorial brightness of the south, which is invasive to the soul. In moments of longing for freedom and nature – and such moments happen to every participant of scientific expeditions when living in a big city becomes difficult – gray rocks, a leaden sea, mighty larches with broken tops, and gloomy thick spruce forests appear before my eyes...

In short, I was happy with the monotonous landscape that surrounded me and gladly fulfilled my task.

However, I received another assignment – to inspect some excellent asbestos deposits in the middle of the Katun, near the great village of Chyemal. The shortest path to this place led me across the highest parts in Altai, across the Katunski Ridge through the valley of upper Katun. After reaching the village of Uymon, I had to cross the Terektynskie Bielki – also a high ridge – and through Onguday again to return to the Katun valley. Despite the need to hurry, forced into long, daily treks, it was only on this road that I experienced the true charm of Altai's nature.

I remember very well the moment when with my small caravan, after a long journey through the Urman – a dense fir, cedar, and larch forest – I went down to the Katun valley. A large, deep bog slowed us for a long time at this point. The horses sank up to their bellies in a lapping, brown swamp, hidden under vegetative layer. We struggled with difficulty about every ten meters, so I decided not to stop the caravan in this place for the night, and instead, we continued to cross the difficult terrain throughout that day until we reached the right bank of the Katun.

The moon rose early over the mountains, and it was easy to make headway. When we reached the edge of the Katun, we were welcomed by the monotonous noise of the fast river. In the moonlight, the river seemed very wide, but when the guide rode his roan horse into the humming, murky water, and the rest of us followed, it turned out that the water did not reach above the horses' knees, so we easily crossed to the opposite bank.

Having passed the floodplain covered with large pebbles, we again came across another swamp called the 'Karagaynik' by the Siberians. Haggard spruce trees were scattered over a soft carpet of moss, and everywhere around were tall clumps on which the prolific hard sedge rustled. In a place such as this, the horses would be forced to be without food all night – so, I decided to move on.

The road led upward, which made it possible to hope to get to a dry place. The path disappeared into the dark black of the spruce forest, and the horses' legs stuck in the soft carpet of moss. We persevered through this terrain for an hour and a half until the forest thinned; now firs and cedars dominated, and the moss disappeared almost completely – but the path upwards persisted and became even steeper. No matter how much we encouraged each other after our already hard trek and troubles of the day, these last two hours of climbing seemed very difficult. Therefore, everyone was delighted when the horses' shoes finally clattered on stones, and the almost flat top of the mountain range appeared. Finally, there was a place with grasses for the horses and a dry place suitable for tents. We immediately untied the horses, set up our tents under huge cedars, and after the usual ritual of absorbing a bucket of tea and smoking pipes, we sank into a deep sleep.

I was awakened by a bright light, so I quickly got out of the tent. A fresh breeze rippled the dark green branches of the cedars that rose up before the entrance of the tent.

Between the two trees, to the left, there was a wide gap. As if seated within a black frame, the light contours of four sharp white peaks hung in it against the background of pinkish, pure light. The air was surprisingly clear. On the steep slopes covered with eternal snow flowed every imaginable combination of light shades of red. A little lower, on the convex surface of a blue glacier, were huge, sloping stripes of navy-blue shadows. This blue foundation further enhanced the impression of the airy lightness of mountain environments, which seemed to radiate with their own light, while the sky that appeared among them looked like a sea of pure gold. Over the next few minutes as I watched, the sun rose higher, the gold acquired a purple hue, the pink tinge of the peaks disappeared and changed to pure blue, and the glacier sparkled with silver.

The metal and wooden bells that hung around the horses' necks – known locally as the botala – rang as the workers shouted under the trees preparing the horses for the journey ahead. While they busied themselves packing and tying leather bags, I still admired the dance of the morning magic light show. After the closed horizon of the taiga paths, the wild rocky austerity of the bare tundra, this was a whole new world of transparent radiance and a delusive play of sunlight.

As you can see, my first love for highlands of Altai's eternal snow exploded, unexpectedly and intensely. This love did not bring me further disappointments either but gave me all new impressions. I can't describe the feelings that were born at the sight of the extraordinary clarity of the blue or emerald water of mountain lakes or the glittering brilliance of sapphire ice. I would just like to say that the view of the snowy mountains enhanced my sensitivity to the beauty of nature. These almost musical transitions of light, shadows, and colors conveyed to the world the bliss of harmony. And I, a mere human, succumbed to a completely different mood in the mountain world, and my discovery, which I will tell you about right now, I owe to some extent to these exalted feelings.

After crossing the alpine part of the route, I descended again into the Katun Valley, then to the Uymonski Steppe – a flat valley with excellent feed for the horses, but the landscape here did not provide me with any interesting geological observations. Once we reached Onguday, I sent my assistant to Biysk with the collections and equipment. A visit to the Chyemal asbestos deposits wouldn't require any special equipment. So, together with a guide and on fresh horses, we soon reached Katun and stopped to rest in the village of Kayancha.

The tea with fragrant honey was especially tasty, and we sat for a long time at a clean, white table in a garden. My guide, a sullen and silent Ojrot – the name for the people who live in Altai – puffed on a copper-clad pipe. I asked the host about the sights ahead of us on the way to Chyemal. The owner, a young teacher with a sincere and open, tanned face, willingly satisfied my curiosity.

"I'll tell you something else, comrade engineer," he said. "Not far from Chyemal, you'll find a village where our great artist, Chorosov, lives. Surely, you've heard about him. He's a grumpy old man, but if he takes a liking to you, he'll show you everything, and his paintings are truly magnificent!"

I recalled the images of Chorosov that I'd already seen in Tomsk and Biysk, especially the 'Crown of Katun,' and 'Chan-Altai.' To see the numerous works of Chorosov in his studio, and to purchase of some sketch would be a good conclusion of my acquaintance with Altai.

In the middle of the next day, I saw a wide ravine as described by the teacher, off to the right side of the road. A few new houses, shining with light yellow wood, were scattered on a hill at the foot of larches. Everything corresponded exactly to the description given by the Kayancha teacher, so I confidently directed my horse to the house of artist Chorosov.

I expected to see a surly old man and I was surprised when an agile, clean-shaven man appeared on the porch with quick and precise movements. It was only after a closer look at his yellowish Mongolian face that I noticed the gray in his wild, unkempt hair and rough mustache. Deep wrinkles lined his sunken cheeks, under prominent cheekbones, while he had a prominent, high forehead. He received me kindly, but I can't say exactly welcoming, so I followed him, somewhat embarrassed.

It was probably only as a result of my sincere admiration for the beauty of Altai that Chorosov became friendlier. His succinct stories about some of the particularly remarkable places of Altai were clearly recalled by me, so precise was his observation.

His studio was a large room with unpainted walls and large windows and occupied half the house. Among the multitude of sketches and small paintings, one caught my attention and immediately interested me. According to

Chorosov's explanation, this was his personal copy of 'Deny-Der' – the 'Lake of the Mountain Ghosts' – and the original, on a large canvas is located in one of the Siberian museums.

I will describe this small canvas thoroughly because it is very important for understanding what followed.

The picture shone with strong colors in the rays of the setting sun. The bluish-gray depth of the lake occupying the central part of the painting breathed a cold and silent peace. In the foreground, by the stones on the flat bank where the green ridge of grass was interspersed with the stains of pure snow, lay a swiss pine trunk. A large, blue ice sheet touched the shore just at the very roots of a fallen tree. Small ice floes and large, gray stones cast greenish, gray-blue shades over the surface of the lake. Two low, wind-torn cedars raised their dense branches as if they were arms raised up to the sky. In the background, snow-white steep hills of jagged mountains with rocky ridges of violet and straw color fell straight into the lake. In the center of the painting, the blue, crumbling wall of the glacier sank into the lake and above it, at a towering height, rose a diamond pyramid from which a veil of pink clouds swirled to the left. To the left edge of this valley, beside the trough with very steep sides that remained from the passage of the glacier, was a mountain in the shape of a regular cone, almost entirely dressed in a snow mantle. The mountain rested on a wide foundation, whose stone terraces, like a colossal staircase, led to the far end of the lake...

The whole picture was full of emptiness and a cold, sparkling purity that had already captivated me on my way through the Katun Ridge. I stood for a long time staring at the true face of the Altai's eternal snows, admiring the subtlety of the observation of the people who gave the lake the name 'Deny-Der' – 'Lake of the Mountain Ghosts.'

"Where did you find such a lake?" I asked. "Does it really exist?"

"The lake exists, and I must admit that it is actually even more beautiful in reality. My merit is in the correct expression of the essence of the impression," answered Chorosov. "This essence was not cheap for me... Well, but to find this lake isn't easy, although it is possible, of course. But why do you need to find it? Is it necessary to mark it on the map? I know you!"

"No, I just to visit such a beautiful place. When you see something like that, you'd even stop fearing death."

The artist looked at me searchingly.

"It has been said, that a 'man ceases to be afraid of death,'" he slowly responded. "You probably don't know what legends among the Oyrots are associated with this lake."

"Apparently very interesting, since they called the lake so poetically."

"Have you noticed anything here?" Chorosov asked as he turned his gaze to the picture.

"I noticed something here, in the left corner, where this cone-shaped mountain rises," I pointed out. "Forgive me, but these colors seem completely unnatural to me."

"Well, look at it even more carefully..."

I began to stare again, and the subtlety of the artist's work was so great that the longer I looked, the more details seemed to emerge from the depths of the picture. At the foot of the cone-shaped mountain, there was a greenish-white cloud radiating with a faint light. The intersecting reflections of this light and the glittering snow on the water formed long strands of shadows, for some reason in the red hues. The same marks were visible in the rock cliffs, only darker up to a bloody tone. In those places where the perpendicular rays of the sun penetrated from behind the white wall of the mountain ridge, long pillars of bluish-green smoke or fumes, like huge human fingers, appeared over the ice and stones, giving an ominous and fantastic view to this landscape.

"I don't understand," I said, pointing at the bluish-green poles.

"And don't try to understand," smiled Chorosov. "You know nature well and love her, but you do not believe her."

"And how do you explain how these red lights in the rocks, these bluish-green pillars, and those glowing clouds?"

"The explanation is simple – mountain ghosts," the artist answered calmly.

I looked at him but didn't notice even the shadow of a smile on his closed face.

"I'm not joking," he continued in the same tone. "Do you think that the lake was given its name just because of its unearthly beauty? Beauty is beauty, but it has a bad name! Oh, even when I painted this picture, I barely managed to walk away. I was there in 1909, and I was still sick until 1913..."

I asked the artist to tell me about the legends associated with the lake, so we went and sat down in a corner on a wide sofa which stood on a thick, yellow-blue Mongolian carpet. From my position, I could still look at the 'Lake of the Mountain Ghosts.'

"The beauty of this place," Chorosov began, "has long attracted everyone, but some strange forces have often brought destruction to the visitors. I also felt the terrible influence of the lake in person, but more on that later. Interestingly, the lake is most beautiful on warm summer days, and that's when its destructive force is most pronounced.

"The story goes, that as soon as the people saw the blood-red light on the rocks and the flickering of bluish-green, transparent pillars, they began to experience strange sensations. The surrounding snowy peaks seem to crush down like a monstrous weight on their heads, and irresistible dances of light rays played out before their eyes. The people became drawn to a round, cone-shaped mountain, where the bluish-green ghosts of the mountain spirits danced around the greenish, glowing cloud. But as soon as they reached that place, everything disappeared, and only the gloomy, bare rocks keep guard. Gasping, barely moving their legs from a sudden loss of strength, the tormented souls, the unfortunates, barely managed to escape that fatal place, but death followed them, anyway. Only a few strong hunters, after incredible agony, reached the nearest yurt. Some of them died while others were seriously ill for a long time, having lost their former strength and courage.

"Ever since then, the notorious reputation of Lake Deny-Der has spread widely, and people have almost stopped visiting it. There is neither beast nor birds there, and on the left bank where the gathering of spirits takes place, nothing grows, not even grass.

"I heard about this legend even as a child, and I was long drawn to visit this country possessed of mountain spirits. Twenty years ago, I spent two days there in utter loneliness. On the first day, I didn't notice anything special, and I worked for a long time doing my sketches. However, thick clouds moved in across the sky changing the lighting, and as a result, I couldn't capture the clarity of the mountain air.

"So, I decided to stay one more day and spend the night in the forest half a mile from the lake. By evening I felt a strange burning sensation in my mouth which made me slightly nauseous and spit all the time. Usually, I tolerate the higher altitudes well, so I was surprised that this time the thin air was affecting me like that.

"A wonderful morning the next day promised great weather. Oddly, however, I experienced a great weakness and had a heavy head as I dragged myself back to the lake, but soon I was absorbed in my work and forgot about everything. The sun had warmed the area nicely by the time I'd finished my sketching, which later served as the main basis of the picture. I pushed back the easel to take a last look at the lake.

"I was very tired. My hands shook, my head hurt, and I was dizzy, and continued to feel nauseous. It was at that moment I saw the spirits of the lake. This ghostly shadow, almost like a cloud, shimmered over the transparent surface of the water. The sun's rays that crossed the lake at an oblique angle became brighter as light does after passing eclipse. On the receding border of light and shadow, I suddenly noticed several pillars of a ghostly, bluish-green color, similar to huge human figures in cloaks.

They stood motionless, to begin with, then suddenly moved quickly before melting into the air. I looked at this unprecedented phenomenon with a feeling of oppressive fear and anxiety.

"The silent movements of the ghosts continued for several minutes, then flashes of the bloody color glared among the rocks. And above all this, floated a mushroom-shaped cloud glowing in a faint green light...

"Suddenly I felt a surge of strength, my eyesight sharpened, and the distant rocks seemed to move towards me! I could distinguish the smallest of details of their steep slopes. I grabbed my brush, picked up my paints, and with wild energy, I tried to capture this extraordinary picture with hurried strokes.

"A light breeze swept over the lake, and instantly the cloud and the bluish-green ghosts disappeared. Only the red lights in the rocks continued to glitter gloomily, scattering on the water in the shadows cast by the rocks. The excitement that had engulfed me weakened, my indisposition sharply intensified, and I felt as if my life force was leaking out of my fingertips holding the palette and the brush. I got a strong premonition that something wasn't right, and it told me to hurry. I closed the sketchbook and collected my belongings, feeling that a terrible weight was falling on my chest and head...

"The wind at the lake increased, and its translucent blue mirror faded. Clouds covered the peaks of the mountains, and the bright, crisp colors of the surroundings quickly dulled. The spiritual and pure beauty of the lake turned into a gloomy sadness, the red reflections in the location of the ghosts extinguished, and only the dark rocks blackened among the snow patches. My breathing became heavy and whistled in my chest, when I, struggling with my loss of strength and an overwhelming sensation burdening me, turned my back to the lake. I struggled along like in a foggy dream, down the path to the place where, by agreement, my guides who'd refused to accompany me to Deny-Der were waiting for me. The mountains swayed in front of me, and fits of vomiting brought me to exhaustion. At times, I fell and lay for a long time, unable to continue, without the strength to arise. I don't remember how I got to my guides, and it doesn't matter. The most important thing was that the box tied onto my back, containing my sketches, was saved.

"My guides saw what was happening to me from afar. They carried me to the camp, laid me on my back, and slipped a sack under my head.

"'You will die, Chorosov,' the senior guide said to me in a tone more like that of an impartial observer.

"And, as you can see, I didn't die, but I felt so bad for a long time. The lethargy and a dulled vision interfered with my living and working. I painted the large painting 'Deny-Der' only a year later, working on it only a bit at a time, between bouts of bedrest. It took its toll and cost me a lot to get the truth about Lake Deny-Der and the ghosts that inhabited it."

Chorosov fell silent.

Quite some time had passed, and I could just make out a small valley submerged in twilight through a little window. I'd been extremely interested in the story, and I had no reason to doubt the words of the artist, but at the same time, I couldn't find any explanation for the wonderful phenomena, preserved in the colors of his work.

We made our way into his dining room. A bright lamp that hung over the table dispersed fantastic shadows, almost as if inspired by his strange story. I couldn't resist and just had to ask how to find the Lake of the Mountain Ghosts in case I was ever to be in that area.

"Aha, this lake has interested you!" Chorosov smiled. "Well, go there if you're not afraid. Write this down."

I took out a notebook and a pencil from my backpack.

"Deny-Der is in the Katunski Ridge, at its eastern end. There's a deep gorge between Chuyski and the Katunski snowy peaks. About forty kilometers upstream from the Argut estuary, you'll find the place where it meets the smaller Juneur River. This place is notable because the Argut twists here and the mouth of Juneur leads to a wide, flat valley. From this river mouth, you go up Argut on along the left bank – count off some six kilometers – and then to your right, you'll find a stream, or if you prefer, a small river, which flows through a very wide valley and cuts deep into the Katunski Ridge. You have to go along this valley. This is a dry place, and the larches spread very wide. When you get in quite high, you will come across a large, steep crevasse with a small waterfall; here the valley turns to the right. The bottom of the valley will be completely flat, wide, and on it, you'll find a chain of five lakes, each distant from each other by some half a mile, and some about a whole. The last, fifth lake, where there is no further passage – is Deny-Der. That's all; just be careful and do not mistake the gorges because there are many valleys and lakes everywhere... Oh, I've just remembered a that will help you! At the mouth of the stream, where you turn from Argut, there is a small swamp, and on its left bank, stood a huge withered larch, devoid of branches, with a trunk split like a devil's pitchfork. If it still stands, it will be a signpost for you."

I wrote down Chorosov's directions, unaware of the significance they would mean to me in the future.

In the morning I looked through the other works of Chorosov, but none of them could match 'Deny-Der.' Realizing the immense value of the painting, I didn't even dare to hint about the possibility of buying it with my very modest means. Instead, I bought two sketches of snowy mountains, and I also received a small pen drawing as a gift, which depicted my favorite larches, reproduced with a deep knowledge of the nature of this tree.

At our parting, Chorosov told me:

"I see how you look 'Deny-Der,' but I can't give you this. I will give you a sketch done by me at the lake. But..." he paused for a moment, "only after my death; right now, it's hard for me to part with it. But do not worry, it will be soon... then it will be sent it to you," the artist added seriously, with his intimidating indifference.

Having wished Chorosov a long life, and myself – to see him again soon, I mounted my horse, and fate, as it turned out, separated us forever.

***

But, as it turned out, a long time passed before I got back to Altai. Four years of hard work went by, and only in the fifth year I was given a longer vacation. Bad rheumatism – an occupational disease of the taiga men – knocked me off my feet for nearly half a year, and then I had to deal with a weakened heart.

Tired of forced inactivity and boredom, I escaped from the southern health resort to a cloudy but nice Leningrad. At the suggestion of the chief management, I took up mercury deposit research in Sefidkis in Central Asia. I hoped to get rid of the disease that plagued me in the sunny lands of Turkestan, and then return to the harsh savagery of the North, which had captivated me forever. This attachment consumed me so completely that I could hardly control the attacks of acute longing for Siberia.

One warm, spring evening while I was sitting at home looking down a microscope, I was brought a package that upset me more than it pleased me. In a flat box made of smooth cedar slats, lay the sketch of 'Deny-Der' – the sign that told me that the artist Chorosov had finished his working life. When I saw the 'Lake of the Mountain Ghosts' again, memories flooded over me.

The distant and inaccessible beauty of Deny-Der filled me with dreadful sadness. I tried to dispel this overwhelming sadness by immersing myself back into my work. I put a new ore specimen from Sefidkan under the microscope, and with a skilled hand, I lowered the tube with the adjusting screw, adjusted the focus with the micrometer, and resumed studying the sequences of the mercury ore crystallization. The polished mineral plate was almost pure vermilion, and somehow, it didn't matter – I couldn't examine it. Subtle shades of colors reflected from the thin section were concealed by the electric light. I replaced the pack-illuminator with a Silverman's side light and turned on the fluorescent lamp – an excellent invention that replaces the sun in the narrowed world of the microscope...

The Lake of the Mountain Ghosts still did not give me peace of mind, and at first, I wasn't even surprised when I saw in the microscope the same blood-red reflections on a bluish-steel background that had surprised me in the painting. It took me a moment to realize that I wasn't looking at the picture but watching the inner reflections of the mercury ore. I turned the base of the microscope, and then the blood-red streaks flickered, dimming, or turning into a deeper, brownish-red tone, while most of the surface of the mineral continued to glisten with a cold, steel glow. Touched by a premonition of an unrecognized discovery, I directed the beam of the fluorescent lamp to the image of the 'Lake of the Mountain Ghosts,' and saw among the rocks at the foot of the cone-shaped mountain exactly the same shades of color that I had just seen through the microscope.

I quickly grabbed the color tables, and it soon turned out that the colors in the patterns...

But why these same patterns here?! I could only say that for minerography – the study of ores of various metals and the same metals – color tables of the most subtle shades of all imaginable colors, numbering around seven hundred, have been created. Each of the shades has its own designation, and the sum of shades creates the spectrum of the mineral. So, it's turned out that the colors Chorosov used in his depiction of the 'Lake of the Mountain Ghosts,' according to these tables, closely corresponded to the shades of cinnabar in different lighting conditions, angles of incidence, and all the other complex play of light in science, called interference of the light waves. The mystery of Lake Deny-Der suddenly became clear to me. I just wondered why it hadn't occurred to me a long time ago, when I was still there, in the Altai mountains.

I called a taxi by phone and soon found myself in front of a fence, behind which the large windows of the chemical laboratory shone. My acquaintance – a chemist and metallurgist – was still there.

"How are you, Siberian bear!" he greeted me. "What brings you here? An urgent analysis again?"

"No, Dmitry Mikhailovich, I've come to you for help. What can you tell me about mercury?"

"Oh, mercury – it is such a special metal that you could write a thick book about it! What do you mean? Explain yourself more clearly!"

"So, mercury boils at three hundred and seventy degrees, and evaporates at how many?"

"All the time, dear engineer, except when under extreme cold."

"Is it so volatile?"

"Extremely volatile for its genre weight. Remember: at twenty degrees of heat in a cubic meter saturated with mercury vapor – fifteen-hundredths of a gram, and at a hundred degrees – already almost two and a half grams!"

"One more question: the mercury vapor itself, does it shine or not, and if so, what color?"

"It doesn't shine itself, but sometimes with a strong concentration of transmitted light, it gives blue-greenish shades. And if there are electric discharges in the rarefied air, it glows greenish-white..."

"Got it! Thank you, I'm extremely grateful."

After five minutes, I knocked on my doctor's door. He's a good, old man, and he looked worried as he stepped into the hall, recognizing my voice.

"What happened? Is it your heart again?"

"Oh, no, no, my heart is fine! I only here for a moment. I wondered if you could tell me what are the main symptoms of mercury poisoning?"

"Hmm, in general, mercury: salivation, vomiting, and as for the gases, I'll go check... Come in, please."

"No, I'm just here for a moment. I'll wait here, dear Pavel Nikolaevich!"

The old man went to the office and returned a minute later with an open book in his hand.

"Here you are, mercury vapor: a drop in blood pressure, strong arousal of the psyche, rapid, intermittent breathing, and the death from heart paralysis."

"This is great!" I couldn't hold back.

"What's great? Death like that?"

However, I only laughed, childishly rejoicing at the bewilderment of the doctor, and ran down the stairs. Now I knew that my reasoning was undoubtedly right.

After returning home, I called the head of Glavka institution and announced that in the interests of our work, I needed to go to Altai immediately. I asked him to delegate Krasulin to me, a young graduate whose physical strength and good head was very necessary for me in my still current and painful condition.

***

By mid-May, it was already possible to reach the lake without any problems. It was at this time, when Krasulin and I, and two other experienced taiga workers, left the village of Yin on the Chuisk Road.

I remembered all the instructions of the late artist about the upcoming journey, and most importantly, I carried my old, tattered field book with the route recorded directly from Chorosov's words in my side pocket.

In the evening, my small unit pitched the tent on a dry rise at the mouth of the valley against a dry, pitchfork-like, withered larch. I felt, not without some excitement, that my assumptions would be confirmed tomorrow – either was the reasoning dictated by my imagination, right? Or the invention of something even more unlikely than the fabulous ghosts of an Oyrot artist? Krasulin was also excited and squatted next to me on the hill where I was thoughtfully contemplating the horned larch.

"Vladimir Yevgenyevich!" he began quietly. "If you remember... you promised to tell me about the purpose of our trip once we got to the mountains."

"I hope that not later than tomorrow we'll discover a large deposit of large mercury, maybe even partially self-sustaining. Tomorrow we'll see if I'm right or not. You know that mercury is usually found in a diffuse state, in small concentrations. Large deposits with a rich content of mercury are known only in one place in the world, in..."

"In Almadena in Spain", prompted Krasulin.

"Yes, Almadena. They've supplied half of the world's mercury requirements for many centuries. Once a tiny lake of pure mercury was found there. Well, I'm hoping to find something similar. That we'll find entire cliffs almost entirely made up of cinnabar here, I'm convinced of this, if only..."

"But, Vladimir Yevgenyevich, if we discover such deposits, this would be a coup in the mercury economy!"

"Yes, it's very expensive! Mercury is also the most important metal in electrical engineering and medicine. Well, now – sleep, sleep! Tomorrow, we'll rise before dawn. It seems that the day will be overcast, and that's what we need."

"Why is an overcast day so important?" asked Krasulin.

"Because I don't want to poison any of you or myself. Mercury vapor is no joke. The proof is that the discovery of these deposits has been delayed for hundreds of years precisely because of the deadly properties of the mercury gases. Tomorrow we'll battle the mountain ghosts of Deny-Der, and then we will see..."

A haze of pink mist clouded the ridges, and the valley had darkened. Only the sharp mountain peaks, covered with their eternal snows, shone for a long time in the invisible rays of the sun... then they also went out. A gray curtain covered the mountains. Stars glittered through the cloudy sky, and I still sat by the fire. Finally, I mastered my excitement and went to sleep.

I don't know why, but I only remember all the events of the next day fragmentarily.

I clearly remember the vast, flat bottom of the valley between the third and fourth lakes. In the middle of the valley, like a plain, green carpet, was a mossy swamp without a single tree, but large cedars rose along the edges. These cedars were devoid of branches on one side while extending powerful branches towards the Lake of the Mountain Ghosts – like mourning banners on high poles. Low, gloomy clouds quickly passed over the cedars, as if they hurried to the mysterious lake.

The fourth lake was small and round. From the bluish-gray water, covered with tiny ripples, protruded a ridge of sharp rocks. Once we passed by them, we then entered a dense thicket of cedar shale, and after another ten minutes, we stood on the shore of the Lake of the Mountain Ghosts. The sad, gray mist obscured the water and snowy slopes of the mountain range. Nevertheless, I immediately recognized this as the temple of the mountain ghosts, which had captured my imagination a few years ago in Chorosov's studio.

Reaching the rocks that shimmered with steel flashes at the foot of the cone-shaped mountain turned out to be a daunting task. However, all the difficulties were immediately forgotten by us when the geological hammer with its characteristic ring hit the first heavy piece of cinnabar off the edge of the cliff. Sloped steps lead further down the cliff to a small depression, over which a light mist curled. The hollow was filled with muddy, hot water, bubbling up from hot springs around the deep clefts, which shrouded the edges of the depression with a mist.

I instructed Krasulin to take a picture of this section of the ore deposit, while I went with one of the workers through the veil of fog to the foot of the mountain.

"What is there, comrade chief?" the worker suddenly asked me.

I looked in the direction indicated. Half hidden by a rocky ridge, a mercury lake gleamed with a dull and ominous glow — the product of my imagination. The surface of the lake seemed to be convex. With indescribable excitement, I leaned over its elastic surface and immersing my hand in the elusive and unyielding fluid, I thought of several thousand tons of liquid metal – my gift to my homeland.

Krasulin, who came to my call, froze in silent delight. However, it was necessary to temper my enthusiasm and hurry my companions to carry out their necessary work as quickly as possible. Already, I'd begun to feel the burning in my mouth and throbbing in my head – the sinister signs of the onset of poisoning.

So, I snapped pictures to my left and right with Leica's camera, and the laborer filled the flasks with mercury from the lake. Krasulin and the second worker hurriedly measured the outcrops of the ore deposits and the size of the lake. It seemed that everything was done at lightning speed, but we still walked back slowly, sluggishly, struggling with the growing feeling of oppression and anxiety. While we were barely walking around the left bank of the lake, the clouds parted, and a faceted diamond peak appeared before our eyes. The slanting rays of the sun broke through the gates of the distant ravine, and the entire Dena-Der valley was filled with a sparkling, transparent light. Turning around, I saw bluish-green ghosts flickering in the place we'd just left. Fortunately, the bank gradually leveled off, and we soon got to the horses.

"Now ride, boys!" I called, turning back my horse.

On that same day, we rode down the valley to the second lake. By dust, the limbs of the cedars seemed threatening and to stretched out towards us, trying to keep us.

At night, we felt unwell, but in general, everything had gone well.

There's not much left to tell. The magic lake has given, and still gives the Soviet Union all the mercury it needs to satisfy all the demands of our multilateral industries.

And I have forever retained the grateful memory of a true artist, a fearless seeker of the soul of the mountains.

DIAMOND MINE

Irritated, the commander-in-chief pushed away the ashtray filled with cigarette butts and looked indignantly at the interlocutor.

The other man, thin, small, and gray-bearded, drowned in a large leather armchair, cowering and clutching his legs. His eyes gleamed through his glasses with uncompromising tenacity.

"The Evenk expedition is working for the third year now – and still no results!" said the chief.

"What do you mean, none? What about the kimberlites?"

"Speaking of that, about the kimberlites. Do you know that the Academician Chernyavsky gave a negative conclusion about them? He said that those deposits were just coarse-grained igneous rock with no diamonds inside. In fact, he doesn't even recognize those rocks as kimberlite. And in general, Sergei Yakovlevich, I personally understand everything. This is a huge, almost unexplored country. Expeditions are expensive, especially after you added detours to it – and there are no results. I strongly insist on the termination of the work! Our institute has many more urgent tasks, and the expenditure of large allocations for this kind of research is at the expense of others. On this end..." The commander-in-chief, frowning in displeasure, threw a cigarette.

The director of the institute, Professor Ivashentsev, sitting in the chair opposite, straightened up sharply:

"You are stopping the business, which should bring in millions to the country, and not only to the economy but also direct income from exports!"

"This business has so far only disappointed. However, I already said that everything is clear for me. My decision is final." The chief stood up.

Next to him, the professor seemed very small and defenseless. He silently got up from his chair and straightened his glasses. Then he muttered something unintelligible and handed the chief a round stone.

"I've already seen this," he said dryly. "The Moyero River, the Moyero River!" Three years I've heard this! And you also showed me this Grikvaitic rock."

The professor hunched over his briefcase, fastening the clasp and lock.

The chief began to feel sorry for the scientist. He approached Ivashentsev.

"Sergei Yakovlevich, you must admit that I am right. But, sorry, I don't understand your perseverance in this matter..."

"Any work," Ivashentsev interrupted, "is easier to manage when you treat it impartially. And I can not be impartial. You see, I am confident in this matter, with all my heart! Only huge unexplored, inaccessible spaces stand between the theoretical conclusion and real evidence. You will say, of course, that this is already enough for failure. Yes, I know, state money and all that!" The professor began to get angry, although the chief didn't even think to protest. "Do you know the iron law of the economics? To earn a million, you need to spend seven hundred thousand! But we, in fact, expect tens, hundreds of millions, just waiting..." And with those words, he headed for the door.

The chief looked after him and shook his head.

Returning to the institute, Professor Ivashentsev ordered his secretary to immediately get the head of the production department for him.

"What is your latest information from Churilin?" he asked when he entered the office.

"The last information was a month ago, Sergei Yakovlevich."

"I know that. Is there any news?"

"No, not yet."

"Where do you think they could be now?"

"Churilin reported on their arrival at Lake Chiringda, from the trading post. They've walked down Chiringrad to Khatanga, and from there they had to cross the peak of Moyero. They may have already completed this route and be approaching the Turin Cultural Base — that was their plan. But a plan is one thing, and the taiga is another..."

"Yes, I know this very well, thank you."

Left alone, Professor Ivashentsev leaned back in his chair and pondered. Before his mind's eye, a map of a vast area appeared between the Yenisei and Lena. Somewhere in the center of it, in the chaos of the low mountains, cut through by countless rivers and covered with a continuous swampy forest, there was an expedition sent there for... a dream. The professor took a stone out of his briefcase — the one which he'd shown to the head of the central board. The small piece of dark rock was dense and heavy. Numerous crystals of pyrope – red garnet – sparkled in small drops over the coarse-grained surface of the sample, and inclusions of olivine were cast with clean, fresh greens. These crystals were clearly distinguished against a light bluish-green background of the mass of chrome-diopside. Tiny cornflower lights glittered here and there. The stone fascinated the eye with its motley combination of pure colors. The professor turned the sample to the other side, where on a smear of white enamel paint stood the inscription: 'Moyero River, southern slope of Anaon mountains, Tolmachev expedition, 1915.'

This grikvaite is typical in South Africa! Neither in the Anaon mountains nor in the valley of Moyero did we find even signs of such rocks. And this year again, failure: Churilin is silent. So, the dream did not come true, Ivashentsev sighed as he thought to himself.

He weighed the stone on his hand, before locking it in the bottom drawer of his desk. Then, with resolve, he picked up the phone of the internal telephone system.

"Send Churilin a telegram: 'If there are no results, cancel the expedition, return immediately...' Yes, I will sign it myself. Otherwise, he won't listen. Where? At the Turin camp. Well, of course, on the radio, through Dixon."

He replaced the handset effectively cutting off the conversation, and all the possibilities for implementing his long-standing dream. He took off his glasses and covered his eyes with his hand.

Ivashentsev had dreamed, at least in his declining years, to mount a study of the deep zones of the earth's crust by drilling special wells. But even the first steps to solving the problem – the pursuit of a dream hidden in the forests and marshes of the Central Siberian plateau – were in vain. Apparently, life had taught him nothing, and in his sixth decade, the professor remained a dreamer, striving for too large a scope of research.

***

Telegraph signals rushed from Moscow to the northeast – over the tundra of the North, the cold expanses of the Arctic Ocean – and reached the high masts of the radio station on a bare island. Two hours later, new radio waves sped south from here, past the Byrranga Ridge, the Pyasina Marshes, and swept over the endless forests. At the Turin radio station, the telephone clattered, and the radio waves were imprinted in a short phrase, clearly written on a blue letterhead.

"Do you have any of the Kravunchan Evenks, Vasya?"

"Why?"

"An urgent telegram for the Churilin expedition. They're at the top of the Korvunchan about now.

"There are no Korvunchanskys, but Innokenty will go to Bugarikht tomorrow. The guy is good, he'll do fifty kilometers extra, if you ask him."

"Let's go look for him together. I'll give him the telegram right away."

***

Twilight fell over the broad valley of the Nikuorak River, three hundred miles from the Turin base camp. The gentle slopes bristled with a spruce forest, gloomily black beneath, while it was still quite light on a flat hill, which blocked off the round swamp from the north. Between the rare larches were four dark green tents, and in front of them on a flattened area covered with light gray deer moss, a bonfire smoldered, barely alight. The thick brown smoke exuded a sharp, stupefying smell of wild rosemary as it wafted on the calm air. On the right side of the site stood a pile of packed boxes, a bag, bales, and saddles. A cloud of midges and mosquitoes hung around the fire, behind the backs of people. Those who sat by the fire tried to keep their heads in the pockets of clean air, which made it possible to breathe and at the same time relieve the persistent irritation from the smoke to their eyes, nose, and ears of the nemesis.

"Tea is ready!" proclaimed a black man, thoroughly saturated by the smoke. He removed a large bucket full of dark-brown liquid from the fire.

Each of those who sat around the fire, armed with a large mug, took a huge piece of Tungus flat cake – a heavy and dense kind of bread concentrate. Moss which blew around landed on the edges of the mugs, covered the surface of hot tea with a gray bloom. The people sipped their tea with pleasure and engaged in small-talk.

A rare and measured distant chime wove through the tinkling sounds of the horse nearby.

"Listen, comrades! That's not ours – let's go!"

The young people rushed to the tents for their guns. The meeting of detachments of one expedition after a long separation was always a solemn moment in the life of taiga explorers. Twilight had not yet managed to deepen as a chain of thin, tired horses appeared on a large clearing of the northern slope of the watershed, sluggishly rising upwards. Scuffed packs, tied with weathered ropes, testified to a long journey through dense thickets.

Shots rumbled. The arrivals responded with a discordant volley. A gloomy, large man approached the tents – the geophysicist Samarin, head of the pendulum detachment. He climbed down heavily from his horse. His neck was somehow wrapped in a dirty bandage. He lifted a black mesh from his face and stepped toward the expedition leader Churilin, a tall, clean-shaven man.

"Hello, Comrade Churilin," Samarin said hollowly, in response to the friendly greeting of the commander.

"That's good, just in time for tea! Well, what's interesting?"

"There is something. It's been a hard journey... I fell ill, lost three horses..."

"What's wrong with you?"

"Some kind of rubbish – a midge bit me, and it's caused inflammation around the bite."

"Dang! Has it scabbed?"

"No, I wouldn't scratch it!" Samarin growled angrily in response to Churilin's reproachful look. "My skin isn't as tanned as yours. Now I don't know how I'll manage on the next part of the route."

Churilin gave the order to give everyone a little of the precious supply of alcohol once the other new arrivals settled down by the campfire. Loud, happy voices interrupted each other as the people told stories about their various adventures.

The expedition leader sat down next to the geophysicist, who, after drinking tea and eating, had finally relaxed a little and rejuvenated.

"Modest Afrikanovich, I'd love to hear of your adventures!" he said.

So, Samarin talked about the route he'd traveled – covering a wide area spanning from the Jerome River to the summit of Vilyuchan.

"By going this route, we managed to cover more than twenty measurements of gravity."

"Everywhere there are quite large positive anomalies – sixty, eighty. But in one place I even did three measurements in a row at short distances. It turned out..." The geophysicist paused.

"Don't torment me, Modest Afrikanovich!" Churilin interjected quickly.

Samarin chuckled and continued:

"It turned out two hundred..."

"Wow!"

"Wait... two hundred and seventy, and three hundred and five!"

"Where?" Churilin exclaimed excitedly.

"Amnunnachi... An extensive low plateau... a continuous swamp to the west of Moyerokan."

"Moyerokana! That's it! Selection made!"

The conversation at the campfire subsided, and the newcomers went to sleep. Only the employees of Churilin, who had already rested for four days, remained at the fire, listening with interest to the conversation between the chief and the geophysicist.

"Well, I tortured you, Modest Afrikanovich," Churilin said. "Please excuse me, but I'm sure you need to rest by now. We've already rested up here so much that we don't go to bed before midnight."

Reluctantly, Samarin rose and folded his last cigarette.

Churilin stared intently at his tired, swollen face for some time.

"It's good to be a geophysicist, Modest Afrikanovich," he said, "precise tasks, clear answers – like you, for example."

"You found something to envy!"

Churilin's face was serious.

"I compared our research. I admire the power of geophysics! I'm a bad physicist and even worse mathematician. Perhaps, therefore, like any unfamiliar scientific discipline, your work seems to be much more significant than mine. Look at least from this perspective: the Stukrat device you use for measuring gravity is set at the intended point. Two short, heavy pendulums, equipped with mirrors reflecting the light from the tiny bulbs, swing steadily inside of it. And that's all. Later, you only need to observe the coincidence of the oscillation period of the pendulum with the course of the astronomical clock – the chronometers. But, of course," Churilin realized suddenly, "before that, you still need to carefully align the device, to observe the stars to check the clock. But, in general, how ingeniously simple! The pendulum swings and barely responds to an increase or decrease in gravity in any given place. And in the hands of the geophysicist, this fabulous sword, invisibly dissecting several kilometers into the depth of the rock mass – this is the eye, showing inaccessible underground depths.

Samarin threw a cigarette butt into the fire and grinned.

"On the contrary," he replied. "I clearly see all the helplessness of geophysics, the abundance of unsolved problems, the imperfection of methods. And your geology seems to me, a clearer, more powerful science that has at its disposal an immeasurably greater number of facts... Well, I'm going to sleep."

With the departure of the geophysicist from the fire, silence fell. The top of the flame was edged with a star wreath, the hissing of the smoke was scarcely audible, and the mosquitoes were inexorably buzzing. Down in the valley, the horses still sounded like a rattle.

"Maxim Mikhailovich… can geophysics easily solve what we have been fighting for so long?" the young geologist asked cautiously.

Churilin smiled sadly.

"I didn't speak about the power of geophysics in that sense. We are looking for diamond deposits. Why are we looking for them here? Five years ago, our director first drew attention to the extraordinary similarity between the geology of these places and South Africa. The Middle Siberian and South African plateaus have a strikingly similar geological structure. Here and there, huge eruptions of heavy, deep rocks broke through to the surface. Sergei Yakovlevich believes that the eruptions were simultaneous in our country and in South Africa, where they ended with powerful explosions of gases accumulated at enormous depths. These explosions pierced through the thickness of the rocks a lot of narrow seams, which became diamond deposits. In the space from Kapa to Congo, hundreds of such seams are known, and undoubtedly, a huge number of them are still hidden under the sands of the Kalahari Desert – enough diamonds for the whole world. And you know how necessary they are in industry and for our business – in drilling. Large companies bought up all the deposits. Of the dozen rich seams, only five are developed. The rest are surrounded by high voltage wires and heavily guarded. It is understandable: to put all the deposits into development would sharply reduce the price of diamonds. In the Soviet Union, no significant deposits have been discovered so far, and if we can find such seams, you yourself can understand how important it is!

"Here, on this Central Siberian plateau, everything is surprisingly similar with South Africa with the same type of mineralization – platinum, iron, nickel, and chrome – all except for the diamonds. Sergey Yakovlevich noticed that those areas in South Africa, in which diamond-bearing seams were found, are characterized by positive anomalies of gravity. It is larger than normal because masses of heavy, dense rocks – peridotites and griquaites – rise from the depths to the surface. Anomalies reach up to one hundred and twenty units. Here, in the first year of work with the pendulum, we immediately caught anomalies from forty to a hundred, and now... now there are anomalies of up to three hundred units. So, here we have large clusters of heavy rocks. But it is still far from solving our question. The pendulum confirmed another feature of similarity to South Africa and gave indirect indications of the areas in which diamond deposits may be discovered. I say 'maybe,' but there are as many chances that they will not be found.

"In South Africa, it is easy to look for - there are dry steppes, almost without vegetation, and with vigorous erosion. The first diamonds were found in the rivers. But here we have a sea of forests, swamps, and permafrost, which weakens erosion. All closed. And after three years of work we still have the same thing with which we began: only a mysterious piece of griquaite found in the pebbles of the Moyero River! This rock, a mixture of garnet, olivine, and diopside, is only found in diamond seams in the form of rounded pieces in blue earth containing diamonds. And so, we've examined the whole of the upper Moyero, surveyed a lot of keys and rivers in the basin..."

There was silence around the dying fire. The interlocutors dispersed one by one, while Churilin sat deep in thought. The last flashes of flame cast red gleams on his dry Indian face. Only his assistant, the black-bearded, gypsy-like, Sultanov remained, sitting beside him, leaning on a bag, and sucking on his pipe.

The bucket of the Big Dipper twisted in the black sky – it was approaching the dead of night.

There is not more than a month left until the end of the field season, thought Churilin, *time only for another short expedition... And if we return again with a failure, the work will probably be stopped. In these vast forested mountains dozens of parties are needed, and dozens of years of research. But, in any case, it's necessary to delay the expedition as long as possible. It's necessary to divide up into small groups to have time to examine more routes.*

Suddenly, Churilin and his assistant were alerted to the sound of some small stones rattling on the southern slope. They pricked up their ears as the faint noise approached. Then a dog with sharp, protruding ears, appeared out of the darkness into the light circle of the fire, followed by the sound of the heavy breathing of a reindeer. An Evenk came to the fire, carrying a long-handled, heavy knife, known as a Palma, in his hand. Leaning against it, he easily jumped off the reindeer, and the deer immediately lay down. The Evenk's round face was smiling.

He inquired where the chief was and handed an envelope with a huge wax seal to Churilin.

Churilin thanked the messenger, invited him to eat and promised two bricks of tea. After stoking the fire, Churilin opened the envelope and, unfolding a piece of blue paper, read it. His eyes narrowed and glittered with an unkind spark.

Sultanov looked at him attentively.

"Bad news, Maxim Mikhailovich?" he asked in a low voice.

Instead of replying, Churilin handed him the paper. Sultanov read it and coughed, choking on too deep a puff. They were both silent.

"Well, this is the end..." Sultanov finally said quietly, staring into the fire.

"We will see!" answered Churilin. "Only silence, Arseny Pavlovich."

Churilin took the telegram and threw it into the fire. Then they sat down by the fire. Sultanov took out a piece of paper and began to cover it with calculations. The firewood prepared for the morning was gone by the time Churilin and Sultanov left the dying fire.

***

Churilin woke the camp while it was still dark, just before dawn the next day, and very soon two caravans dispersed in different directions.

One, with twenty-eight horses, stretched out in a long chain between the firs in the valley of Nicuorak heading south towards home, accompanied by the sounds of merry songs.

The remaining four people – Churilin, Sultanov, Peter, their worker, and their guide Nikolai – with five horses loaded to the limit, gave two farewell volleys. They watched the other caravan as it departed for a few minutes before they turned and began to go down the hill in the opposite direction. There, behind rows of monotonously diffuse mountains, the cedar forests of the high plateau in the top of Luluktakan were black...

***

The movement of a pack caravan through the taiga, trekking through unexplored areas, across the 'blank spots' of geographical maps... some would think it to be more romantic than conquering unknown frontiers! However, only thorough organization and firm discipline can ensure the success of such an enterprise. And this means that usually, nothing unforeseen happens: day after day, measured stretches of monotonous hard work, calculated far ahead by the clock. One day differs from the other most often by the number of obstacles overcome and the number of kilometers traveled. During a hard hike, the soul seems to sleep, the impressions of new places slip by hardly touching feelings, and are only mechanically marked by memory. Then, in the easier days or after the evening rest, and even more correctly – after the end of the hike – a chain of impressions forms in the memory. The experience of intimacy with nature enriches the researcher and makes him quickly forget all the adversities before it beckons and calls to him once more.

The hot days came. The sun poured its heavy, dense heat, onto the soft, mossy surface of the swamps, exuding a steamy atmosphere from the moist fumes of rotted moss. The pungent smell of wild rosemary resembled the smell of spicy fermented wine. The heat did not deceive: the senses, which had been sharpened by prolonged communion with nature, sensed the approach of a short northern autumn. Its barely perceptible imprint lay on everything: on the slightly brownish needles of the larch trees, the woefully lowered branches of birches and rowan trees, the woody mushroom caps that had lost their velvety freshness...

The mosquitoes were almost gone, but the midges, as if anticipating their impending doom, rampaged and formed into shimmering reddish-gray clouds.

Churilin's small caravan had now been walking through the vast swamps of Khorpichekan for a long time.

A soulless stillness reigns in the heart of the taiga. The wind is rare here, and a welcome guest when it arrives and drives away the annoying midges. However, while they were on the move, the midge wasn't a terrible problem, following behind the travelers like a cloud. But it was worth stopping from time to time to look around, record observations, and to give the horses a rest, and this was when the cloud of midges would immediately envelop them, stick to their sweaty faces, climb into their eyes, nostrils, ears, and get under their collars. The midges would climb under their clothes, bite their skin around their waist, on the back of their knees and ankles, and cause enough annoyance to bring tears to nervous or impatient people. Therefore, the midge acted as a kind of 'accelerator,' which determined the speed of work at random stops and minimized any delays. And it was only during a long rest when the smoky fires were lit, or a tent was put up, it became possible to take a leisurely look back at the path just traversed.

The horses' hoofs clattered, and the belts and the rings of packs on the saddles creaked. A huge swamp was ahead hidden in the greenish haze of vapor. The weathered branches of dry larches rose above rare and stunted spruces. The concentrated silence in which the detachment moved was sometimes interrupted by languid swearing addressed to this or that horse. However, the horses, well versed in the taiga over the summer, labored on in good faith. Hanging their heads, they walked in a line without any leashes. Evenk Nicholas, in soft wet leggings, a stick in his hand, and a bandana over his shoulders, somehow moved in a crouched position with his knees continuously bent, and quickly crossed ahead of the caravan.

Sultanov walked behind them all. Drops of sweat fell on his opened notebook, and midges stuck to it, leaving vague, pink spots of blood on the pages.

"Are we far from Horpicekan?" Churilin asked his obligatory evening question to the guide.

The cold night had forced everyone to move closer to the fire, spread out on a small dry hill.

"I don't know, we don't go there," answered the guide. "I think it's far away."

Churilin and Sultanov exchanged glances.

"Twenty days already, and we are turning around Amnunnachi," Sultanov said quietly. "Actually, Khorpichekan is the last river."

"Yes," agreed Churilin, "there is no longer any identifying landmarks. All Amnunnachi is a continuous swamp, a low, flat plateau. If Horpichekan doesn't show anything, we'll have to turn around with nothing. Without horses, we could stay... we'd have enough winter."

It was only on the second day that they managed to reach the mysterious Khorpichekan – an unremarkable river with dark water, rapidly flowing between the winding banks. Heavy stems of dense grass hung from the high banks, almost to the water's edge. At a width of not more than three meters, the river was deep.

The firewood from the willow and the bird cherry burned poorly; the bonfire hissed and smoked strongly, dispersing the midges. This inconvenient stop was necessary but what could a deep, marshy river, devoid of any outcrops of bedrock, show? Even pebbles – an indicator of the composition of rocks in the upper reaches of the river – did not gather on a viscous, muddy bottom.

This evening the moon did not shine on a gloomy swamp: the arrival at Khhorpichekan coincided with a change in the weather. Rare dim stars flickered, showing the movement of invisible clouds. By midnight, the silent swamp came alive – the wind whistled, and a rare spell of rain began to fall.

In the morning, the cold mist rose quickly: a sign of bad weather. Without the sun, the gloomy terrain became even more gloomy, the reddish area of the marsh grew gray, and the waters of Khhorpichekan seemed completely black.

Sultanov poked a long pole at the bottom.

"We 'll have to dive!" he declared.

Groping into a shallow spot, where the stick had rested against some stones under the liquid clay, Churilin first undressed and then plunged into the icy water.

"Here are three stones for you!" he shouted, climbing back up onto the bank. "I'm going to get dressed in the tent before the midges eat me. Well, Arseny Pavlovich!"

"The carbonaceous shale and diabase, ancient basaltic lava," said Sultanov, peering into the tent a few minutes later. "All the same!"

"No, I cannot quit this matter!" Churilin looked at Sultanova. "We'll go to the top of Khhorpichekan, to the center of Amnunnachi. I have some kind of a... premonition: there is something here, or our whole undertaking has been in the pursuit of the unrealizable... Let's reorganize, without wasting time."

"Uh, and so tired!" Sultanov laughed, tying a tent rolled up in a bale. "Just think, what a month! In the evening, untie everything, layout it out, gather it all up in the morning and tie it up again. And repeat every day..."

* * *

For six days, under a continuous drizzle, the caravan moved to the northeast. All traces of people, the winter migrations of Evenks disappeared; not a single chopped tree was seen by the small party. The top of Horpicekan hid in the thicket of a dense fir grove. Looking back, before entering the thicket, Churilin could see almost the entire distance they'd covered over the previous two days behind him. The drizzle had cleared for the past few hours, and the atmosphere, saturated by the wet evaporation shimmered, giving the vast swamp space a ghostly appearance.

Churilin and his comrades became wary: two large moose crossed the swamp nearby. They walked calmly without seeing the people. The tall legs of the animals moved leisurely, but their sweeping stride easily and swiftly carried their massive bodies through the swamp-soaked with water thicker than moss. The front elk threw back its huge horns, lifted its head and looked with some disdainful glance at the submerged bogs. The animals disappeared behind the uneven gray comb of dry larches.

"It's a shame to watch!" said Sultanov. "On such long legs, no swamp is scary. You could do two hundred kilometers a day!" and he looked at his feet in heavy boots with dismay.

Churilin laughed, and the guide broke into a smile, although he didn't understand what was being said.

"Meat, however, will be here!" said the Evenk cheerfully.

Churilin continued to feel anxious – time for work, in fact, was no longer there. They moved forward at the expense of the time required to return. Still, the small detachment trekked deeper and deeper into uninhabited swamps, remote from large rivers.

The center of Amnunnachi completely corresponded to this Evenki name: it was a completely treeless plain covered with hummocked dry grasses, on the gray-yellow surface of which dark patches of mossy glades stood out. The plains gradually decreased, swept away by a barely visible brush of low forest. Only to the left, the horizon was closed by a blackening flat line: there the terrain apparently had a steeper decline, and distant mountains jutted out. Soon the sky was filled with a leaden veil, and the rain began to fall again. The vast space of impenetrable swamps, in which the four people were lost, crushed and oppressed them, bringing forth thoughts about the inadequacy of human strength. No matter how much they'd like to get out of here, they knew that only weeks or months could free them from this captivity. And it was no coincidence that Sultanov envied the moose: even the most strongest of men, with his feet most used to walking on a soft moss cover, squelching mud, clinging grasses, and rosemary spikes, could cover no more than thirty thousand steps. And if they need half a million steps to get out of these marshes, no amount of shouting, beating in anguish, calling anyone they wanted – nothing would help them. Thirty thousand steps and not one of them can be wrong. Otherwise, hitting between bumps, roots, the cracks of stone boulders... a fragile bone will crack. Then – death.

The caravan turned at a right angle to the left, toward the distant valley of Moyero. There was nothing visible behind the net of rain, so for days on end, they walked by compass direction only. Churilin and Sultanov barely spoke, the worker and Evenk also remained silent. At night, the hungry horses stirred restlessly, as they pushed around the tent. Sometimes there was a hoarse, short roar of a moose – the time of autumn battles between the males had begun...

***

At the turn of a freshly made path, Churilin saw a caravan ahead, with the horses stopped and huddled together.

"Maxim Mikhailovich! Come quickly! Voronok ran into it!" cried Peter, with desperation in his voice.

Churilin approached. A young black horse known as Voronok had already been freed from his pack and saddle and stood aside. A shiver ran across its skin, his hind legs bent.

"It stumbled with both of its legs – and onto a stump," Sultanov explained gloomily.

Blood ran down the left posterior leg of the muscle in a broad stream. The horse staggered and hastily lay down.

"What should I do, Arseny Pavlovich?" Churlin asked after examining the wound.

"What else is there we can do?" Sultanov turned away and went to the side. "Only I can't..."

Pity for the animal hurt Churilin painfully. But the caravan was stalled, and Churilin, slightly pale, took the Berdan and engaged the bolt. He lifted the barrel slowly up to the ear of the horse. Peter, up to now frozen in woeful immobility, darted forward and grabbed the Berdan:

"Maxim Mikhailovich, do not shoot! I tell you, Voronok will recover, he can follow us..." Tears streamed down his cheeks.

Churilin willingly yielded to Peter's requests. The load carried by Voronok was distributed among three other horses, and its saddle was loaded on the fourth. Voronok lay and stretched his neck, watching the caravan disappearing into the distance...

To the right, on a steep hillock, a small stream emerged from the vague light mud of Talik.

"Stones, Maxim Mikhailovich!" and Sultanov pointed to a small hill in the middle of the stream.

Large rounded pebbles with a red coating of iron shone through the water.

"I'll check it out." Churilin stepped into the stream. "And you tell Nicholas that today we will go before dark.

Sultanov hurried to the guide. Evenk, having listened

to the order, frowned, but nodded his head and announced that he also knew: we must hurry.

Churilin's voice called out from the stream:

"Stop, Arseny Pavlovich!"

Sultanov's heart began to beat faster. He rushed back. Churilin waved a piece of stone and couldn't utter a word of excitement. He silently thrust a stone fragment at Sultanov, then went back to feverishly throwing one after another stone out onto the bank. Sultanov looked at the fresh split of the rock – and shuddered with joy. Blood-red crystals of pyrope appeared on a mottled surface mixed with olive and blue-greens of olivine and diopside grains.

"Grikwait!" shouted Sultanov, and both geologists began to fiercely crush the stones that Churilin threw to them.

The viscous, dense rock could hardly withstand being hit by a hammer, and each new split opened the same mottled coarse-grained surface. Sultanov also climbed into the brook to look for new stones, and only when a different kind of fracture appeared before the geologists – a dark, almost black surface with green dots – did Churilin straighten and wipe the sweat from his face...

"Phew!" sighed Sultanov. "Almost all the pebbles are grikwait. And this is not kimberlite?"

"I think so," Churilin confirmed. "From an undisturbed part of the intrusion, formed where the magma gets trapped between layers of the earth.

Churilin's hands, rolling a cigarette, trembled.

"These are not pebbles, Arseny Pavlovich," he said quietly and solemnly. "Such stones are too large for a small brook."

"So, the stream has washed away..." Sultanov hesitated.

"... the eluvial placer of the gruquaite rock! These deposits formed here and have been exposed from the ground by weathering, not from the actions of streams, which carry away the lighter materials. Thus, we can consider this to be the immediate place of their formation," Churilin completed. "Remember, because grikvaitovye fragments are found in African seams in the form of boulders, they are rounded during the eruption."

For the first time in many days, Churilin smiled broadly and lightly.

"So," Sultanov drawled. "So, we need to get to the top of the stream, where the spruce trees... Turn back!" he shouted to Nikolai and Peter.

Evenk, squinting, carefully watched the cheerful faces of his superiors, and Peter slapped Bulan on the rump:

"We go back to Voronok, you idiot!"

***

The blows of an ax resounded hollowly through the silence of the dark forest. Soon, a felled spruce tree collapsed with a crash, and another fell behind it.

Tired people sat down to smoke.

"Our Voronok is getting better, he's only limping," said Peter as he walked over to look at the horses. "Didn't I say that? Only, the horses are getting thin, they're hungry — the grass around the camp has been all eaten up."

The hill was the home of owls. The curious-eyed, intelligent birds sat on the branches near the camp in the twilight and, bending their heads to one side, watched the people with their bright yellow eyes. At night, their cries eagerly spread in the thick of the branches, adding to the cacophony of the moose roaring in the swamp.

The fog, which had settled in during the evening had become a widespread blanket of frost by morning, and the swamp sparkled and flickered. It was still dark under the fir trees, and in the pale light of dawn, fallen tree trunks could be seen covered with fungus growths. The mushrooms wavy ruffles clung onto the stumps and roots and bloomed in all sorts of shades of red, green, and yellow, emitting a putrid smell, while during the night, cast a subtle phosphoric light.

The people rummaged in the ground, fiercely digging hard into the sticky clay with their pickaxes, only occasionally devoting some time to sleep and eat. They didn't have enough of the right tools, and the permafrost soil made it very difficult. Only huge bonfires laid out in pits, an old exploration technique, forced her to yield. Then another enemy appeared – water. Two pits had to be abandoned: they hit the bottom of the taliks and instantly filled with water.

Churilin expected to meet the bedrock at about two or three meters from the surface. However, this insignificant depth was reached only with great difficulty.

Another pit was laid at the very top of the hill. Smoke from the fire filled the spruce grove, spread over the shaggy branches, and its long blue tongue crawled out onto the swamp and mixed in the distance with the cold, damp mist.

The guide brought over another dry spruce trunk on his shoulder and threw it into the fire before he resolutely approached Churilin.

"Chief, we need to talk. The horses will soon starve, and then us. The flours running out, oil too. I can't go hunting, and you have to work. This is bad, very bad business – we have to go soon!"

Churilin was silent – the guide had merely expressed aloud the same thoughts that had long tormented him.

"Maxim Mikhailovich," Sultanov suddenly suggested, "let him and Peter lead the horses away, and you and I'll finish the hole. We only have enough tools for two anyway. And then we can go back along the river, by raft..."

Churilin quickly took a step toward his assistant. He looked carefully at his thinner face, overgrown with a black beard, and eyes reddened from smoke and insomnia and turned away...

"You will go with all the cargo directly to Sottir," he said calmly after a few minutes to the conductor and the gloomy Peter. "There, in the village, hand over the horses. I agreed on everything in the spring with the chief of the polar station. I'll give you a letter so that you can be provided with food, and Peter will be taken to Djergal. There, let him prepare a boat and wait for us. Maybe we'll have time to raft along the Khatanga to the airport. Nikolai will get provisions in Sottyra – let's give him the money now, and let him return to his home. As you reach Moyero, leave all the food you can allocate in a conspicuous place. Mark the path with notches and cuts, which we will follow. How far is it from here to Sottyra?

"I don't know." Evenk shook his head. "I'm guessing about three hundred kilometers."

"Well, and Moyero is fifty."

"No, you can't walk to Moyeros from here, the trek is too long with many obstacles. If you go through the mountains, that path is shorter, with fewer problems."

"Well, one hundred kilometers?"

"A hundred, one hundred and twenty, however, you'd get there…"

***

It was very lonely and quiet on the spruce mound. Where a tent had once stood was now a large pile of firewood, with a bonfire burning in front of it, smoking a little from the rain.

At night, Sultanov woke up from the cold. His whole body ached, and he didn't want to get up because of the pain – it seemed simply impossible to move his hand. With great effort, Sultanov rose and woke Churilin. He quickly got up, drank a mug of tea, and began to look in the darkness for a small scraper, lying somewhere near the fire.

The flame of the campfire flared up, animated by a new portion of dry firewood. It was completely dark in the pit, which was already around two and a half meters deep. Churilin dug a pile at random, scooping up clumps of clay with his hands into a bucket, which Sultanov occasionally lifted up on a rope.

Afraid of flooding, the geologists did not thaw the permafrost with fire. Instead, they preferred the more reliable method to work directly in the frozen soil, even though it was painfully slow. Already, a quarter of a meter of water filled the pit, and each blow of the rock hammer was accompanied by a loud splash.

Sometimes, Churilin felt that he'd been working bent over this close, damp pit for many years. For long periods, he only heard the dull crunching of rocks, the clinking of the bucket, and was digging with his torn, swollen fingers in the icy, liquid mud.

"Enough for you, twenty-five buckets already! Now it's my turn!" Sultanov shouted from the top just at the moment when Churilin felt that he could no longer raise the latest bucket.

He climbed out of the pit by pushing against the wall with his feet and hands and sank heavily on the wet clay.

Sultanov disappeared into the pit, and from there, his muffled voice was heard:

"Looking good! Well, you have the power, Maxim Mikhailovich! Another quarter of a meter is left, small pebbles are already tinkling... No, then clay again."

At the same time, Sultanov felt that the clay had changed to a different kind: it was still dense and came away in large pieces, but the unyielding, sticky viscosity had disappeared.

Bucket by bucket the excavated clay hill increased. The long autumn night was already coming to an end when Sultanov weakly and hoarsely shouted from the pit:

"The stones have gone! The last one is huge!"

The last bucket seemed incredibly heavy to Churilin. He extracted a sticky, cold and heavy piece of rock, and broke it with a hammer by the fire. The dark, dull rock in the flickering light of the flame was no different from the diabases they'd found throughout their journey.

"Well?" Sultanov asked impatiently.

"I don't know, it's dark," Churilin answered, not wanting to upset his comrade, and threw pieces of stone onto a pile of dug clay. "Come out, you need to sleep. Six o'clock, dawn will be here soon.

***

They wanted to sleep for a long time. But the time passed inexorably fast, and at nine o'clock the two geologists were already back on their feet and preparing a meager breakfast.

"No matter how hard the work is, we need to reduce our portions," Churilin said gloomily. "There's not much flour in the bag."

Sultanov grinned and was silent. Then, raising a mug of tea, solemnly recited: "The destruction is true ahead... and the one who sent us to the terrible deed – without a heart in an iron chest..."

"What's even worse is that no one sent us, and there's no one else to blame."

"What the hell is holding us here?" Sultanov said quietly, his head down.

The comrades slowly trudged back to the pit. Sultanov suddenly seized Churilin's elbow with his fingers.

"Maxim Mikhailovich! Yellow earth!"

On top of a pile of excavated rock lay some kind of special, grainy but at the same time dense clay of a reddish-yellow hue. Churilin hurriedly picked up a stone that had been split the night before. It was a heavy, greasy-to-feel blue-black rock. The outer layer of the stone was soft and of a lighter, a bluish-gray hue.

"Water, Arseny Pavlovich, more water!" whispered Churilin. "Yes, get it out of the flooded pit. Pour out the tea, damn it! You'll need a second bucket. You start washing the yellow rock, bring it to the tray, and I'll do the stone fragments."

"Really..." began Sultanov.

"Wait!" Churilin snapped abruptly.

Slowly, as if not in the least worried, Churilin began to wash all the extracted pieces of solid black rock, cleaning off loose crusts and dirt.

Forgetting everything in the world around them, the geologists went about their own business. Suddenly Churilin uttered a muffled exclamation and hastily took out a folding magnifying glass from his breast pocket. Sultanov threw the tray and ran. On the bluish-black background of a small piece of rock, there were almost three transparent crystals the size of a pea. The triangular sides of their faces were not absolutely smooth, but nevertheless brightly gleamed. Each crystal represented two tetrahedral pyramids connected by bases. The geologists stared intently at the crystals. In the deep silence of the forest, only the intermittent breathing of people could be heard.

"Diamonds, diamonds!" Sultanov choked out.

"Yes, typical octahedra, as in South Africa," Churilin said. "Pure clarity, not bluish. According to the local nomenclature – second-grade of the highest class; the so-called first – Cape. That's it, Arseny Pavlovich, our business is done. It's your..." Churilin couldn't finish, and instead squeezed Sultanov's hand, which was soiled with clay.

He wearily sat down on the mud and tea-spattered rosemary.

"So, this red clay is the 'hallowed ground'—the yellow land of the African mines," said Churilin. "Top quality, and also, diamond-enriched seams. A few meters below will be the 'blue earth' – the 'blue gruel.' This is from a black one, pieces of which we found in the yellow earth. Think what's a few more meters below. It's a less degraded, less oxidized kimberlite rock. And our spruce hill, undoubtedly contours around the boundary of the diamond seam. Such hills often help in South Africa in the search for diamond deposits, showing the upper, expanded part of the seam projecting to the surface, but hidden under the soil. And remember, my dear Arseny Pavlovich, the main commandment of the African diamond hunters: 'where there is one pipe, look for a few more. They are never alone!' Now we need to rinse all the dug up yellow earth and carefully select samples. To carry them, we'll have to give up part of our food. Then we must mark this area with our identification post, the reper – and at dawn, we leave from here: our lives are now especially precious."

Sultanov last shook the tray for the last time and poured all that remained after washing a ton of yellow earth onto a sheet of clean paper. There, on the white sheet, were scattered small crystals – columnar, prismatic, polygonal – red, brown, black, blue, and green. These were diamond-associated ilmenite, pyroxene, olivine, and other persistent minerals. And among them, like small pieces of glass and yet not similar to it with their strong brilliance, stood out small crystals of diamonds. There were white, clear water stones, and were covered with a rough brown crust. Some crystals had a pinkish or green tint.

"Look here, except for the octahedra, it's a rhombic-dodecahedron." Churilin used a match to separate a green dvenadychedra. "This kind of diamond is distinguished for its extraordinary hardness, even for this stone. In Africa, such diamonds are found mainly in the Faorsped seam. And this side," – and he pointed with a match to a rounded grain of black color – "is a cluster of tiny diamond crystals formed by an intergrowth of microscopic crystals, you know, called a 'board.' I measured the diameter of our hill," Churilin went on. "This diamond seam isn't small, not less than a quarter of a kilometer across. True, there are more in South Africa; for example, Dyutoytspan, which is nearly seven hundred meters. It is no longer a seam, but a whole volcanic vent."

Sultanov looked thoughtfully at the hill. He tried to imagine a huge seam, which almost went to a depth of several kilometers and filled with precious blackish-blue rock with diamonds. And it was here, in a marshy, gloomy plain, under moss and mud, barely covered by the shell of permafrost!

Churilin was also silent. He poured diamonds into the pouch, wrote labels to pieces of rocks, carefully wrapped the samples, and began to draw out a detailed plan of the field.

The geologist did all this without any enthusiasm. It was as if now that he'd achieved his goal, all his previous aspirations had disappeared somewhere. The fatigue was too great...

Sultanov sketched a tall stump in the form of a pillar, and, heating up his knife, he burned several letters and numbers into it. Soon the reper, their identification post, was ready – a tall spruce with chopped branches and a crossbar at the top.

***

The path straight through the mountains wasn't easy: it crossed many small valleys, and it was necessary for them to overcome up to fifteen passes a day. The geologists walked mechanically, without words and thoughts. The small portions of food weren't enough to cover the huge expenditure of energy. They'd begin their trek each day with the first glimpses of the morning light and only ended long after midnight. The bright yellow needles of larches drooped low, and the forest was saturated with water from continuous rain. Everything was quickly drenched through. In the evening, they'd smoked for a long time around a strong fire, and the next morning they'd be once again saturated with moisture within the first hour of the journey. The water flowed through the marshes and covered a quarter of the tall hillocks, between which at the slightest wrong step, they'd fall into the water up to their waist. The thin ice crunched under their drenched boots. No game was encountered on the way – the mountains seemed to die out, and they'd toss their packs from side to side, as the weight alternatively squashed their shoulders with a useless load.

On the morning of the fourth day, Churilin and Sultanov climbed a steep path. Ahead of them, at the top of the pass, a reddish-gray haze of mist parted, revealing to the travelers an extensive gentle descent formed by a scattering of huge acute-angled stone blocks. In the distance, stood a dark blue cliff spotted with reddish stain, and on the opposite slope of the valley was a large river.

"Well, that's Moyero!" sighed Churilin, before he crouched on a large rock, and hunted around in his pocket in search of the last crumbs of makhorka. "How did they go with the horses? The last one is at the top, and then nothing is visible."

"We'll go straight down to the marker in the valley and then down to the river," suggested Sultanov, "then we'll go back up. We're sure to find their traces somewhere."

***

The head of the production department of the Institute entered Ivashentsev's office and silently sank into the chair.

"I'm seriously worried about Churilin," the professor said worriedly. "This man is too stubborn to be cautious. Samarin arrived a month ago, and Churilin and Sultanov stayed in the taiga. It is necessary to send telegrams everywhere, where possible, with requests: to Sottyr, to Tura, Khatanga, Chiringdin base of Soyuzpushnina..."

And so, from the high masts of the radio station of Dixon Island, the radio waves rushed through the ether over the taiga again. Interrupting and resuming again, they carried the same question: "Khatanga, Sottyr, Tura... Tell me urgently whether there is news of the expedition of Glavmintsyrya engineer Churilin..."

The radio waves reached the furthest alluvial outposts, but both geologists, of course, didn't know and didn't feel that space saturated with questions about their fate. They carefully balanced on the slippery, lichen-covered surfaces of huge stone slabs, jumped deep gaps between boulders, and clambered along the narrow edges and sharp drops.

The scree stretched for several kilometers over an incredible chaos of broken stone — a solid dead field, covered with gray bones of mountains. It was as if the forces of the earth's crust that collided in a terrible battle and had been smashed, mutilated, sprinkled with mountain tops, and then fell over here as defeated skeletons, exposing their naked sharp ribs...

"Sergey Yakovlevich! Sottyr reports yesterday that Churilin's guide and a worker arrived with horses; the geologists remained in the taiga. Here is the telegram."

The professor fiercely banged his fist on the table.

"I knew it! They'll perish for nothing! Send a telegraph to Sottyr... Hmm, who will give it to them though? An expedition must be equipped..." Ivashentsev was worried and began to shuffle through papers on his table. "And, most importantly, stubbornness is something useless: in three years we haven't found anything, and in one extra month you won't achieve anything.

***

"Well done! Look, Arseny Pavlovich: they prepared a lot of dry wood and a raft from the spruce trees. Well done! Enough for about a week. Well, it doesn't matter: the river is fast, it will carry us well. Well, let's go. One, two...!"

The small raft rocked on the water, turned and, guided by poles, quickly flowed out into the middle of the river. Here, the Moyero River wasn't deep yet, and long, smooth pebbles flashed quickly beneath the raft. Both geologists felt joyous relief for the first time in many difficult days. Their knapsacks didn't crush their overworked shoulders anymore, and their blistered feet and tired legs enjoyed a rest, while the river carried their raft at a leisurely speed of at least six kilometers per hour. Perhaps this was the main joy – to sit, smoke the tobacco left by Nicholas, and occasionally straighten the raft with an occasional prod of the poles, while at the same time enjoying the knowledge that they were advancing ahead – that with endless path decreased with each passing hour.

At last, they could afford the luxury of thinking, remembering that there is another world. The splash of water, the gurgling of its murmur over the narrow pebble beds, the rapid movement of small waves – everything seemed to be full of joyful life after the oppressive silence, monotony, and stagnant air of huge swamps.

The Moyero River meandered its winding passage through the valley, and the low banks sailed by. Soon, the wide floodplain was left behind. The forest came right down to the river's edge, hanging over its channel like dark, high walls. The raft sailed on as if through a corridor between dense spruce. Many trees, washed up by the river, leaned towards the water. In the distance, the forest corridor seemed to narrow; the tops of the forest trees on the opposite sides of the bank leaned towards each other over the water, which lost its lively shine, to looked gloomy and cold.

A huge, recently fallen tree spruce lay across the river, almost touching the still green tops on the broad left bank. The geologists took the raft ashore, and jumping into the water, dragged it over the pebbles and around the tree. Then came a few more of these tree obstacles which slowed their progress, but it all seemed trivial to Churilin and Sultanov... that was until a sharp turn of the river, and they suddenly heard a loud murmur and splashing blows.

"To the shore, quick! To the shore!" cried Churilin. "Dam ahead!"

But it was too late – the raft was going too fast. The pole stuck in the bottom of the river and broke with a snap, and the raft, like a blind man, rushed straight towards a high pile of tree trunks blocking the river.

To the right, where the jumble of trees was less, the water loudly rushed under the dam. The branches and thin trunks sprung and vibrated under the pressure of water, producing characteristic bursts, similar to the blows of a giant roller.

Sultanov and Churilin rushed to the rear end of the raft and seized the precious sacks, an ax, and their rifle. At the same moment, the raft dived under the dam, stopped, and began to rise vertically, sinking deeper into the water. A strong push jolted the comrades forward, but they managed to jump onto the dam. The water roared, billowing behind the raft, blocking part of the narrow passage. Without losing a minute, Churilin and Sultanov began chopping at the trunks, taking turns with their one ax. After two hours of hard work, they managed to free the raft, and with the help of a rope, pulled it closer to the shore, where the water was waist-deep at the edge of the dam. Struggling with the icy water that had knocked them off their feet, the geologists lifted the raft higher and forcibly pushed it through a hole they'd cut through thick, slippery logs lying under the water at the edge of the dam. Further on the path was free, but alas, only for another one and a half kilometers before another forest dam appeared in front of the raft again! This time, it was an even wider pile of white logs, between which thick branches and deeply buried roots protruded out from the water.

***

A large bonfire burned on the whitish sandbar. The raft was pulled up onto the shore. Churilin and Sultanov sat facing the river, turning their wet backs to the smoking fire. Above the sand, the shore rose steeply, and the dry grasses on it shone in the bright sun, which roused clouds of midges.

Sultanov suddenly got up and walked in the wrong direction. He was nauseous; his stomach refused to accept the food he'd just eaten. Churilin watched his assistant anxiously – he also felt unwell. Wearied by the exorbitant work, long malnutrition, and insomnia, the heart either pounded hard and rarely or quickly and feebly fluttered, demanding rest – a prolonged rest.

The dark fear of the tenacious grip of the wilderness filled the explorer's soul. Swimming about four kilometers of the river was necessary. And at this point, it had taken them two days to only swim seven kilometers through the crevices. Seven kilometers! They only had enough food left for four days, and that with only the smallest of portions. And how much more hard work was to be done by their shoulders in cold water: to cut thick logs, sit down, drag the raft... They knew they had no more strength left! It was unlikely that they would last even one more day. Who knew how many more dams or obstacles were ahead – one or a hundred?

Sultanov returned to the fire and lay down on the sand. Churilin moved the bag under his head of his friend and knelt beside him.

"Lie down, Arseny Pavlovich, I'll go on." He pointed to the left, where a pile of intertwined gray logs piled up behind a wide sandbank and water sparkling in the sunlight.

Sultanov sat down.

"Maxim Mikhailovich, that's what..." He hesitated. "If I get really sick, then you go alone. It's necessary, it's necessary to save someone. I'm serious, I'm not joking!" Sultanov was angry at seeing Churilin's smile.

"Give it up, my friend! Rest, and everything will pass. If we go out, we'll go together!" Churilin said loudly, without finding the confidence he needed in his tone. "Well, I'm off!" And, lifting the rifle, he slowly trampled through the sand and crisp pebble shallows to the intersection of a steeply curved spit.

Churilin wanted to go farther down the river to check out the valley below the crest.

The fear that gripped him wouldn't pass, no matter how Churilin tried to cope with it. He wanted to quickly return to the familiar world of maps, books, scientific research, give his country the riches hidden under the moss and the permafrost of Amnunnachi, to have time for quiet, calm reflection behind a microscope, for conversations with comrades. Was it really possible to return to the place where there are no midges, always wet clothes, acrid smoke, and a hopeless race ahead, forward?

Churilin crossed the river and turned along the bank.

He walked and thought about Sultanov: *What makes people go to such unprecedented, unknown feats? If we don't make it, will anyone know about this man's staunch heroism? The experience will be quickly erased, forgotten, it will seem like a bad dream... Who is seriously talking about dreams? And if we don't get out, no one will know either. More than that: they will say – they died from ineptitude, carelessness. And Sultanov there, back in the distant world, thousands of kilometers away... a life, happiness, a beloved woman, who has been waiting for a long time, anxiously and impatiently.*

To his right, on the opposite bank, he heard a noise. Pebbles crunched, the dry grass rustled softly. Churilin woke up, looked, and his heart pounded wildly.

Under the ledge of the bank, plunging a hoof into the water, stood a huge male elk. Its powerful body seemed completely black from a distance. The wide horns, like the palms of a giant with spiky, pointed fingers, were light, and between them, facing the direction of Churilin, the large ears stuck out. It peered at the frozen geologist, tilted his head exposing his horns, and gave a hoarse bellow. Churilin did not stir, painfully gripping the strap of the rifle in his fist.

The elk turned and immediately became different — lean, hunchbacked, on tall legs. As part of the nature of the animal and its readiness for a swift run, one could feel the latent energy of the cocked spring. A powerful, horn-nosed head rose, a thick, black beard stretched out on his throat, and a long nape showed even sharper. Then the elk spread his legs wide, jabbed his nose in the water and entered the river. Churilin jerked the rifle off his shoulder. The elk made a light jump onto the short. Churilin released the safety catch with a click, and he sent a bullet into the long neck. The elk stumbled, fell, then jumped up again. The thunder of the second shot flew across the river, and the animal disappeared into the bushes. Beside himself, Churilin rushed to the river, raising his rifle high over his head. The current knocked him down, but he coped with it and was soon on the opposite shore. A blackish-brown body could be seen ten meters from the water in the tall grass.

Churilin cautiously approached him and made sure that the beast was dead. The elk lay with his head thrown back on his horn; its front legs bent at the knees. The magnificent power of the animal was felt in a motionless body.

Churilin was not a real hunter. He bent on one knee, and stroked the muzzle of the moose, regretting what had happened. Whatever it was, sixteen pounds of excellent meat changed the fate of geologists.

Churilin straightened himself, and leaning on the rifle, looked around and saw on the river one more dam ahead, a quarter of a mile below. Further along, the river was hidden by a dense forest, which seemed like a dark brush. However, this brush in one place was lower in one place, and there was a mountain slope that came close to the river.

If the river goes to the gorge, there will be rapids, but the dams will end, thought Churilin.

He quickly gutted the moose, took his tongue, heart, and a piece of meat. Then he marked the place with a high pole and moved across the river along the upper bank, having carefully examined it on his way earlier.

The abundant meal of meat at first weakened the travelers even more, but by the next morning, Churilin and Sultanov had noticeably cheered up.

***

On the last leg, the Moyero took on a large river on the right. The valley narrowed, and the peaks of the spotty mountains, black and yellow from the autumn larches, descended to the river, causing everything to accelerate. The dull, leaden surface of the water seemed to breathe, gently rising and falling. Boulders towered like ramparts. The sandbanks, trees, and black ravines quickly swept back. Here the rocks came very close and the waves frothed – the whole river became covered with troughs and sharp foamy crests. The water flooded the raft as it ran through the turbulence, but after a few alarming minutes – the raft made it through and back onto regularly moving, spacious water.

The rapid movement invigorated the tired men. Finally, they were fully embraced by the joy of the victory.

It will take a little time – but thousands of people will go to where they both languished in the captivity of forests and marshes. The power of labor will dissect the impenetrable spaces with roads, clear forests, and drain swamps. The noise of cars and bright electric light will break the dark silence of the taiga.

***

"Sergey Yakovlevich, a telegram from Khatanga. Probably from Churilin."

"What? Quick, pass it here!"

The professor hastily opened it and read the telegram. It fell out of his hands. "Well, I never… Go, everything is alright with them, they've made it back safely."

Left alone, Ivashentsev re-read the short text: "Everything that we've been looking for has been found. We're coming back by plane. Churilin and Sultanov are healthy."

Professor Ivashentsev stood up and bowed low to the telegraph form, which he gently placed on the table.

FAKAOFO ATOLL

A small bright hall was overcrowded. Among the diversity of civilian attire stood the distinguished blue uniforms of sailors. Slowly examining the hall, Captain-Lieutenant Ganyeshyn noticed someone's energetic gestures from a distant row – friends were inviting him over to an empty seat beside them. Ganyeshyn smiled and made his way between the rows of chairs.

"Even you came!" Captain Isachenko said, squeezing Ganyeshyn's hand. "Is the whole fleet here?"

"What for?" Ganyeshyn asked.

Tkachov appeared and handed over a report.

"This is what, Tkachov? The one that is unsinkable?"

"On the contrary, from flooding," Isachenko quipped. "Commander of the Northern Fleet patrol ship."

"Ah, yes," Ganyeshyn said indifferently. "And what kind of report?"

"Ho! What a joker!" Isachenko exclaimed, and the sailors around them laughed.

"Well, so enlighten me," Ganyeshyn smiled good-naturedly.

"Today is the final session of the Academy of Sciences session devoted to maritime affairs. Well, Tkachov caught an unusual reptile, and the commander ordered him to bring this to the attention of the scientists. Tkachov is a brave commander, but he's not an amateur about the reports. But, it's starting," Isachenko broke off. "You'll find out soon enough."

The president judge rang the bell. A fair-haired middle-aged officer with sharp-featured face confidently stepped onto the platform. The Order of Nahimov decorated his carefully ironed uniform. The sailor looked around the hushed hall and began his speech, often and carefully touching the upper hook of his collar in agitation. Soon, however, he mastered himself and began to speak calmly and simply.

Ganyeshyn had sailed more than once in those places being mentioned, so he listened to Tkaczov with particular interest. As soon as Tkaczov said: "My ship was patrolling for five days on the open sea, around the thirty-second meridian, in our opinion, in the fourth region," a picture of the gloomy, leaden sea appeared in Ganyeshyn memory...

The expanse of water was difficult to judge in the cool, misty air. The horizon was hidden, and therefore it concealed dangerous surprises... The appearance of a German submarine, which was going 'full speed ahead' on the surface was something totally unexpected. Evidently, the Germans did not expect a Soviet patrol boat here either, so far from the shores, and before the boat submerged, Tkaczov managed to get close to the enemy.

Depth charges were dropped into the sea, with gigantic splashes, a little ahead of the place where the submarine had just disappeared. They'd been set to explode close to the surface, and pillars of water rose as they did, with glimpses of red lightning and clouds of black smoke. As an experienced fighter, Tkaczov immediately determined the probable section where the enemy was likely to be, and that's where he ordered his ship to go.

When the ship sailed to where he estimated the submarine had hidden, Tkachov ordered the bombing and the ship to be stopped. Lieutenant Malutin handed the hydrophone headset to Tkachov, while continuing to turn the amplifier dial. The undefined sound of the sea heard through the headphones, did not reveal the presence of an underwater enemy. Tkachov understood that the submarine had heard their ship stop above them, and stopped their engines too.

Nodding to the lieutenant, Tkachov yanked the telegraph lever. The engines roared into life, and the motors roared like a waterfall in the hydrophones. The telegraph rang again. The ship instantly stopped, and in the echoes of the ship's movement, Tkachov caught the elusive, distant sounds of the submarine's engines.

"Hard to port!"

There was an even, dull noise from the depths. Tkachov imagined exactly how far under them the submarine was, trying to sneak away by confusing them by starting and stopping their engines. After a few seconds, the submarine stopped their engines again, and the noise of the motors stopped. But Tkachov already knew the bearing, approximate depth, and the direction of their opponent's escape. The nimble hands of the explosive experts set the hydrostatic fuses to a depth of ninety meters – the explosion of heavy depth charges is more effective upwards than downwards, into the depths. The two-barrel cannon was no longer needed: now heavy bombs could be dropped directly from the gun carriage. Tkachov set the telegraph lever to 'full speed ahead,' and the ship surged forward, with the powerful machine raising a huge shaft of foam behind the stern. When the speed of the ship reached fifteen knots, Tkachov alternatively pressed the release levers of the right and left gun carriages. Depth bombs, similar to gasoline barrels, splashed their several hundred kilograms of weight softly into the foamy water behind the stern, slowly rolling one after another – all seemingly innocent, all new, black smooth barrels, all rolling in a continuous chain of the gun carriage.

The patrol boat moved in a wide arc, leaving behind large, blackish water eruptions without fiery flares, in its wake. Tkachov monitored the distribution of explosions, continuously calculating the size of the range and the coverage area. *Just one more, to be sure*, he thought, pressing the right lever of the bomb launcher. *It's not going anywhere... it won't dive to the bottom, because it's almost a kilometer deep*.

The lieutenant, who watched the stopwatch, shrugged in surprise. The time required for the bomb to sink was over, but there wasn't any explosion yet. A minute passed – and nothing. Tkachov ordered the ship to turn back to listen to the submarine in the bombed area.

"Gavrylenko!" cried the Lieutenant to the chief bomber. "How did you set the fuse on the last mine?"

"Just like all the others, to ninety meters, Comrade Lieutenant!"

"Apparently, the fuse must have failed. Strange, this is my first case..." Tkachov said in surprise.

At that precise moment, a low rise of water appeared just half a chain away from the right side of the bow. A very distant explosion was heard from the depths, which was then immediately drowned out by a strong splash of a wave smashing against the bow. The ship rocked. Tkachov grabbed the railing.

"What time, Lieutenant?" he called.

"Two minutes and forty-five seconds," Malutin replied.

"Wow! so it means it sank to almost half a kilometer, which is why the explosion was so weak. Clearly, it's a defect in the fuse... Oh, we got them!" Tkachov suddenly shouted, glaring at a huge oily stain spreading over the crests of the small waves.

The engines fell silent, and again the sensitive underwater hydrophone ears began to catch the sounds of a struggle for life on the defeated enemy boat. He could hear the noise of motors, not only uneven but also intermittent. They would fall silent, then it was heard again...

They dived, probably their rivets are leaking, thought Tkachov. He sent two more bombs along the new bearing while watching the foamy surface of the water through his binoculars.

"Left, stern, object!" A seaman's voice pealed behind him.

Astonished at the discrepancy of the bearing he'd just chosen, Tkachov turned abruptly, aimed his binoculars at a vague red spot near the place where the last bomb had been dropped, and almost recoiled from surprise. Through the magnifying circles of his binoculars and the haze of the smoke, he could make out the outline of a huge, reddish-brown body among the steadily rolling waves. It was some kind of animal of unprecedented size and color. It seemed to him that the animal had a large body, huge fins, and a huge round neck – the head and tail were hidden by the waves. The strangest thing was its smooth, red skin, with some wrinkles in places and folds of a deep-red color, turning into dark brown.

"To the right of the bow – air bubbles!"

The voice of the signalman brought the Commander back to reality, and Tkachov focused again on the fight against their underwater enemy. Thousands of air bubbles dotted the surface of the waves. After a minute, Tkachov's ship stood over the place where the air was escaping, listening to the depths.

Suddenly, the water boiled from the large amount of air that rose up from immediately below them. At the same time, a short, dull, and slurred rumble could be heard in the hydrophones. The crew silently watched. The ship had already lost its speed and stood upside to the wave. A few minutes passed, and the last air bubbles disappeared. No sound could be heard from the depths through the hydrophone. Only the oily stain was spreading wider, smoothing the pointed crests of the waves.

Somewhere far below in the sea depths, a broken submarine, unable to ascend, sank deeper and deeper into a kilometer-long abyss, and the merciless pressure of water pressed the air and oil out of it.

Tkachov gave the command: 'full ahead,' and took the handphones of Malutin.

"Make a note of this, Lieutenant, one more. But just to be sure, let's wait a little longer, let's listen... Oh, but what about that monster?" he remembered. "Quickly, let's find him!"

In the place where the unknown creature had emerged, the seafarers were disappointed: no red monster could be seen. As far as the eye could see – only the cold waves were visible.

Tkachov angrily rubbed his watery eyes.

"Am I mistaken? No!... Comrades! Who else saw this... well, this creature that emerged out here?" he said to the ship's crew.

Many sailors immediately spoke up, and among them, Foreman Gavrylenko, who swore that it was nothing, only a sea serpent stunned by their bombs.

"No, that was no snake," the whistleblower Epiphanov protested. "I saw it: it had a thick, wide torso, and there were flippers too – what kind of serpent is that then?"

"Well, it's still not a fish nor a sea animal... more like an underwater reptile," Gavrylenko insisted, standing his ground.

Gavrylenko warned Tkachov that he believed the animal had been stunned or killed by one of their bombs and rose to the surface.

Eh, it's a shame that it drowned! If only we could've caught that animal... thought Tkachov, *because otherwise, who will believe us?*

As if hearing the captain, Lieutenant Malutin, answered the unasked question.

"It's a deep-water reptile," he said. "A deep-water creature, and our last bomb, the one with the broken fuse, killed it. It reached the depth of five hundred meters, and the animal swam out from those depths. Maybe he drowned, or maybe he just woke up. Anyway, I managed to..." and Malutin pulled a camera out of his pocket. "I don't vouch for quality, but I snapped five times. Luckily, I put on a telephoto lens."

Tkaczov was delighted with the lieutenant's resourcefulness, never thinking that he'd have to give a lecture in Moscow because of those photographs.

***

The specialists developed the photos of Lieutenant Malutin with the utmost care, and yet they were still not sharp enough: the gray day, slow shutter speed causing under-exposure, and the red color of creature – all these circumstances were not favorable.

Tkaczov was summoned to the commander, to whom he had to outline all the circumstances of the case and show the pictures. He received an order to go to Moscow for the maritime session of the Academy of Sciences.

"It doesn't matter," the Commander said to Tkachov's statement that no one would believe him. "We have a duty to explore the sea and inform scientists of such extraordinary events. And if the scientists don't believe what the nine honest sailors have seen, then we can't rely on their authority..." With those jocular words of the Admiral, accompanied by the favorable murmur throughout the rest of the room, the officer finished his brief lecture and started to show the photographs. The lights went out, and a blurred image appeared on the overhead screen.

The bright and dark bands of the waves stuck in the picture cut across and covered the uncertain contours of the convex neck, on which a low crest loomed. The great bulk lay diagonally in the water, and the slightly brighter belly was covered from the top on one side with a bizarrely curved fin. The neck began with a very thick base, wrinkled with deep transverse folds, and apparently, it was very long.

Slowly, one after the other, all five photos were shown, but Ganyeshyn couldn't imagine the animal; the impression was elusive, uncertain. The lights turned back on. Dozens of people who tried to identify the animal from the blurred pictures shared their impressions in a whisper. The allure of the unknown, felt by all people, had disappeared, but some of the excitement remained. This 'something,' as Ganyeshyn determined, was the consciousness of the reality of what happened – the captured, elusive mystery of the sea. Ganyeshyn gladly noted with pleasure, how the eyes of the serious scientists and stern commanders seated in his row, glittered excitedly. It was as if a dream had touched all those in the hall, raising and uniting the most diverse of people.

There was a movement at the table on the podium. A very tall, old man with a large gray beard appeared on the platform. The room fell silent – many people had heard of the famous oceanographer, who had bought glory to the Russian maritime sciences.

The scientist bowed his head, and two large locks of hair fell over his huge forehead framed by his thick silver hair. He looked around all those gathered there. Then he placed a large fist on the edge of the rostrum, and his powerful bass rose loudly, reaching the farthest corners of the hall.

"That's Georgie Maksymovich!" Isachenko whispered to Ganyeshyn. "With such a voice, you can command a battleship during a storm, not give speeches at lectures."

"So, he commanded," said Ganyeshyn.

"Comrades!" said the oceanographer in the meantime. "I am very glad that I heard Captain Tkachov's amazing report. The presentation of his lecture couldn't arrive in a more timely manner than at our final meeting. We are too accustomed to the existence of unexplored mysteries of the sea, and many issues of oceanography are still considered unresolved even today. I think that everyone present has heard about the experience of the brave American Professor Beebe, who dropped to a depth of a kilometer in a steel ball, called a bathysphere. Beebe observed huge animals swimming in the unimaginable darkness in front of his windows, too large to be viewed in full in relation to the small range of his spotlight and the small field of view of the quartz illuminators. Do you know that just before the war, a huge fish – known as a Latimeria of the coelacanth species – was fished out from the eastern shores of Africa? This species had been considered extinct on the surface of the earth since the ancient geological era, about one hundred million years ago? And now, the unknown reptile, discovered in the Barents Sea by Captain Tkaczov, gives us one more confirmation of the mysterious life existing in the depths of our oceans. It's still just a shadow that flashed before us, but the shadow of something real, that really exists.

"Despite the ongoing war, the fleet and our scientists continue to deepen knowledge about the sea. But victory is already near, comrades, and I hope that soon I will see you in the post-war maritime session when our possibilities will increase immeasurably.

"I turn to you in the name of science, comrade seafarers! Our fleet has a great future ahead. Armed with technical knowledge and the enormous production power of our homeland, after the war, in peaceful working conditions, you can render great assistance to the enormous importance of science."

The scientist paused, sighed loudly, and his voice thundered even stronger than before.

"Many people think that we know the sea, and of course, we've studied its surface well. We already know the exact location of currents, winds, temperatures, salt content, even the nature of waves in different seas. We all know, for example, that the Indian Ocean has the steepest waves. The Arctic Ocean is distinguished by gigantic waves with unusually long fronts, and the Atlantic gives the highest waves. I don't need to list all oceanography achievements here – you know them as well as I do. But as soon as we turn from the surface of the ocean to its depths, we immediately feel our weakness.

"Of course, we know the general location of sediments on the ocean floor. The invention of an echo sounder immediately moved forward the study of the seabed topography, and the moment is near when we will know this surface as well as we do the surface of the land. But the thing is that the very bottom of the ocean, the structure, and composition of its bedrocks, are completely unknown to us. I won't be exaggerating if I say that we have studied the surface of the moon much better. Imagine the ocean as a stone dish, filled with water, with sediment on the bottom. We don't know this stone vessel completely, and for now, we don't have enough knowledge to examine it.

"The seas and oceans occupy about seventy-one percent of our planet's surface. Therefore, geology in its study of the earth's crust, so far, has been limited to the study of only twenty-nine percent of this area. No wonder then that the most important, basic geology issues that will enable us to achieve significant power over the riches of the interior of the earth can not be solved without examining the seabed in geological terms. We need eyes and hands in the most terrible depths of the seas. You young commodores and engineers, think about it.

"I will allow myself to hold your attention for another five minutes. In the middle of the Pacific Ocean, north of the Samoan Islands, there is the group of coral islands known as Tokelau, some of which are low atolls – ring-shaped coral islands, often with a lagoon in the center. There are many young people among you who, I think, have not seen a real atoll. And a low atoll, that is, an island which stands very little above the surface of the sea is an unforgettable sight. As one of the old captains aptly put it, the low atoll is a ring of uninterrupted noise, fog, and foam of the waves frantically beating around its shores. The white ring of foam, covered with a rainbow from a shiny cap of the sun's rays refracted in the mist, is surprisingly beautiful from a distance, against the shining blue surface of the sea. But close up, such an atoll looks harsh, and at high tide, perhaps even scary. The even waves that oscillate around the surface of the ocean, suddenly grow near the atoll itself, rushing with a roar and slamming at the atoll with a tremendous roar. And if you find yourself on a low atoll during a hurricane – stock up on your courage. The thick clouds will block out the sunlight, and the sea will become immediately dark, angry, and formidable, furrowed by black clefts among the giant waves. Waves, rising higher and higher, will rush onto the atoll, flooding and crushing everything in its path. Only one or two small areas of the coral ring will remain undamaged, and a man, half-strangled by the wind, stunned by the roar and blinded by splashes, will seek salvation on them. Horror can fill the souls of even the bravest, overwhelming them with the fear of seeing an island sinking, as if drowning in a terrible solitude in the middle of a raging ocean.

"So, among the low Tokelau atolls, there is one called the Fakaofo atoll. It's a small island of only three-hundred-meters in diameter, yet six hundred inhabitants live on it – many more than on the neighboring islands. At high tide times on Fakaofo, only a dense, gray-green dome of a thick coconut tree grove protrudes above the surface of the sea. The Fakaofo Atoll lies nine degrees south of the equator, in the path of constant hurricanes. And yet, while hurricanes flood the neighboring islands, the inhabitants of Fakaofo feel safe. These bronze-skinned native Polynesian sailors surrounded the island with a wall of large segments of coral reefs, and inside they made an embankment, raising the surface of their island almost five meters above the level of the tide. Thus, the natives, without any help of machinery, created a safe haven for themselves. What courage and deep, age-old knowledge of the ocean they must possess, in order to counter the formidable power of the elements with the weak forces of simple human hands!"

"Fakaofo atoll always represents for me, a perfect example of the power of man and his power over the sea. And I have told you about this atoll to show you, my companions, what can be achieved with the simplest of means. Can we, armed with all the power of modern science and technology, fail to achieve a final victory over the ocean – power over its depths?

"That's all I wanted to say. Let me hope that some of you will leave from here at least with the dream of overcoming the depths of the ocean. And the dream of a wise and strong man is already very much.

The scientist's thundering voice fell silent. The silence that prevailed in the room seemed unusually profound by contrast. The speech had captivated the sailors, and stormy ovation broke out in a wave around the hall when the chairman started to say something. During the scholar's speech, Ganyeshyn felt his thoughts, experienced impressions, and sensations of his youth, far removed from him during the war, now moved in his soul again.

***

The drizzle, driven by the wind, beat at the ship. The horizon was approaching quickly. Dusk was falling as if a large amount of ash had been immediately shaken into the air and night was coming fast. The ship rocked smoothly, vibrating steadily to the rhythm of its engines. One of the men on watch closed the portholes of the navigation room and the lights burst into brightness.

Ganyeshyn slowly walked along the bridge. His headache subsided as if it dissolved in the damp, cool ocean breeze. These pains, a consequence of an injury he'd suffered in the Great National War, still bothered him, even though several years had passed. Leaning on the railing, he stared into the darkness. The ship's white superstructure appeared in an obscure mixture of darkness and the ship's lights.

The door banged. The bridge's deck was cut briefly by a wide band of light – someone had left the navigation room, spotted Ganyeshyn in the darkness and addressed him.

"Comrade Captain of the first rank, another sharp blip. Would you like to see?"

"Look, Fyodor," interrupted Ganyeshyn, "enough with the titles. I've said this quite often."

"True, rightly so," laughed Shchytov, the commandant of the hydrographic ship, "but the habits of wartime are hard to break…"

The officers entered a brightly lit navigation room, glistening with polished wood, instruments, and mirrored windows. It was a pleasant transition from the cool darkness and the infinity of the sea to the warm comfort of the room. The feeling of coziness was enhanced by the soft sounds of a violin flowing from the loudspeaker located in the corner of the navigation room.

A midshipman stood in front of a large screen of an echo sounder. He turned to the people entering and stood at attention when he saw Ganyeshyn. Ganyeshyn smiled again; somehow, he couldn't quite get used to the respectful attitude of his fellow workers. Now, in peaceful times, it seemed completely unnecessary.

"Continue your business, midshipman!" Ganyeshyn took off his raincoat, captain's hat, and took out his pipe.

"I… I, actually, enjoy it," the confused midshipman replied quietly.

"Oh, so you like our new sonar?" Ganyeshyn looked at the young man approvingly. "And what, in your opinion, is it better than the Hughes; the latest model?"

"How it can be compared!", exclaimed the midshipman. "First, the depth range. Ours takes every depth without any angular displacements; it has tremendous sensitivity, has very accurate automatic consideration of corrections, and most importantly, an immediate chart of echography, our courses marked right there on the tape."

"Very good... I see that you've already fully acquainted yourself with our device."

"Comrade Sokolov is an enthusiast of deep-sea measurements," interrupted Captain Shchytov. "However, maybe we should look at this irregularity on the tape before the tape escapes."

Ganyeshyn took the pipe out of his mouth and went to a large disk, where an orange peephole burned in the center, and a thin arrow shook, surrounded by a triple ring of graduations and numbers. It was a pointer to the depths of the echo sounder, and beneath it, in a black rectangular frame, behind some shiny glass, was a bluish tape of an echograph – an instrument that continuously drew the profile of the seabed beneath the ship's path.

High-frequency sound vibrations emitted from the bottom of the ship, penetrated down into the inaccessible depths of the ocean and, returning through a complex system of amplifiers, would force the needle to oscillate, drawing the profile line. The midshipman pointed to the appropriate place of the tape. Here, between a thick line which marked the bottom of the ship and the slanted marks of the distance traveled and directional changes, ran a smooth line of a gentle ocean floor, suddenly interrupted by a sharp break: the pointed underwater peak rose almost two kilometers from the four-kilometer flat-bottomed depression of the ocean.

Ganyeshyn smiled in satisfaction.

"That makes fourteen such 'blips' we've found already! No wonder I'm here with you..."

"Admit it honestly," the commandant of the ship turned to Ganyeshyn. "Do you need these underwater 'blips' for a new device?"

"You guessed, you guessed!" Ganyeshyn turned to Shchytov. "Let's sit down because I've already walked about twenty miles along the bridge. My new device has already passed all the tests, and we'll try it at work as soon as we return. I can tell you now, even if the midshipman listens – we do not make any secrets about the principle of the device. My instrument is adapted to see underwater to the greatest depths, based on the principles of a television. The greatest difficulty of the task lies was to illuminate sufficiently large spaces so that, due to the huge absorption of light rays in the oxygen-rich deep waters, the TV was not like looking through the eyes of a short-sighted person. I've achieved good results by creating a 'night eye' – a device so sensitive to light rays that very little light is enough for it to get a picture. Next, I used a double spotlight with two simultaneous beams of rays: one with red and infrared rays, the other with purple and ultraviolet. You know that water absorbs the red, long-term rays; shortwave rays go much deeper – ultraviolet rays reach up thousands of meters from the surface of the ocean. However cloudy, or murky water scatters light, and in those cases, shortwave beams are easily absorbed, while long-wave beams penetrate such waters better. The right combination of the longest and shortest wavelengths in the beam of my projector's light is suitable for various conditions that may occur in the depths of the ocean. Such a device, lowered into the depths, transmits an image through the cable upwards by electric waves, which turns into a visible image on a special screen. The angle of illumination and angle of view of my apparatus is very wide: dual lenses, which can be moved apart as in a rangefinder, give a broad stereoscopic picture. This device sees wider and more clearly than human eyes... What? You look disappointed, Fyodor," Ganyeshyn smiled. "You thought my invention was different?"

"No, no," Shchytov began to justify himself, with a guilty look on his face. "I just don't quite understand what we can do at such great depths. Of course, such 'eyes' are important for any rescue operations, but in these cases, the depths aren't great, and such a complicated camera isn't needed... When we immersed it, we just saw some rock or fish – and that's all."

"It's a lot to start with, Fyodor."

"Yes, but what next?"

"Next? 'Hands.'"

"What?" The Captain did not understand.

"First, 'eyes,' and then 'hands,'" repeated Ganyeshyn. "For the time being..."

"But there are no 'hands' yet."

"No, not yet. They're still in the drawing stage right now."

"Eeh," Shchytov was delighted. "It's good to have such a bright mind. I wouldn't say no!"

"I don't know, Fyodor, sometimes it's hard when you've been fighting for years to do it..." answered Ganyeshyn thoughtfully, standing up and stretching. "To think about it is one thing, but to fulfill it... sometimes a trifle can make you crazy... Well, it's time I head off," and Ganyeshyn threw on a coat.

"Just a minute." Shchytov stopped him. "Soon, we'll be at the Twin Isles, and you wanted to capture the western end of the Aleutian Ridge. Agattu Island is nearby. Where do we turn?"

"I don't remember right now," Ganyeshyn replied, thinking. "Where is their lighthouse, I think at Cape Dog? It's range?"

"Eight miles," prompted Shchytov.

"Well, it's close. About twenty-five miles ahead of Agattu, we'll head northwest to the end of the Aleutian Ridge. And then again along the meridian, fifty miles west of Attu, lying on the very edge of the Twin, from the Commander's traverse... How far are we now from Agattu?"

"Almost seventy miles," said the midshipman.

"Yes, the line of our course goes more to the west. So, to the turning point... forty miles. Well. Wake me up when we turn back."

The door slammed behind Ganyeshyn. Shchytov and the midshipman remained alone. Almost an hour had passed. The tape of the echo sounder crawled along without hurry. The bottom gradually decreased; already the depth under the keel was five kilometers. With great accuracy, the engineers maintained the ship's course for hours, because the accuracy of seabed mapping depended on it.

Shchytov smoked for a long time while he reflected on the personal fate of a group of people who were once united together by a great war. Either his tobacco was too strong, or he'd smoked too much, but he soon felt a familiar pain in his chest and went out to the bridge. The rain was still falling, and wind gusts were still breaking and foaming the crests of the waves. Suddenly, it seemed to Shchytov that something flashed and instantly disappeared, far ahead, just before the bow of his ship. Almost simultaneously, the hoarse voice of the watchman called out:

"Lights dead ahead!"

It took another five minutes for the faint flickering to turn into a bright light of another ship. Minutes passed, but there was no sign of side lights. No more than two miles separated the ships when Shchytov gave his order.

"Attention, the stern light is ahead of us!"

"Will we overtake, comrade Captain?" asked the watch assistant.

"Of course, that one barely moves."

"But what about the course on the measuring equipment?"

"No worries, it'll take some deviation..."

The ships approached each other, continuing in the same stream of the wake. The assistant took the ships horn. Two short, low, and strong sounds swept out over the dark sea. The rudder propulsion clattered, and the ship's bow rolled to the left.

A small night lamp burned in Ganyeshyn's spacious cabin. He'd taken off his jacket and shoes and lay on an ottoman. He'd decided not to undress and lie on the bed because he knew he had to get up soon. He was thinking about his new camera. The deep-water TV was ready, and the inventor had no worries about the outcome of the final tests. The first part of the task he'd set for himself was accomplished. A few years ago, an old scientist who was now no longer alive, had talked about victory over the ocean, about the Fakaofo atoll. He'd spoken not only about the 'eyes' but also about 'hands.' So now it's time for the 'hands.' Ganyeshyn visualized a complicated, telemechanically directed camera, drilling like an auger into the bottom of the ocean under the eye of a television set. The basic principle was to work without any hermetic closures; with low-voltage, high-ampere electric motors that work perfectly in water, and they'd been invented long ago. Water should be for these mechanisms as natural an environment as the air for our earth machines: then a huge pressure won't be a problem – that's what the secret of success lies in!

The broken noise of the siren vibrated in his cabin. Ganyeshyn mechanically listened to them: two short – a left turn. *We are overtaking someone.* A meeting of ships on the high seas always excites the soul of a sailor. Ganyeshyn jumped up and began to pull on his boots.

On the bridge, Shchytov and the assistant saw a red sidelight, and above a top light – of an even stronger red light.

"Trawler," the assistant said quietly. "It was not a stern light, but a circular top-end, and above – a tricolor lantern."

"I see, I see," Shchytov replied. "Do you see that? Watch signalman, to me!"

A light flashed on the indistinct and unknown vessel. Short flashes alternated with sharp, long rays that evoked feelings of anticipation.

"They're calling us," grumbled Shchytov. "Eh, here it is."

Three short flashes were replaced by one long one. In the darkness of the night, the Latin letters flew, one after the other; asking for help – an SOS.

A breathless signalman with a signal lamp appeared on the bridge, with Ganyeshyn arriving at the same time.

"Tell Sokolov to stop the echo sounder!" ordered the Captain.

For a while, the two ships exchanged light signals across the dark night over the ocean. '*Recovery*,' 'San Francisco,' '*Amethyst*,' 'Vladivostok.'

"We have a kilometer of rope cable," Shchytov grumbled to Ganyeshyn. "Can we spare it?"

"Very good! Let's get closer, maybe we can help them with something more."

"Searchlight!" ordered Shchytov.

Agile legs clambered on the deck. Before they powered up their searchlight, the ship sent one last light signal: 'A scientific oceanographic expedition.' Then the powerful searchlight of *Amethyst* pierced a wide, bright light into the dark night. At the end of it, a black, low ship with a far back tilted chimney appeared.

"Let it stand still, we'll approach," the captain decided. *I don't know what their maneuverability is...* he thought. The searchlight went out, and the signalman quickly carried out the order. Then the *Amethyst* turned on the light again and began to draw closer to an awkward-looking American.

"Interesting! They are also oceanographers, like us," Ganyeshyn spoke briskly after the distressed ship gave light signals that told him there was an oceanographic expedition on it. "I wonder what happened to them?"

The *Amethyst* sailed to the American ship as far as the waves allowed it, settled alongside it, and then Ganyeshyn, who spoke some English, took the bullhorn. From the brief words exchanged, and the words muffled by the splash of waves crashing against the sides and the wind, the Soviet sailors quickly realized the tragedy of what had happened. It concerned a large bathysphere – a steel ball recently built to explore the greater depths, and which had already been successfully descended several times. On the last descent, however, the hoist rope with the electric cable broke off, and the steel ball remained at a depth of three thousand meters, the greatest depth for which it was designed. The bathysphere was equipped with a paraffin float and should have floated to the surface independently after the cable broke and when the power supply to the electromagnets was interrupted, because the magnets no longer attracted the heavy iron load, thus the bathysphere floats. But this time, it didn't surface – and there were two people in it – the engineer who'd built it, John Mills, and a zoologist, Norman Noors. The air supply would only last for sixty hours, and they'd already spent forty-eight hours in fruitless attempts to hook the bathysphere with grapples made with specially designed brackets. If the sphere was whole and the researchers were alive in it, they only had about twelve to fifteen hours of air left.

The Soviet sailors stood silently on the bridge.

The large cargo boom of the American ship protruded overboard and nodded with its nok – the front part of the crane – as if it was pointing to the waves that had swallowed the steel ball.

"It seems that they are not fine," Shchytov said quietly to Ganyeshyn. "It's almost impossible to find it in waters three kilometers deep out in the open sea! There are no markers without a coast... Yes, I wouldn't want to be there."

Ganyeshyn didn't reply, but frowned and glanced over at 'Recovery.'

"Fyodor Grigoryevich, get me a lifeboat," he said unexpectedly.

Shchytov noticed his determined, stubborn look.

The Americans, when they saw the boat dancing on the waves, quickly lowered the ladder. Ganyeshyn was soon surrounded by a group of people on the bridge. His calm and resolute eyes, looking out from under the peak of a military cap, covered with a yellow hood, encouraged people exhausted by the struggle.

"Who is the commander?" Ganyeshyn asked in a low voice.

"I am the second-in-command, Captain of the vessel Penland," introduced an American who stood opposite Ganyeshyn. "Our Commander is there..." and Penland pointed to the sea.

"Let me ask you some questions," Ganyeshyn continued. "Forgive my brevity, but we have to hurry if we want..."

"Do you want to help us?" someone asked in a clear voice.

"Yes, but do not interrupt me," Ganyeshyn said dryly, "I'm talking to the commander."

"I'm listening," the American captain quickly replied.

"How many trawling cables do you have?"

"Two, with yours – three."

"What length is the cable that remains attached to the bathysphere?"

"That's the misfortune, sir, that the cable broke very near the place where its attached to the ball. The cable is over a mile long down there, but the bathysphere has a device which, when torn off, immediately separates the rope at the place of attachment. So, you can't count on getting hooked on the cable; only the brackets remain."

"Is there a radio in the bathysphere?"

"There is, but it doesn't work now, because it was only powered by the cable."

"According to your calculations, do they still have air for twelve hours?"

"Twelve to fifteen. That's all they can maximize with the toughest savings."

"Yes, the situation is very serious... And what do you want to do next?"

"Continue searching by the same means – there's nothing more we can do. Two planes will fly from Macdonald Bay on Agattu. They'll be here in the morning and bring improved grappling devices. On the day of the catastrophe, we radioed a ship equipped with an electromagnetic device, to help us in our search for the bathysphere. This ship is coming with all possible speed and may be here tomorrow. That's actually our last hope," Captain Penland finished, lowering his voice and approaching Ganyeshyn. "Two more ships trawled with us, but they've gone to Macdonald Bay."

"Thank you, Captain. I hope we can help you. Please, show me your winches and lifts."

Ganyeshyn and Penland descended onto the large deck, cluttered with coils of cables with a huge winch in the middle. The electric lamp swayed alongside the mast, illuminating the various items accumulated there.

"I think the situation is hopeless, sir," said Captain Penland quickly as soon as they left the bridge. "Judge for yourself: a terrible depth, the open sea, no possibility of either finding the right bearings or throwing a buoy. I've done everything that I can. I haven't left the deck for two days now. There, on the bridge, is Mills's wife, the hydrochemist of our expedition. I didn't want to express my opinion around her."

"Did she ask me?" And, having received an affirmative answer, he regretted that he'd reacted so sharply. "We will mark from the bridge the probable area where the bathysphere is, and I will be grateful for your complete information... Another question, Captain," said Ganyeshyn after a brief pause, while they squeezed themselves carefully through the littered deck. "Why did your researchers decide to go down here? In the open sea?"

"Here is one of the rare places where there are many steep underwater cliffs, and the bedrock is completely exposed from sediment. One of the objectives of our research is to study the igneous bedrock in the depths of the ocean, but somehow it went badly..."

Ganyeshyn did not answer. He ran lightly up the steps onto the bridge.

"Now we're going to search. We'll put the buoys out."

"Why the buoys?" several voices were heard at once.

"You will see," Ganyeshyn smiled slightly. A small hand touched his sleeve. The sailor turned around and saw huge, glistening eyes that were strained with excruciating tension.

"Captain, please tell me honestly, is there any hope of saving them?... Can you do it?"

"Hopefully, if the bathysphere isn't damaged," Ganyeshyn answered.

"My God!" exclaimed the American.

Ganyeshyn gently interrupted their exchange.

"Excuse me, time does not wait," and with that, he turned to those gathered on the bridge. "The Soviet hydrographic ship *Amethyst* will proceed immediately with the rescue operation. This, of course, does not exclude your work, but now, I ask for you to trust us and move away from the place of immersion of the bathysphere. I have devices that are extremely useful for this present situation, but the main device is located in Vladivostok. I will bring it here by a fast plane, but it will still take at least five to six hours – the distance is very great. During this time, we will try to find the bathysphere's exact location and mark the place with a buoy. Thus we will facilitate the rescue work after the arrival of the plane when we will have only seven hours left. You will have to raise the bathysphere because we don't have such powerful winches and cables. That's it... Give a signal to our ship to turn off the searchlight, and light your own. I'm going back to the *Amethyst*.

Previously invisible behind the strong light it had been throwing, and now under the glow of the *Recovery*, the *Amethyst* shone with its snow-white grace. The distinct silhouette of the ship, the lightness of its superstructures, harmonized with the power of the slanting backward chimneys – a sign of the strength of the vessel.

"Is it a hydrographic ship?" Captain Penland shouted. "It looks as graceful as a swan!" Indeed, the white, glittering lights of the ship did make it look like a giant swan prostrating itself on the water, preparing for flight.

"This is a navy hydrographic ship," Ganyeshyn emphasized, then he raised his hand to his hat and left the bridge. His boat quickly sped through the wide corridor of light. The American sailors silently watched him go, slightly surprised by the sudden appearance of Ganyeshyn and his confident orders.

"He must be an important person to the Russians, sir," the first officer finally said. "And if he can save the bathysphere..."

"I do not know if he can," answered Penland, "but just look at their ship!"

Although silence reigned once again on the *Recovery*, this time the general mood was different. Now there was a subconscious belief that this beautiful white ship, that so unexpectedly emerged from the ocean night, and this man with the intelligent, decisive gaze, extending a friendly helping hand to them — would really be able to help.

Meanwhile, Ganyeshyn and Shchytov wasted no time and went directly to the radio room together. A converter bellowed, lights of neon flickered, sending conditional call-signals over thousands of kilometers of ocean. He tapped the key for a long time until the radio operator turned his sweaty face to the officers.

"Vladivostok is responding."

"Well, the fate of these two poor people will be decided now," Ganyeshyn turned to Shchytov. "If we manage to reach the Admiral... What if he's away though?"

The device tapped away, then fell silent, then the characteristic Morse crackles were heard again. Ganyeshyn listened intensely to the apparatus's galloping dry language. He waited, just like the ship swaying alongside them, and those two men locked in their steel coffin on the ocean floor. What would the answer be? The *Amethyst* crew had already prepared everything to save the Americans.

The headquarters stated that the Admiral was at sea on his ship. Again, call signs were sent out over an immeasurable distance to a powerful new battleship, and somewhere over the airwaves, they found the antenna of a formidable ship.

"'*Marshal*,' responds," announced the radio operator shortening the name of the liner out of habit.

"Finally!" Ganyeshyn breathed a sigh of relief. The device succinctly, precisely, and clearly tapped the request and fell silent.

A few minutes of tense waiting passed – and in the code of dashes and dots, the sailors heard: "I give the order, I wish you success."

Shchytov led his ship to the opposite edge of the area where the bathysphere was believed located.

"Prepare the deep-sea buoy, two thousand seven hundred meters!" the first officer ordered.

A grapple was immediately hooked up and a glimmering shell, similar to an aerial bomb, was thrown overboard. The sailor tugged the rope, and the projectile disappeared almost without a splash, into the greenish black of the sea. After a quarter of an hour and fifty seconds, according to the first officer's stopwatch, a slightly steaming object popped out above the waves in the light of the *Amethyst* searchlight, opened like an umbrella, and a tiny white dome lay on the water and bobbed on the waves. The Soviet ship signaled to the American to hold onto a floating anchor and stop their engines.

"I want to avoid the slightest resonance of their motors," Ganyeshyn explained to the midshipman, standing at the echo sounder and slowly operating scales and regulators.

"Could I ask you a question, sir?" the midshipman began timidly. "Do you really think we can use an echo sounder to find the bathysphere?"

"Of course. Didn't you know that the pre-war sensitive echo sounders detected submarines and sunken ships? Hughes' echo sounder, for example, drew the contours of the *Lusitania* with an echograph – even the layout of the superstructures was obtained – and this was at a depth of fifty fathoms... The size of the bathysphere, given to me by the Americans, of course, can't be compared with the *Lusitania*. The sphere is only a three-meter ball, on top of a mushroom-shaped float of two meters in height, but our echo sounder is much more sensitive and emits polarized echoes."

"And... the depth?" the midshipman asked carefully.

"And the accuracy of regulators?" Ganyeshyn jokingly answered him in the same tone, and again leaned over the device looking into the tables of oceanographic sections.

Meanwhile, the Americans watched the Soviet ship constantly, as it appeared in a band of light, then disappear again, showing red or green lights.

"Look, they put the buoys out," the first officer said animatedly when during the second pass of the *Amethyst* in front of the bow of the *Recovery*, a white mushroom object swayed.

"They've apparently invented deep-sea buoys. Such things have long been used in underwater warfare and it's all a matter of durability. They clearly have achieved this, that's all. Very simple."

"All things are simple when you know how to make them!" the first officer muttered in response to his captain.

Hour after hour, the white ship crisscrossed a small area of the sea marked off in a square by four buoys. The wind died down, and the surface of the water became oily and smooth. The people in the bathysphere only had enough air for another ten hours... Again, heavy hopelessness hung over the American ship, and all the people gathered on the bridge and on the deck, did not take their eyes off the *Amethyst*, as if their very ardent desire could help in its search.

As they watched, the *Amethyst* showed a green light, then again turned back towards the *Recovery* and passed to the very left edge of the area designated by the buoys. As the Soviet ship got closer, its sharp nose grew, then another hundred meters – and again it took a hopeless turn to the north.

Suddenly, the barely audible noise of the *Amethyst's* engines stopped. In the silence of the night, even the telegraph bell could be heard, and the captain's voice resounded, issuing an order. In the unfamiliar fluency of Russian speech, only one word was clear: "buoy."

"They found it! They found!" exclaimed Mill's wife excitedly.

There was confusion on the American ship, and this showed in the revival of the exhausted people. An indefinite expectation is easier to bear than the already realized failure. But shortly, the already familiar voice from the *Amethyst* calmly reported through the megaphone:

"The bathysphere is found!"

Dozens of voices from the *Recovery* deck responded with a joyous exclamation.

In the navigation room, Ganyeshyn filled his pipe and half-closed his overstrained eyes. During the four-hour search, the echo sounder's tape was covered with a series of curves that succeeded one another, but not a single projection broke the smooth line of the rock profile. The ship had moved very slowly, and the monotony of the results lulled attention, and it had been necessary to keep vigilance all the time by sheer force of will. In the vicinity of the last turn, the echograph pen, which had up to that point flowed smoothly, suddenly jumped, and a tiny curve barely lifted above the flat line.

"There it is!" Ganyeshyn shouted happily.

The first officer rushed to the bridge like an arrow. The telegraph clanged twice – 'stop' and 'back.'

"Buoy, two thousand eight hundred meters!" Shchytov shouted, and a heavy marker fell from the left side.

"Hurray! We have managed to do this!" Shchytov congratulated Ganyeshyn a few minutes later in the navigation room.

"Well, not so much," Ganyeshyn replied wearily, "we've been searching back and forth for four hours. There isn't much time left, but we have to wait. I'm going to rest on the couch before the plane..."

"Can I interrupt, comrade Captain?" The first officer stood in the doorway. "The Americans are asking if they should try to hook the bathysphere now?"

Shchytov looked at Ganyeshyn who, without opening his eyes, replied: "Of course, in this current situation, we shouldn't neglect any chance."

Amethyst gave its place at the buoy to the American ship, and floated away a small distance, lightly swaying as if resting. Tired sailors went to their cabins while both commanders remained in the navigation room. Only the sailors from the watch watched the American ship. There was a clank of winches, a whistle of steam and a screech of ropes; the Americans were operating again, inspired by the success of the Soviet seamen.

Ganyeshyn and Shchytov were woken up at the same time by the drone of an aircraft.

"No, it's not ours," Shchytov determined.

It was dawn. Dampness and cold penetrated under his clothes, sobering up the sleepless captain. From the bridge, the sea seemed unusually lively – two seaplanes swayed near the sides of the *Recovery*, and a little further distance away were two warships – a long, gray, high-cruiser, and a squat patrol ship.

"The population is increasing," grinned Ganyeshyn. "There should be ours here soon also. I will go to the Americans, see what and how..."

This time, when his boat approached the *Recovery*, there were welcoming cheers. However, the faces of the people who met Ganyeshyn were gray and gloomy. Although they'd tried consistently for three hours, they'd failed to catch the bathysphere; they couldn't even hook it with a cable. Only seven hours remained to save those trapped deep in the ocean.

"The ship with the electromagnet device hasn't come yet," Captain Penland said to Ganyeshyn, "but it is less necessary now after your remarkable intervention. How to capture the bathysphere at this damned, unthinkable depth? Apparently, the cables get diverted... perhaps by some currents in the deep layers of water. The buoy also doesn't give the exact location."

"It may deviate," said Ganyeshyn, glancing at Mills' wife approaching them. He turned to the young woman and saluted.

The American's eyes met his gaze with an expression of such hope that Ganyeshyn felt sad.

"We worked all this time..." tears and pain sounded in the words of the young woman. "But this terrible depth is stronger than us. My only hope now is for your help again..." she sighed heavily. "When do you expect your plane?"

Ganyeshyn raised his hand to look at his watch.

"Airplane? It's here!" he immediately said loudly and happily.

Everyone raised their heads. Indeed, the plane, which, due to the noise of the working winch, they couldn't hear, was now descending, moving the sky and the sea with the growing drone of its engines.

"It is nosediving to make haste," Ganyeshyn realized.

A narrow plane with high wings, whipped up water spray, turned and soon, calm and silent, swayed next to the *Amethyst*.

The morning fog, as if frightened by an airplane, thinned revealing a clear, blue sky. The sun played on the heavy, oily waves, illuminated the snow-white of the *Amethyst*, and it sparkled with hundreds of blinding lights on its copper parts. Ganyeshyn looked from the plane to the *Amethyst* as if he saw this beautiful ship for the first time. He smiled.

"We'll see the bathysphere soon," he said to the Americans.

The American woman, having suppressed an exclamation, took a step towards Ganyeshyn. He guessed her thoughts.

"If you want, I will show you my device with great pleasure. We'll go over right away," he offered.

Ganyeshyn asked Captain Penland to wait for the TV to be installed, and after finding the bathysphere, to immediately approach Soviet ship and act on its signals.

At that same time, on the *Amethyst*, a mechanic brandishing a wrench gave a speech to their engineers and fitters.

"The speed with which we assemble this machine," he said, "will determine whether or not we will be able to save those men below, who have only six hours of air left. And another thing: if we save them, it will be a miracle made by the hands of Soviet sailors."

"And it will be a real miracle!" one of the engineers said. "I worked as a diver, so I understand what it means to get such a small capsule from a depth of three kilometers... but I think we can do it."

Captain Shchytov wasn't surprised by the arrival of the guest. Mrs. Mills was invited to the navigation room, and Shchytov immediately seconded the midshipman, who knew English well. The wife of engineer Mills listened absently-mindedly to his explanations, and often glanced through the window of the cabin, to where she could see the work that was taking place on the deck: some bases were screwed together, cables were dragged, and boxes were unloaded from the plane.

Ganyeshyn briefly looked into the navigation room, and the young woman immediately rushed to meet him.

"Oh, please forgive me, but your device seems to be very complicated. They may not be able to assemble it in time, because..." and she silently pointed to a large clock, screwed into the bulkhead.

"Another six and a half hours are at our disposal," answered Ganyeshyn. "The device is really complicated, but our sailors can do this quickly – but I won't hide that it's incredibly difficult work. Have faith in our sailors, Mrs. Mills, you can trust them."

Yet another agonizing wait stretched ahead for the tired, young woman. If only she could help in preparing this mysterious device! Time was running out. Suddenly, a terrible roar stunned her. That was too much for the strained nerves of the young woman.

"My God, what is it?" In exhaustion, she leaned against the bulkhead.

"It's a siren. Ours is indeed very loud," the midshipman explained matter-of-factly. "*Amethyst* gives this signal to tell us that the instrument is ready, and the search begins."

The midshipman was not mistaken. Immediately, Shchytov appeared and invited Mills' wife to go down. The television set was temporarily installed in a dark laboratory. The deep-water part of the apparatus swayed on the boom as it was swung overboard, and a huge coil of cable was inserted into the winch. The ship slowly sailed towards the buoy that marked the place of the bathysphere.

"Lower?" Shchytov asked Ganyeshyn as he appeared on the deck.

"I think it's time."

"Aren't you scared?"

"Of what?"

"Well, you never know what... The device has just been assembled and hastily installed. It could fail. I worry too..."

"No, it has been tried and experienced many times. Lower it boldly, faster!"

The camera quickly disappeared into the waves, and the cable ran for a long time through the counter of the coil until the wonderful 'eye' finally reached the desired depth. The cable was attached to a shock absorber, which mitigated the ship's roll, and at the same time, in the darkness of the laboratory, Ganyeshyn switched on the current. Mills' wife, beside herself with excitement, looked at the oval screen, which suddenly turned from black into a bluish glow. Ganyeshyn threw abrupt words to Shchytov, incomprehensible to the American woman – they were orders from him to the team which was then transferred to the deck, to the winch.

As soon as the camera reached the depth of fifteen meters above the bottom, Ganyeshyn pressed two white buttons on the right side of the screen. Down there, tiny screws that rotated the device were set in motion. A black shadow appeared in the blue light of the screen, and it immediately became clear that this glowing blue was the deep transparent water, in which the slightest misting of the sediment was showed as a swarm of microscopic silver dots, reflecting and scattering light. The view of the ocean floor on the TV screen was unusual. A person who had fallen onto another planet would probably also be amazed and unable to understand what they saw. Ganyeshyn, who had mastered the view of the depths of the ocean during previous tests of his camera, carefully directed the instrument. The black, slightly swirling hump on the left was a flat ledge of a rocky bottom. Further to the north, the bottom decreased slightly, because the reddish reflection of the bottom in the front disappeared, cut off by the same silvery blue glow.

By manipulating different levers, Ganyeshyn changed the projections of a clear image. As he turned the instrument slowly, the image on the screen also changed. At first, a black wall appeared in the distance, which took on a red hue under the intensified spotlight, and then details began to stand out in it: a huge slanting crack, a bulging ledge... but then the TV turned, and the gloomy rocks disappeared in the shimmering blue of the previous lighting. In the depths of the screen, misty, sharp 'teeth' appeared. What they were, became clearer as the camera approached, and eventually became a solid base in the blue-blackness background in the darkness.

"The limit of illumination," explained Ganyeshyn, "is about one kilometer."

The high teeth of the underwater ridge looked gloomy, barely visible in the eternal darkness and coolness of the underwater world.

The camera made a full circle — a rocky bottom extended everywhere, covered with a layer of silt, that glistened in the rays of the spotlight, like an aluminum powder. The view of the ocean depths gave the impression that something hostile lurked in the deepest darkness that surrounded the field of view of the camera. It was a terrible world of silence, darkness, and a cold alien world to the earth's surface, motionless, unchanging, devoid of hope and beauty.

The bathysphere was nowhere to be seen.

Did we miss the buoy so much? flashed through Ganyeshyn's head. *For half a kilometer! Oh, clearly, it must lie in this hollow!*

He started tilting the camera lens down. A vague dark spot appeared on the edge of the frame. Ganyeshyn quickly turned the lever. The blur moved to the center of the screen. He zoomed in and enhanced the picture. Its indistinct outlined edges sharpened, and the black color began to appear red again. The young woman behind Ganyeshyn made a faint cry and immediately covered her mouth with her hand. An egg-shaped capsule stood in the center of the frame, which now seemed like a translucent glass. The clarity of the image was so great that a piece of dangling cable could be seen hanging above it, the thick loops of the rescue buckles, and a gleam on the porthole, which looked back at the sailors like a brilliant garnet-red, mysterious eye.

"The bathysphere has portholes on all four sides, which means they already see us," Ganyeshyn explained to Mills's wife. "Now the most important thing is to see if they are alive..." Ganyeshyn hastily recovered his words. "Let's try to talk to them."

He snapped something and put his long fingers on the button. Depending on the movement of his fingers, the screen went out and flashed again. All those present in the room realized that extinguishing and re-lighting the searchlight, Ganyeshyn sent Morse code light signals to the window of the bathysphere. He repeated just one question many times before he turned the light off and waited for an answer in front of the darkened screen. Everyone in the cramped cabin held their breath, restraining any excitement of hope for a response. The screen remained black. A minute passed. Slowly and ominously time stretched into the second minute, and then a bright, turquoise light appeared, disappeared, flashed brighter and spread in a wide blue circle – a silent answer that shone up from the ocean floor.

"They are alive! Notify *Recovery*. Let it come up to hook the cables onto the bathysphere!" Ganyeshyn shouted happily. At that moment, the blue light flashed like a signal lantern. "They say…" Ganyeshyn turned to Mills' wife, but he heard only a sigh and a soft fall of her body.

"Carry her to the navigation room! Get the doctor!" Shchytov ordered the approaching people. "The poor thing couldn't stand anymore. She's waited almost three days, she was tired… Well, what's their message," he turned to Ganyeshyn.

"They say they're both alive, they save oxygen as much as they can, but they won't last more than another two hours. The bathysphere is good, the ballast did not break off…" Ganyeshyn was reading light signs flashing on the screen. "We can't understand how…? You won't understand, wait," said the sailor aloud.

A siren from the American ship was heard. The lowering of the cables with grapple handles had already begun. The blue circle disappeared from the screen, and the TV spotlight flickered. Ganyeshyn informed the people in the bathysphere that they'd started the rescue.

Another hour passed by watching the TV screen constantly. Whistles, shouts in a megaphone, the noise of the American ship's engines, the hiss of steam, and the rumble of the winches was heard over the sea. The people trapped in the bathysphere had only one hour of life left – sixty minutes – when for nearly the past sixty hours, efforts by hundreds of people had failed.

The victory came suddenly and unnoticed. Huge grapplers lowered according to Ganyeshyn's instructions, hooked on a side buckle. A siren of the *Amethyst* roared loudly, and at that precise moment, the engineer of the *Recovery* winch reversed the clutch. Slowly, the slack, huge, arm-thick sized cable went taut, and the drum creaked from tension. A flexible steel cable, woven from two hundred and twenty-two wires, weighed sixty tons together with the bathysphere – three times more than the permissible load.

The cable held. In the blue light of the TV screen, the bathysphere swayed, straightened, jerked up, and slowly began to rise. Ganyeshyn, manipulating the lenses, watched it for a while until it disappeared, then turned off the power, turned on the light in the lab, and after waiting a moment for his eyes to adjust, he went out onto the deck. The television was no longer needed. All the attention was now focused on the *Recovery's* winch, which was slowing drawing up the immense burden from the deep. Captain Penland stared intently at the evenly coiling reel, calculating the speed of the lift in his mind – only forty minutes remained before the fatal period.

"We won't make it! They'll suffocate..."

Taking a deadly risk upon his shoulders, Penland ordered to accelerate the lift. Among the strained silence, the winch rattled quicker – and the drum began to rotate faster. A few more minutes passed. Suddenly the sharp whistling of the steam cut the monotonous clatter of the winch. The winch then did a few quick turns, and a pale engineer stopped it quickly.

"The cable...!" someone shouted with fear.

The horror gripped people on both vessels, before they all rushed as one, to stretch their necks and peer overboard. A cold sweat poured over Penland, his throat went dry, and he couldn't gather his thoughts. He couldn't give any command, and he didn't know what to command.

Suddenly a huge, blue, ovoid object jumped out of the slow-moving, frothy waves, disappeared into a column of splashes, and after a second it bobbed lightly in a white circle of foam.

It suddenly surpassed the ballast of the bathysphere, which then jerked up, causing the automatic opening of the grippers, which freed the device from the weight of the cable. An eruption of victorious cries broke out everywhere, drowned out immediately by a powerful roar of four sirens. The vessel threw into the expanse of the ocean, the news of the new victory of human reason and will.

Ganyeshyn stood with his legs apart and looked intently at the bathysphere he had saved. Shchytov put his heavy hand on his shoulder.

"Leonid Styepanovich, the Admiral asks about the results."

"I'm going now. You give the order to raise the camera... And how's our guest?"

"I sent her back, she is needed more there," Shchytov smiled. "Although, she looked everywhere for you... apparently, she wanted to thank you."

Ganyeshyn weakly waved his hand and headed for the radio cabin. The bathysphere had already been towed to the *Recovery*."

Leaving the radio cabin, Ganyeshyn saw Shchytov again.

"I want to tell you this," said Shchytov sternly and seriously, "about your TV... I've wrongly thought of it..." Any further words he said were drowned out by the roar of the engines of the Soviet aircraft rising up.

Ganyeshyn firmly shook his friend's hand.

"What do we do next?" asked Shchytov.

"What?" Ganyeshyn was surprised. "We'll pull up the camera and go on our way."

"Won't you go there, to them?" the Captain exclaimed. "I ordered the lifeboat not to be lifted..."

"No, I won't go."

"Well, you are just amazing! Aren't you interested in meeting those survivors? Don't you have any questions you want to ask them? After all, they also research the bottom..."

"Sure, I'm curious. But you know..." Ganyeshyn jokingly winked. "There will be thanks. The engineer's wife looked with such eyes... but meanwhile, we will run quickly and escape!"

The people on the ship of the American expedition were so busy raising and opening the bathysphere, that they didn't notice the white Soviet ship quickly picked up its lifeboat and the camera. As the *Amethyst* was about to leave, it asked about the health of those rescued, and received a reply that "they are weak, but out of danger." It then turned around and began to gain momentum.

The Americans looked at the actions of the *Amethyst* with bewilderment, and it was only when the signal of the traditional farewell appeared on the halyard of the Soviet ship – they understood what it was all about. The signalman from *Recovery* desperately waved the flags, but *Amethyst* increased the speed, and only the powerful horn of the siren and the waving sailors' hats sent a friendly farewell. The rescued researchers, officers, and sailors, all stared as one after the white ship that was getting smaller and smaller in the sunny distance. Suddenly a resounding roar of guns rolled over the green waves: the cruiser saluted the departing *Amethyst*. Again, and again, the guns thundered. On the *Amethyst*, the flag with the red star was lowered, and then the stars and stripes of America soared.

The Soviet ship went on as if nothing had happened, with its engines roaring and slicing through the waves of the Pacific Ocean. Ganyeshyn watched TV, dreaming of a soft bed. It cost him a lot to save the American bathysphere. The voice of Shchytov came from the bridge:

"Leonid Styepanovich, come, the Americans are calling." There was a friendly mockery in the captain's words. "Technology can reach you anywhere, even from the depths of the ocean."

The Americans called *Amethyst* by name, without call signs, and the name of the gem persistently sounded over the airwaves. The radio operator tapped out kind words of gratitude, a request for the name of the commander who led the rescue operation, admiration for the unprecedented work of the Russian sailors, and the miraculous invention. A sharp click of the *Amethyst's* call sign, characteristic of a powerful radio station of a new battleship, suddenly intervened in the dry crackle of the radio from the *Recovery*. The radio operator got the answer, and Ganyeshyn listened to clear signals, greeting the American expedition and the crew of the *Amethyst*. The Admiral was especially satisfied with Ganyeshyn. After answering to Admiral, Ganyeshyn gave a command to the radio operator.

"Communication to *Recovery*, to the head of the American oceanographic expedition Mills: 'The Admiral of the Soviet Pacific Ocean fleet has just conveyed to you congratulations on the rescue and wishes for further success in your bold work."

Five minutes later, Ganyeshyn was fast asleep in his cabin.

***

The autumn Vladivostok rain was poured in an uninterrupted stream and lashed at the high window of Ganyeshyn's office. The seaman was re-reading a letter from the two American scientists he'd saved a month and a half ago, intending to answer them. The shrewd scientists had sent a letter to the Admiral, asking him to pass it onto Ganyeshyn, who wasn't difficult for the Admiral to find.

'Only a person, who has spent sixty hours in hopeless despair on an inaccessible ocean floor can understand what you have done,' the scientists wrote. *'For several hours, we struggled to separate the ballast stuck to the bottom of the bathysphere with a screw jack, slowly suffocating, and drenching ourselves in our sweat in the icy cold. It is impossible to convey what we experienced, having already fallen into a resigned indifference, faced with our inevitable fate, to have suddenly seen the light in*

our windows and understood your signals... From that unforgettable moment, we now live with a firm faith in the infinite power of man, in his bright future, in the fact that there is no loneliness even in the most daring quest not yet understood by the world...'

After reading the letter, Ganyeshyn began to write his response.

'It is difficult for me to answer the question of how I achieved such results in conquering the depths of the ocean. Perhaps the main thing here was in the exact orientation of the tasks set and, of course, in the enormous material possibilities. The direction was first given to me by an old scientist, who several years ago called upon us seamen, to help science find the 'eyes' and 'hands' that could reach the ocean floor. He also showed us what a person is capable of in the fight against the sea when he spoke about the extraordinary Fakaofo atoll. The financial means was given to me by my homeland.

'I only developed the idea and turned my focus away from lowering a person into the depths of the ocean, and instead replaced it with a device that wouldn't need air and was resistant to the terrible pressure. Thus, was developed my camera and TV – the 'human eye' lowered to the bottom of the ocean floor. My drilling tools, which we use to obtain specimens of rocks from the seabed – are the outstretched 'hands.' I remember the deep-water creatures: some of them have eyes placed on long antennae; that's what gave me the idea to use the television.

Ganyeshyn wrote for some more time, he pondered some more, then quickly finished:

Therefore, I believe that your gratitude should not be addressed to me personally, but to my homeland, my people. Because what would I be or any other man without a homeland, without the support of a large number of people? Alone, even the wisest and the most distinguished person would have remained only a dreamer. Support: help from the government, a huge fleet team, various people from the scientist to a locksmith – all that which is my homeland – led to those achievements that seemed almost supernatural to you. And this is only the beginning because we are still moving forward.'

Ganyeshyn finished the letter, stood up and went to the window. Water trickled down the glass panes, through which a distant, rocky headland, overgrown with oaks was visible.

THE TRAILS OF OLD MINERS

The mining engineer Kanin told us this story. He sat leaning comfortably in the chair and spoke as if to himself, not addressing anyone. This was his story...

***

I would like to tell you a simple story from the life of the former, passionate miners, who made a very strong impression on me.

Twenty years ago, in 1929, I researched old copper mines near Orenburg, now known as Czkalov. Here, for almost as long as humans have endeavored, the mining of copper ores had been carried out, with the mines forming an intricate labyrinth of tunnels hollowed out over a vast expanse into the depths of the earth. These mines had been closed for a long time, and nothing remained of their above-ground buildings.

On the expanses of the steppes, on the slopes and ridges of low hills, stand large heaps of bluish-green stains – these are the dumps of waste ore – large heaps of worthless ore bordering large funnels – and in some places, you can see the hollows of old, failed, buried shafts. In places, these dumps and funnels completely cover vast fields of several square kilometers. Such a land, in the words of the local grain-growers, is 'spoiled,' and cannot be plowed; therefore, the unearthed sections have become overgrown with feather-grass, and the shafts of the mines, with stunted cherry trees. Even at the height of summer when everything around is already burned out, and the steppe lies brown in the whitish haze of scorching heat, the hills with remnants of old mining operations are covered with flowers. These greenish-blue heaps of ore dumps sprinkled with dark cherry foliage and golden, swaying feather-grass, create fantastic and beautiful combinations of delicate colors. Like watercolors of talented artists, these small patches of color look like islands on a brown steppe of stubble and fallow land.

It's good to rest at this place after a monotonous journey on a hot, dusty road. The wind stirs the feather-grasses, and whistles through the bushes. It brings to mind times of the past when these now deserted and abandoned areas were once the busiest places in the whole steppe. One could hear the shouts of boys, the clatter of horse-drawn carts, covers of shaft hatches banging, cranking wheels creaking, wheelbarrows and ore carts thundering, and women chattering as they sorted the ore manually. All these people have died long ago, but deep under the surface of the earth, countless underground passages remain, silent and dark, as permanent monuments to their labor.

I managed to get to explore many such old excavations. For more than two months I climbed through them, sometimes with an assistant but mostly alone, because my assistant was afraid of dangerous places. I went there to do an underground survey and to search for any abandoned ore reserves and collect samples of it. In these places, the rocks are dry, surprisingly stable, and many excavations have been standing for hundreds of years, almost without any deterioration.

All the archival plans, maps, and data on the Orenburg copper mines accumulated since the 18th century was lost during the Civil War. Therefore, the labyrinth of old underground works had to be rediscovered, traveling through them at random as if in an unknown land.

The study fascinated me so much, that at one point, I didn't go up to the surface and see the light of day for two whole days; I was so absorbed in trying to figure out some big system of workings. The darkness and silence of the maze of seams, like an interstate labyrinth that writhed in all directions, and the shaft stations of the overburdened mines dangling threateningly from a great height – all this had a special charm for me. With the monotony of clockwork, drops of moisture fell in wet passages, and occasionally, I'd hear barely audible sounds of rushing water escaping from some upper levels to the lower levels.

Carrying my flashlight, compass, and notebook, I barely crawled through some narrow cross-cut passages or irregular tunnels that connected one system of excavations to another. Sometimes the passage, buried with sand as a result of the penetration of surface waters, was so low that I had to crawl along it, curling into a ball. Sometimes, crawling like this, I'd feel an uncontrollable urge to take a deep breath, but as soon as I'd start to do this, I'd immediately be filled with the sensation horror as I'd eerily feel hundreds of thousands of tons of rocks pressing on me from all sides, with an overwhelming, incredible force.

And how interesting it was unraveling the methods of exploiting the ore's seams, as applied by the former mining companies, tracing, and determining the age of the workings – from those simple but deformed walls created with manual tools, to the smoothed pickaxes of the mid-nineteenth century works, then the wide and direct, but newest walls forged by explosions! Even stranger are the very narrow passages, mined according to the outline of the ore deposits; low drifts of the 18th-century excavations, and regular, simple shafts and sloped corridors of prehistoric times.

I could make out those scars made by a pickaxe, gloomy and blackened over the course of time, the remains of old covers, piles of boulders fallen from the ceiling, and evenly arranged structures of wall supports – all illuminated from the deep darkness of the smooth wall by the shifting light of my flashlight.

Huge black trunks of petrified trees, sometimes even with branches intact, make a striking impression. Giants of long-extinct forests now turned into iron and flint lay across the workings, and often the course curved around such a tree either from above or below, unable to penetrate its hard body.

I could tell a lot more about the underground expeditions that I made this summer, but I've only briefly outlined them to give you an idea of the situation of everything that happened.

I lived in the village of Gornyj, located in a deep valley carved out by a small river, nestled between high hills. The last foreman of the old mine – Kornit Polenov – also lived in my village... a ninety-year-old man but still robust, and a former foreman of the owners of the Paszkowi mines. The old codger lived in a tiny house on the other side of the road, opposite to where I lived, and almost every evening he sat on a bench near his house, staring motionlessly at the high hills where the ore dumps of the mines rose in front of him.

At the very beginning of my work, I asked the old man about various mines, which he knew and remembered perfectly. However, I quickly noticed that the old man hid many things from me, using his old age and weak memory as an excuse. I tried to encourage him, assuring him that it would be wrong if he didn't tell me everything he knew – all the mines should be worked again, and the more information about the ore resources we gathered now, the sooner and more effectively the long-dead enterprises could be developed.

The old foreman remained silent, but I could see he hid a cunning grin in the depths of his eyes. He once said: "Many engineers came here, everybody asked questions, they wrote things down, they promised a reward, they even promised me that they would make me the manager of the works... They talked a lot, but how many years have passed? They come, they look, and they never start the work. And none of these visitors ever went into any of the mines – it was too dirty, damp, and well, dangerous, of course – not their affair to go there. I know this!" And then the old man fell silent, stroking his broad beard with dignity.

I understood that deep down Polenov harbored a grudge against all those hurried and superficial geologists who had appeared in this area, and instead of wanting to do a genuine study, limited themselves only to inquiries, pulling out information from the old man with irresponsible promises never fulfilled. So, I stopped further inquiries, especially after I heard what assistants said about the old foreman: "The old man is like a stone: he will resist, and you'll never get the information you want out of him."

I continued my work day after day, at times using full climbing gear to descend into the semi-collapsed shafts, as I searched for new available mines. I gained real respect among the local residents – descendants of the old miners. I forgot to say that the Gornyj village itself was established by the mining boards of two companies; Bogojawlenski and Archangielski – and its inhabitants were known to the surrounding peasant population as the 'rudniki,' which simply meant 'miners.'

To unwind after work, I'd often visit the foreman, sit down next to him, and we'd smoke together well into the long steppe evenings. I didn't ask him about the mines anymore. I'd chat with Polenov about old times, about the life of the serf mountain people, the old miners, and about the old ways of working. The old man became more and more accessible, animated, and told me a lot, making me admire his perceptiveness and accuracy of expressions. My underground 'exploits,' knowledge of the history of local mining and ancient mining terms, touched the heart of the old foreman, and he treated me much more favorably.

I noticed that the old man was waiting for my questions about the mine. Sometimes he started a conversation about these or other properties of the ore, recalling a few unknown names of shafts, but I didn't ask him anything deliberately. I knew that the old miner would not stand for it... but seeing me as a passionate man about my job, he would share his knowledge with me.

It ended in August. The sun was still warm and bright, but in the cold winds had begun to blow in the steppe. I'd descend down to the village in the evenings, veiled by a bluish haze from dozens of chimneys, and the bitter smell of smoke from the kiziaku was particularly pleasant. The smoke meant warmth for a cold body, food, a good cigarette, and the ability to stretch out on a bed – in a word, everything you needed to turn a tired worker into a sleeping bear...

The conversations with Polenov stopped – the days were shorter, and I often returned in the dark. Only sometimes, when the weather or my work on accumulated notes kept me at home, would the tall, stooped figure of Polenov appear in the doorway of the room I occupied. Stroking his yellowed beard and looking around with his sharp eyes, the foreman would declare: "I missed you, Vasiljicz. We haven't talked for a long time; are you still walking around the shafts like a madman?"

"Sit down, Kornilycz," I'd reply. "Nastazja Ivanovna will give us tea, and they brought me good sweets from Yegorjevsky," I'd say, knowing his weakness for sweets.

Grunting, the old foreman would sit down at my desk, while I'd continue to draw a plan or profile. Slowly a conversation would begin, and we'd both enjoy each other's company so much that we'd stay up late into the night. I recently found out that Polenov was the last of a whole generation of serf-wardens of the copper mines. His knowledge and skills had been passed down to him from generation to generation. In the primitive mining industry, the foreman was at the same time a mine surveyor, an engineer, a sampler, and a drilling director – in a word, a universal mining specialist.

Being brought up in the practice of working underground ever since childhood meant the development of a particular flair for the Polenovs, about which the old man talked about.

"Now these theodolites, you know, geodetic measuring instruments," he said to me one day, "have come, compasses... Today, you calculate and correct forty times, until you're sure that the excavation is planned correctly. If you need to examine a vein, find out where it goes, you immediately start to use the entire mining geometry: plot, calculate. But we — my father and I — somehow worked without all that. How? We'd walk underground, try the ground, and feel where the digging should be done, especially if it connected with an old job or tunnel. This mining sense never deceived us. I suppose we saw the results. Occasionally, I had less of these feelings — and sometimes I had to work with a compass — but still, sometimes I clearly knew that the instrument was wrong. I couldn't find any mistakes, but I knew, the compass was wrong. I'd walk, I'd feel the rock, where the veins were directed, where the seam was enlarged. You begin to develop intuition, and such confidences develop, that I could directly order: 'Beat this with a crosscut here!' And I always guessed correctly, and why? I can't explain it myself. Have you seen the Petrowielikan Shaft? It was surveyed by English engineers who came down from Mikhailovskaya, and they missed it! A lot of work went to waste! So much for the tools!... I can also feel the water underground in the same way. I can feel when we were closer to the water layer, where the limestone lies under the sandstone... I know a lot of things..."

And indeed, the old man was right in his own way, but he forgot that his mining practice had to be taught for many years. With instruments, any person can master the art of laying works in a relatively short time.

But nevertheless, I believed him, and as I listened to him, I often recalled the Freiberg mountain masters, the founders of the mining skills of the fifteenth century. They also had the same knowledge passed down from family to family, from one generation to another; mining knowledge that included the use of instinct, impressions, and clairvoyance under the ground. These masters developed a six-sense of underground space and direction, allowing them to not need the precision of measuring instruments and the schematics of mining geometry. Without the help of mineralogy and chemistry, these old miners were able to predict where the rich ore sections were or where it decreased, according to the most subtle shades and elusive changes in the rock – in a word, they were perfectly orientated in the diverse fields of ore assessment and development. And I also thought that it was such a loss to the history of mining, that the simple and faithful methods were now forgotten, those that had required the development of observation and a kind of spiritual acuity of a man. At some point, people began to believe less in the wonderful possibilities hidden in human nature and neglected the nurturing of true masters – masters in the beautiful, ancient meaning of the word.

One Sunday, I decided to suspend my fieldwork and take stock of my current research. I laid out my maps, and then looked sadly at them because in the vast terrain of the Ordynyn Mines there was only a small section I had left to investigate, and one vast, unknown space that divided the explored areas of the Lewski and Smiezny Mines. In a word, all those spaces on the map spoiled my joy of the great and interesting work I'd done over the last summer.

My thoughts were interrupted by the arrival of Polenov. Wearing a new red coat and high boots, the old man looked noble, festive, and much younger. I immediately noticed that he was excited about something. In response to my usual invitation to sit down, the old foreman threw off his coat and sat on a stool.

"Semyon said that you are going to leave, Vasily?" he asked immediately.

"I will be leaving, Kornilycz," I replied. "It's a pity, of course: I liked both the mines and your company, but it's time to finish the work – they'll demand a report from me soon."

"It's too soon to leave, Vasiljicz. Although you have researched a lot, you haven't seen the most interesting places yet," he pressed me.

"I know, but I can't get to them. These are the oldest excavations, completely collapsed from above. I'll have to make do with what I could see."

The old foreman frowned and remained silent. I surreptitiously looked at him, expecting him to tell me something.

After a short silence, Polenov shook his head and spoke calmly.

"Okay, Vasily, I'll help you a little... Do what you must, but you need to see a few mines..."

"Well, thank you, Kornilycz!" I responded. But I couldn't help but ask again, why he'd never helped me before? "You kept saying that you don't know, that you forgot..." I said to him.

"I, Vasiljicz, wait when I meet a person before I decide whether or not he should be or not should be helped," the old man answered. "And I have watched you and now feel you are as close to me as a brother. A real rudniki. And you have a great love for your good work... Well, you didn't just want to talk about it! Tell me this: have you been to the Myasnikovsky mine?"

"I have, Kornilycz; I know the area well."

"You may think you know, but you don't know everything. You only walked through the upper levels; but our name for it is 'Ordynska Dacha,' where there is a water section in the top strata's. But in the lowest, on the bottom level, there is a vault that goes all the way down into the valley – and you have not been there."

***

So, according to the old foreman's instructions, I penetrated the lowest levels of the ancient Myasnikovsky mines and spent a whole week exploring huge chambers between the left massifs of the abandoned ore of the copper conglomerate.

I made a lot of new discoveries, which we need not talk about here because they weren't of any interest to anyone else but the specialists.

Finally, a momentous day arrived when Polenov agreed to accompany me to the Ordynska Mine; a vast underground system, located on a high steppe plateau, just to the south of the Gornyj village.

The foreman demanded that I wouldn't take anyone with us and I was not to let anyone know about our journey. Also, on his advice, I took a shovel, a pickaxe, a long, strong rope, two thick bars, and a supply of candles and food. Polenov promised to lead me to the shaft, 'through which you need to jump,' and after that, I would have to go myself and outline a plan for research. According to his calculations, I would have to stay underground for about two days.

In the darkness of the pre-dawn, accompanied by the wind whistling through the dry grasses, we headed up the slope, past the high, white ore dumps of the Smiezna Mine. The equipment we took was quite heavy, so I was happy when the old man said that the entrance was near the village. The infinite and mysterious steppe in the dawn twilight, the anxious look of the old foreman, and our stealthy exit created a somewhat sublime mood. Everything, however, turned out to be very simple. The old man turned left in the middle of a mound, and after passing through some overgrown wormwood, we soon found ourselves among a multitude of partially shattered shafts, dumps, and collapsed tunnels of the well-known 'Right Mine.' On hot summer days, I often wandered around its heaps, trying in vain to find a way to the deep excavations beneath the steppe surface.

The foreman made his way confidently to a high heap in the shape of a regular cone. In front of the heap, there was a hopper of a badly buried shaft, overgrown with bushes. Reaching it, Polenov looked around scowling, muttering to himself under his breath. Then he signaled me to stop, and he slowly began to climb the heap. He stood on it for a long time looking down, and for some unknown reason spreading and bending the fingers of his big hands. I looked at him and thought about what memories must have been going through his mind right then.

"Well, Vasily, it must be here," the foreman finally said to me, coming down from the heap. He knelt down and parted the bushes with his hands. And there, among the branches, appeared a small hole of a collapsed shaft through which only the child could have crawled.

"If the excavation hasn't collapsed, we'll soon get through!" he said.

Then, without saying a word, I threw my backpack off my shoulders and grabbed the shovel. The earth that covered the entrance was loose and gave away easily, and after half an hour I'd managed to expand the entrance to the point that it was possible to crawl into it. After preparing the candle and matches, I stretched out on the soft, damp soil accumulated at the entrance, and with a skillful movement and my head down, I slipped into the narrow channel. I pulled myself down a slope for a few meters on my stomach, with dust and dirt showering me before the passage suddenly widened. The upper part was now free, and it now became possible to go further on by crawling. I stopped and lit a candle. I could hear the voice of the old foreman above me, asking me how it was going.

"Perfectly, Kornilycz!" I shouted. "Come on! And don't forget the backpack!"

I soon heard the sound of a backpack rolling down, and old Polenov coughing. We took a lantern out of the bag, left the shovel at the entrance to the expansion, and soon passed the 'tail' of the earth, washed down into the mine from above. We could walk now, almost straightening. The shaft was dry. The light of the lantern cast a yellowish reflection on the walls that went far off into the black darkness. The old man walked slowly ahead.

It was good for me because following him allowed me to operate with a compass and note the direction and distance. The shaft was long and narrow. My back had started to hurt from being hunched over when we reached the shaft station.

"You won't find anything to save here," Polenov grumbled. "Everything is buried completely. You'll have to dig horizontally through here..."

It was at this point, I realized that the old man wanted to dig through to a passage that connected the big shaft with its neighboring tunnel, and so, without delay, I got to work. Luckily, the ground in the corner of shaft station didn't stick tightly to the wall, and it was without any real difficulties, that we soon crawled through a narrow gap into another passage. This passage led us to a small shaft, which wasn't completely buried. At a small depth from the mouth of the shaft was a wooden roof binding, which had collapsed down. A square well led up and down into the black darkness, almost two meters wide. We'd already reached quite far into the hillsides, and the stratum of rocks hanging over us must have been very large.

"Now, where are you, Kornilycz?" I shouted to the foreman, bending over the shaft.

Without answering, he dropped a stone down, and soon the distinct sound of a splash was heard – there was water below. Disappointed, I looked at Polenov, but his face was calm.

"Well, Vasiljicz, now the most difficult part begins: it's necessary to go down."

"Where?" I asked, astonished. "To the water?"

"Eh, you call yourself a miner! Or are you afraid? Remember, I told you that there will be a shaft through which you have to jump. And this is it! Sixty feet below will be a big horizontal shaft in the middle, and we need to get to it. Initially, I wanted to go through a large shaft over which we would have to jump. Well, now you will go down, swing and jump in the second-level station shaft. Attach the rope to your waist with a loop so that it doesn't release. But you don't need to learn that, because I know you've had some good practice of late. You understand my plan?"

"I understand everything, Kornilycz." I replied. "Sixty feet is a trifle!"

So, I unrolled the rope I'd brought, and I put a loop on the strong bar that I'd taken with me. Then I looped and dragged through it a double-folded rope to create an abseil in a manner known to mountaineers and called 'dulfer.'

During my preparations, Polenov crouched on a sack near the shaft and gave me instructions on how to go further. My main task was to get to the huge excavations of the deepest shafts of the region – to the Szczerbakowska Mine.

"Give me the paper, I'll draw you a map," the old man said to me.

Keeping our heads close to the lantern, like two conspirators, we conferred in low, soft voices at the edge of the black hole in the old shaft. The deep darkness and silence enveloped us. We were so accustomed to it, that when something made a brief sound somewhere at the end of the passage, it seemed deafening to us. I turned, and almost knocked over the flashlight; the foreman stood up and rested his hands on the sand. He stretched his neck and peered out into the impenetrable darkness that filled the opposite end of the tunnel. The sound was like the rustle of crumpled paper. Rising, the sound turned into a muffled rumble and ended with a dull thud. After a few seconds, a wave of air hissed along and reached us, extinguishing the lantern and candle. Then everything subsided, and silent darkness reigned once more in the underground. Guessing what had happened, I hastily groped for the matches in my pocket.

"Well, Kornilycz?" I asked the foreman, and my voice sounded hoarse and uncertain. I lit a candle. The old man's face was stern but calm; only his lowered eyebrows and pursed lips indicated the imminent danger.

"It's always like that in these collapsed shafts..." He didn't finish but quickly got up and took the candle. "Let's go, Vasily, let's see... Only slowly."

We went back through the recently completed tunnel, and very soon our footsteps were suppressed by soft sand which covered the excavated floor in a thick layer. I looked at Polenov; he nodded. The layer of sand had thickened, and some large pieces of rock had appeared in it. Moving forward, we had to lean down lower and lower. Finally, we got stuck at an embankment of stones and sand, that had closed the drift hole tightly.

The matter was absolutely clear: a vacuum had settled in the great collapsed shaft. Hundreds of thousands of tons of earth had collapsed and cut off our way back... We were at one end of a huge underground system, with many kilometers of underground walkways, that went deep into the steppe highlands. The further away, the mines became deeper and deeper, and all of them were collapsed. But even if some of them were open, would it be possible to climb through them from a depth of a hundred meters? The feeling of mortal danger that overwhelmed me when I heard the rumble of the collapse didn't leave me. A swarm of thoughts about life, work, relatives, a beautiful, bright, sunny world, which I will never see again, flashed through me... I lit a cigarette and greedily dragged on it. Tobacco smoke clung low in the damp, cold air. Having mastered my nerves, I turned to Polenov. He was gloomy but calm, and he watched me in silence.

"What will we do, Kornilycz?" I asked him as calmly as possible.

"It strongly presses from above; perhaps the whole tunnel has caved in," Polenov said frowning angrily. "We disturbed it ourselves when we were digging. We knew that it had been hanging by a thread for a long time. There's nothing we can do. We won't be able to dig ourselves out because it will fall again. So, we'll go back to the shaft, I think. We have nothing to gain on staying here."

So, without saying a word, I followed the old man. His calmness amazed me, although I understood that throughout his long, hard-working life he had seen a lot and had been in serious danger more than once.

I don't know how much time we sat in silence at the edge of the shaft: the old man was deep in thought, and I smoked nervously. And I jolted involuntarily when Polenov broke the silence.

"Well, Vasiljicz, as you can see, I have to climb with you. I don't fear to die – a year earlier or a year later... But you don't want to, and you shouldn't: you are needed for our common cause." Then he asked how many candles I brought along.

"All three packages," I replied.

"I like it!" he said. "This reserve will be enough, but as we descend, extinguish the second candle – we have a long road ahead... Can you abseil me? I'm heavy," and a faint smile passed over the stern face of the old man.

"I can abseil you, Kornilycz, don't worry!" I responded. "But how will we get out of the depths of the Rozdzestwienska or Szczerbakowska Mine? Here, perhaps, they will find..."

"Who the hell will find us here?" The old man interrupted me sharply. "It would be like looking for a needle in a haystack! We didn't tell anyone where we were going. Look, this is what we'll do: we'll go to Staroordynski – it's a sure way; from Gorny you have to count about six kilometers through the old, dry excavations. There was once the only passage up through Andrieievsky Ninth – Andriej Szawrin was the first to pass through this cave. He discovered it, and that is why the 'rudniki' have named this passage after him. Besides him, me, and one more person, no one knew it was there, and that was seventy years ago. Well, let's get ready; abseil me down first, then you follow. Then pull the rope; it will be useful again..."

***

A few minutes later, Polenov hung in the black well of the shaft. I watched as the lantern attached to the old man's chest moved lower and lower, as I slowly released the rope from under my feet.

"Stop!" The old foreman's voice boomed from below. "We've reached sixty feet!"

So, I turned the rope quickly through the bar, then I saw the foreman push his feet off the wall of the shaft, sway a few times and then he disappeared. A barely perceptible light flickered somewhere down the opposite wall of the shaft. Then the tension on the rope loosened. It was my turn. I dropped my backpack first, then I started to slide down myself, pushing my legs away from the shaft walls until I reached the height of the middle-level shaft. Somewhere deep down, on the lower level, water splashed from the falling gravel I knocked loose. Imitating the foreman, I swung and jumped into the start of the shaft, guided by the lantern light. The foreman stood upright, leaning hard against the sandstone wall, gasping heavily — the ziplining had completely exhausted him. Taking my time, I slowly released and reeled up the rope, placed it on my backpack, prepared the compass, and finally lit a cigarette, to give the old man time to recover. We stood in a large cross-section of tunnels and, unlike the rest, had quite high ceilings. We walked freely, without bending, to a distant path in the subterranean depths, completely cutting off any possibility of retreat. I trusted the old man completely. The most complicated labyrinth of excavations from various times past could again come close to the surface. With knowledge of all the details of the locations of the ancient and new excavation systems, we could still be saved — and this knowledge was possessed by Polenov, the last of the surviving Master of Mining of a bygone era.

The path was tiring and long. We passed through the large, well-organized excavations of the Aleksandrov mine without much difficulty.

Then we crawled for a long time through a low, partially collapsed tunnel, that had been built two hundred years ago. Finally, we reached the long tunnel of the English concession. After passing through this, we came to an entire system of large chambers where there were numerous small diggings of completely excavated ore. This was where we expected to find a crossroad that connected those excavations with the excavations of the neighboring Szczerbakowska Mine. This mine's entrance was about four kilometers from the village, but we covered a much longer distance underground, and the old foreman was completely exhausted. I put my leather jacket on the damp floor of the chamber, and Polenov slumped onto it in sullen silence. However, after we ate, and I gave the old man some chocolate with a good sip of brandy, Polenov noticeably cheered up. I decided not to rush the old man, so I lit one more candle and settled back comfortably on my backpack, and looked around while I smoked a cigarette. The ceiling of the chamber barely gray in the dim light, and the uneven, receding walls of bluish layers were speckled with black spots – the charred imprints of ancient plants. It was more humid here than in the excavations that cut through the sandstones, and the stillness was broken by the steady sound of dripping water. In places, black bands of interlayers, enriched with copper brilliance and carbon 'soot' of fossil plants, sharply outlined the rock in the remaining pillars. Other protrusions of the walls were made up of sapphire and green stripes of oxidized parts of the ore deposits.

On the left side of us, the uneven, cracked ceiling of the chamber rapidly descended to the curved, semicircular gallery, where three low openings blackened. One of them was to take us further on our journey.

I'd just lit a second cigarette when Polenov said he was ready to move on.

"Rest, Kornilycz," I replied to him. "There's no hurry, it's still night above us."

"Oh, yes…" the foreman agreed. "We're about halfway, and now it will get even harder."

"And what is the way we'll go, and who is this Shavrin who discovered it?" I enquired.

"Well, it's some passage – you'll have to see for yourself, but I can tell you about Shavrin; he was my friend."

And then, accompanied by the monotonous sounds of dripping water, the old man began his story.

"It happened shortly before the abolition of serfdom: in the fifty-ninth year. At that time, I was an eighteen-year-old youngster, although due to my skill and training I already worked as a foreman. Andryushka Szavrin, who was two years older than me, was also a mining leader. We both worked on the Buranowa branch of the Czebienka mine – you know, where the birch grove is now, at the descent to Uranbasz, and where the then Wierchotorski management of the mine was situated. Opposite, on the other side of the river, there was the management of the Woskresienska Mine. I made friends with Andryushka… and fondly called him Andriei. Everyone got along with him, he was an excellent guy! He wasn't very handsome, but he was strong with a proud bearing, and at the same time wise and gentle – really, just one special person! He liked his mining work very much. Even while still a child, he often went through old excavations with his and my father: they studied, on behalf of the management, whether there was anything left to excavate. He learned the mining profession well, he read a lot of different books and – unlike his companions – after work he'd like to sit up late into the evening in the steppes and think about things... Everything would be fine. Andriei worked hard, beyond all praise, but he was proud. Well, showing pride was frowned upon by our manager, especially if he was one of those harsh bosses like our Afanasyev was. The Paszkowscy counts, to which we were assigned, intervened little in the mining industry. So, the manager did what he wanted.

"And moreover, Szavrin made friends with his neighbors from the Woskresien office. Their manager – Thomas Richard - always praised him and tried to persuade him to work in his mine. But how to leave? If Andryushka was a government worker, something more could be done... Andryushka often spent time among his neighbors and learned many unnecessary things that didn't match his position. But this was only half the trouble. Andryushka was a calm character; but when it came to Nastya, everything changed in him. There was one girl, the daughter of Fierapontov, a carpenter. She was pretty... long braids, high chest, slim like a stately pine. And she was a good singer, one of the few. She was known for her voice in all mine offices. Andryushka was in love with her, and she with Andryushka. Together, when their love was unleashed, it wasn't just ordinary – they walked like enchanted ones! As soon as evening would come, my Andryushka would rush to the Pokrowska Mine, to his Nastya. The manager found out, and he got very angry.

He'd already been watching this girl for a long time, and he wanted her for himself or for his son. One day, he called Nastya to his house. He lived in a large white house on the farm near the Wierchotorska Mine's office back then. This house hasn't been preserved: it was burned during the revolution. It stood in a big orchard on the edge of the pond. Anyway, the manager gave an order for Szavrin to immediately get his things together and go with the next day's wagon train that took the ore to the factory in the Ufimska province. This meant that he was sending Andryushka to the Ivanovska Mine, which the Paszkowscy had recently bought out from Dema. Andryushka found out about it, and his eyes darkened. How could he be parted from Nastya?! Not thinking much, he ran to Nastya, and he found out that the manager had requested her. And it was already beginning to get dark... Andriei wasn't stupid: he realized immediately that it wasn't without purpose that he was being sent away... So, he set off at full speed to the farm, and it's a long run to there from Pokrowski! The whole way uphill! It was already dark when he reached it. He quickly crossed the fence unseen and lurked in the bushes under the manager's windows.

"And it was just at that moment that the manager had begun to force himself on Nastya. The girl, however, resisted – but it was all for nothing! He threatened to even send her to Siberia, to even kill her! Afanasyev finally became overcome by rage – he wasn't used to being disobeyed. He called for two servants, and the girls were compliant! They helped him strip off her clothes and locked her naked in a dark closet to give her time to change her mind. But Nastya was a strong girl, and while they were dealing with her, she made a lot of noise. Andryushka heard the noise, climbed onto the ledge, and looked through the window, just in time to see his Nastya naked and being dragged out of the room. Everything in his soul cried out, and he told me later that he simply lost his mind and didn't remember what happened next. Apparently, he unhinged the window frame, jumped into the room – which was Afanasyev's office – and went straight toward the door through which Nastya had been pulled out. Afanasiev saw him and reached for his rifle that hung on the wall. Only, he didn't have time to reach the gun. Andriei grabbed a heavy object from the table and hit the manager in the teeth!"

The old foreman chuckled as he continued.

"Afanasyev always was proud of his teeth – they were as white and as large as a gypsy, and Andryushka knocked them all out with one blow. The boy was always strong, and the devil had entered him, so it's clear that the manager fell over with his mouth gushing blood. Andryushka would have finished him off right then and there, but he heard Nastya's voice. So, he left the manager and rushed to look for her. By this stage, an alarm had been raised throughout the whole house. And that Afanasyev... he was strong, too, so he quickly recovered and shouted: 'Help!' The security guards from the office and the caretakers all came at once: they acted like animals, not people! They attacked Andryushka, knocked him down and bound him. Afanasiev looked at Andriei, holding a handkerchief to his mouth, just howling, unable to say a word. Finally, he choked: 'To the granary with him, we will finish it tomorrow!' So, they locked Szavrin in the granary next to the forge and put a guard by the door. And all this time, Andriei's sweetheart still sat in the manager's house, also locked up, awaiting her fate. That's how their happiness changed in one moment, and it was lost!"

It was at this point that he unexpectedly broke off his story, and said: "Well, good... we've rested, it's time to move on," then he coughed and got up from the ground.

It was easy to walk through the wide tunnels and extensive Szczerbakowska excavations. The air was heavy here. The flame of our lantern barely flickered, not giving even the opportunity to discern the passage ahead. Here, at the deepest depth, there was almost no natural ventilation through the complicated system of excavations and airways of half-buried shafts were almost non-existent. It was difficult to breathe, and I was seriously worried about the old foreman. Soon a huge mound of large boulders loomed before us, the slope of which went up high.

"That means we have to go up this slope," Polenov said to me. "We have to do it very, very carefully, Vasiljicz..."

So, we carefully climbed our way up, from stone to stone, avoiding hundreds of gaping crevices, selecting only the most secure of the rocks that were stuck tight, and slowly we inched our way to the top, some fifty meters above. I tried my best to make it easier for the old to climb. Although we eventually reached our goal, it seemed very poor to me. The wide shoal excavation had settled completely, and huge slabs of rock several meters thick had separated from the ceiling. There was a wide crevice between the new ceiling and the settled slabs, no more than half a meter high, leading to a new unknown. Some fifty meters of rock still separated us from the surface of the earth. At least here, however, there was a pleasant draft of air, and it was possible to breathe deeply. The flame of the lantern flared and burned brighter. We rested for a long time, lying on a smooth plate that reminded me of a large ice floe. The movement of the air flickered the lantern light and cooled our hot faces.

I broke the silence.

"A good draft, Kornilycz," I said. "There must be some excavation ventilation shafts nearby."

"It is close, but not for us. Do you know where this wind comes from? From the great Pokrovsky Mine, from where water was fed into the village of Syrta. The second level roughly coincides with this here; there was even a cross connection, but we wouldn't get through that – the village was all but flooded and is now submerged. No, our path is now to the right, to the Wierchotorowski branch – now known as Miasnikowska Nowa. Well, enough! Let's move on, I've rested enough..."

The crevice was relatively easy to cross despite its sinister appearance. Once we left it, we moved into a narrow passage, then further on through a large regular excavation, then a few more narrow passages that took us twenty meters higher. Then there were low, irregularly shaped, curved passages, which steadily turned us to the southeast until they took us into a wide and high cavern.

Eventually, looking happier, the foreman told me:

"Here we are, Staroordyn. This shaft goes around like a ring, and the tunnels lead off it like the spokes of a wheel. In the middle there will be a large chamber – that's where we have to go... Here's the tunnel, we have to climb into it..."

The low, vaulted gap of the passage blackened on the left side above the chamber floor. It was necessary to crawl on all fours again, and with sharp pains in our tired knees, we moved along a slightly inclined, narrow passage. I began to get tired out from crawling.

Then the tunnel ended abruptly, and we entered a huge, almost round hall. No matter how high I held up the lantern, we couldn't see the ceiling, and it was only when I lit the candle that we saw its grooved ceiling at the height of more than ten meters above us. Huge, black pillars formed a colonnade, supporting side ledges that disappeared off into the darkness, slanting diagonally from the ceiling to the walls of the hall. The floor was level and clean. Opposite the exit of the tunnel, there were high heaps of abandoned ore left over from the excavations.

"What a miracle!" I exclaimed in delight, looking around. "I just can't understand how this construction has survived for a hundred years."

"It's not so strange," he replied. "First of all, all the oak beams are fixed. And they survived because there was no pressure. Touch this construction, and you will see."

I walked over to the nearest black pole and touched it with my finger. At first, my finger entered a damp, black crumb – like pushing through butter – but in the depths, I felt solid wood. Looking closely, I noticed that the wood was a dark blue color in places, while in others, green – that meant that it was thoroughly saturated with copper salts.

We settled down to rest against the piles of ore. My watch showed four o'clock in the morning: we'd been underground for twenty-one hours. Fatigue was taking its toll.

"How much further do we have to go, Kornilycz?" I asked the foreman while I put out some food.

"Now it's simple. We will go to Czebieniek – and then to the shaft in Ordynska Basin, above the source, to the forest."

"Well, we've come so far! You are a legend, Kornilycz!" I blurted out.

"I never thought that I'd ever come back here again before my death... After Shavrin, I was last here with my son fifty years ago..."

"You know what, while we eat and rest, tell me further what happened to Andriei," I asked.

"Is there any booze left?" asked the old man.

I froze. Then I made another suggestion instead.

"Chocolate is good; when you eat it, you'll feel full of energy."

"In our day, we didn't know that," he replied and then ate in silence.

Only after he finished, did he speak again.

"Well, good, listen further..." he started. "So, Andriei wallowed in a granary with his arms and legs tied, and we didn't know anything... Either he hadn't been tied very strongly, or the boy's rage was so great, that during the night he managed to free his hands from the fetters. And he was cunning! With a small stretched, he pulled himself up onto the thick beam, directly above the door, and from there he screamed wildly! The watchman got scared and called for help. They decided to see what happened to Andryushka in there; had he lost his mind or had the boy died?... Holding up a lantern, they opened the door and stepped into the granary... Andryushka jumped from above on the last one, who stood by the door with a rifle, knocked him off his feet, and ran out into the steppe! They shouted after him: 'Catch him! Hold on!' They fired gunshots out wildly into the dark...Where was he? It was as if he just disappeared into the earth. As it turned out, he really did hide under the ground. 'Help me, earth mother!' he'd whispered into the night. And she helped." The old foreman nodded to himself as told his tale.

"The next morning, I had to go to work. I got up before dawn. As my mother set the table, she said that something bad had happened with Andryushka. Already, the news had spread: that the manager had taken Nastya away, and the fact that Shavrin broke his teeth and ran away into the night, and no one knows where he is. But what happened to Nastya, no one knew. The news shocked me, and not feeling good, I went to work. I kept thinking what would happen now, and how to help Andriei? We worked in Chebice, at the very edge of the allotment. I climbed to the sixth face to check. As I walked along, deep in thought, I suddenly heard Andryushka Shavrin's voice. Because I'd just been thinking about it, hearing his voice surprised me, so I stopped dead in my tracks. I looked all around, and then I saw an old excavation connection. I shone my lantern towards it, and there was Andryushka waving his hands.

"I looked around and couldn't see nobody else, so I dimmed my lantern and went straight into the tunnel! And there, in the depths, was a passage which intersected with the old Ordynski mine. I followed Andryushka. I bombarded him with questions, but Andriei only shook his head and said that there wasn't time – he must save Nastya and himself.

"'About you, though,' he said, 'they know that you are my friend and they will follow you, so you can't stay here for long. Tell Kostya Siłajew' – this was his second friend – 'that I want to see him tonight night; just you two, no one else. Meet me at the Ordynska Basin, at the spring where the four large birches stand, and tell him to bring as much food as possible – enough to last for a few days. I will expect you there and then tell you what to do next. And remember, that you or Kostya must meet up before the evening with Nadyezda. She can try to let Nastya know that I am alive and will free her quickly. She can't let the old thug win, and she should wait for messages from me...' That was it. He stopped speaking.

"I gave Andriei all the food I had with me, and he disappeared in the Ordynski excavations. I quietly got out of the mine and went back to the previous place, but all my thoughts were focused on finding an excuse to see Kostya. Fortunately, I needed new wedges, and our forge was in Wierchno Ordynski, where Kostya worked. I ran there quickly – and I succeeded: I found Kostya and told him everything... We arranged to see Nadyezda, and to meet later at the large outlet in the Vlach, where we would make our separate ways to the rendezvous location. I was relieved in my heart and returned to the mine. Once there, all I could hear was talk about Andryushka and Nastya. Officials and guards rode their horses across the steppe trying to catch Andriei – even hunting dogs were released.

"The manager was ill and bedridden – it was clear that Andriei had to hit him hard. He'd promised a great reward for whoever caught Szavrin, and he'd deliberately rode to

Kargala on horseback to notify the police, and from there to the police chief in Orenburg to obtain the search warrant to look for Andryushka everywhere, and put him in chains.

"After returning home, I prepared a bag, and then little by little, I shoved as much of any food I could get into it, without my mother seeing. Then, I waited until everyone fell asleep. It was a good thing that there was no moon, and the nights were warm and dark. I went with a restless heart. I was afraid for Andryushka. I didn't know what would happen next.

"The steppe was quiet and empty. Somewhere off in the distance, I could hear riders scouring the area in a rush to find my friend. I walked up the narrow path to the Volkov rail tracks. A huge carriage was barely visible on the hill. Something nearby moved in the bushes, and Kostya appeared out of the ground. He also had a bag with him. Quietly, like two wolves, we made our way through the impenetrable darkness. We went down to the basin, and just in case, we avoided the road, and instead cut through the bushes and up the mountainside...

"Whispering, Kostya told me how he went with Nadyezda. He said her face had changed, and she paled, but she promised that she'd arrange everything. She came from the manager's house at dusk, breathless. She didn't manage to see Nastya, nor could she tell her anything, because they still keep the girl locked up. From the conversations she overheard at the house, she only learned that the manager was very ill, and he'd sworn that as soon as he was better, he was going to personally find Andryushka, and take revenge for his ugliness.

"While Kostya told me all this, we approached our meeting place. At the spring, we turned to the right – there was an empty, sandy place, surrounded by bushes, and above it a small grassy hill where the four old birches stood. We sat under the birches, surrounded by quietness. I made an owl's hoot, then listened, then repeated the call. And suddenly, out of nowhere, Andryushka stood right in front of us! His appearance was so unexpected that we were startled.

"We told him everything, while Andriei sat quietly listening, deep in thought.

"'My beloved brothers,' he said. 'You are now the only hope I have. If you don't help me, then I'm lost, I will die. Nastya too – the manager will ruin her. If you want to help me, there is no time to lose. First, I will show you a place where not only Afanasyev, but the devil himself will never find me. Bring me a sheepskin coat or blanket, a water bottle, and a woman's dress... Then, take this card to the board of the Woskriesienska Mine - to Richard. Put it in his own hands and wait for an answer. Then bring the answer here and put it... I will show you where... And one more thing: you know the old, small mine near the farm? There, large opencast works are carried out, and there are a few tunnels in it that are small and crumbling. So, the middle shaft will lead to an underground passage, and the excavation will go more and more to the right as far as the remaining pits after the small cross-sectioned vertical excavation. These are in the Ordynska Basin itself, in the bushes. It will be necessary to crawl along this tunnel and clear the passage to one of the vertical cross-sections.

Only the ground, mind you, rake inside. Tell Nadyezda that I will be waiting for her in the evening after tomorrow in a grove at Zaowrazny – it isn't a problem for her to go there, and you also come when you finish work. Only tomorrow, bright and early, give my paper to Richard, and in the evening, I must have an answer.'

"Szavrin suddenly fell silent and began to listen. So did Kostya and I. We could hear a horse's trot coming up from the valley below.

"'Well, my friends,' Szavrin whispered, 'We have to hide; they're looking for me.' He grabbed my hand and the bags, and we slipped off into the bushes.

"Behind the bushes was a large old tunnel, called Ordynska. The entrance was wide and so high that one could ride in on horseback, while the tunnel itself was short and there was no way out.

"'Where are you, Andryushka?' I whispered to Szavrin. 'They're sure to look into this shaft.'

"'… and then they will go away…' he whispered back.

"'All right! Sure, they will look… But hurry up, because we noticed them too late because we talked about them too much…'

"'And you're right. You can hear the horse's hoofs quite well from underground, and they're quite close.'

"And the truth was, we could hear the clatter of horse's hoofs very well when underground. I knew this tunnel well. Inside, there were three passages – the middle one was the longest, some fifty feet – and that's where Andryushka led us. At the end were several smaller crevices, and we climbed into the left one.

"'Up above our heads, is a narrow gap of just four feet high and less than two feet wide,' Andryushka whispered. 'At the end of this passage, it meets up under the mountain, inside the Ordyn mine. Spread your hands forward, then pull your legs up, and at the end, you can stand.'

"So, that's what we did and just in time, as we could already hear voices at the entrance of the tunnel. We scrambled through the passage which turned back over the shaft. It was very narrow in there and was impossible to see from below anything at the top. Once we all crammed in there, Andryushka moved two large pieces of rock and placed them into the hollow behind us, completely closing off our way back. Now, even if they found the gap and looked down it, all they would see was a dead-end wall. The passage at the back of the hollow we hid in was wider now, so all three of us sat down quietly above the hole and listened. We could hear them thoroughly searching the tunnel, rummaging everywhere, as they approached closer to where we hid.

"Suddenly, something faintly flashed between the stones – someone had put a candle right up to the crevice we hid in.

"'So, there's no passage there?' I heard someone ask, but I didn't recognize his voice.

"'See for yourself. We know every crevice and tunnel here,' Rybin, the Pokrowski foreman answered. 'Can't you see, or what?'

"And we sat hidden on the other side of the rock wall, poking each other. Eventually, the uninvited guest left, and with a sigh, we struck a match and lit a candle. Andriei took us to his shelter.

"As it turned out, there were a great many Ordynany excavations – and nobody knew anything about them! You know how it was among the Ordynans: narrow passages without bracings, that are structured as firmly as chimneys. We abseiled into the great excavations, where the Ordynans had created a large chamber – this was where Andryushka was based.

"And he showed us the way to the Staroordynska Mine, to this great hall where we are now sitting – and no one knew anything about this place."

I looked around at the great Ordynany excavation which was the size of a large room, only slightly lower. In the center lay smooth sandstone slabs, arranged by Ordynancy. The old foreman continued with his memories.

"We took out supplies from the sacks: candles and flint, and lay them on the slabs, making a note of where we left them. Then we crawled through the shafts to the top, reached the tunnel again, pulled out the stones, and climbed out. Andryushka immediately sealed the entrance behind us. We listened carefully, ensuring that no one was around, and then we ran home without looking back. We came at night, and we still had time to sleep...

"Well, Vasiljicz, we've probably had enough time to rest now. Enough of this fairytale, let's get out..."

At the southern wall of the hall where we were sitting, gradually rose a supporting beam, made of timber, in the shape of a cage. A person could enter it by a ledge along the wall. A narrow cross heading went up, and by pressing my back against the walls and using my legs for support, I reached the second ledge, just under the chamber's vault. This ledge was very narrow. It was necessary to lie on my side, facing the wall, and shuffle for several meters to the left, to the outlet of the prehistoric shaft excavation. Once there, I pulled on Polenov's line. There was no way to straighten up, so I had to crawl on in the same way, feet first. Polenov crawled just behind me, puffing. The accursed excavation stubbornly rose up, and it seemed to have no end.

Just when I thought that the bones in my elbows must be about to break through my skin, my legs lost support, and I jumped out onto a flat floor like a frog. This was the underground chamber in which Shavrin hid seventy years ago. The smooth walls, characteristic of the prehistoric excavation of the bronze age, had oval shapes; the ceiling was dome-shaped, and the floor was concave like a basin. In the middle of the chamber, I saw the smooth sandstone slabs, which the foreman had told me about. Looking around the chamber, I found two bronze pickaxes, destroyed by the passages of time, and a few pieces of copper alloy. I also found pickaxes, one piece of the alloy, shards of some vessels and a skull, in the adjacent drift – I later sent them to the Russian Museum in Leningrad. The foreman illuminated the area with the lantern and rummaged around the floor, muttering something under his breath.

"Look, Vasily," he said, pointing the lantern behind one of the great slabs.

I saw a blackened but well-preserved oak barrel there.

"A barrel for water. Kostya dragged it here... and here's Andryushka's knife..." The old man lifted a rusty piece of a knife from the floor and put it in his pocket. "Everything is as it was as if it was only yesterday..." Even in the weak light of the lantern, I noticed how youthfully the eyes of the old man shimmered. "Eh, such a busy life! It has passed like one day..."

The old man didn't want to hurry. He went around the excavation with the lantern and sat for a while on the stone slab without paying any attention to me. I used this time it to look at the excavation and several of its outlets.

Eventually, Polenov called me to go on, and once more we were crawling through pipe-shaped, narrow passages again. We gradually climbed higher and higher while steadily heading in a south-east direction. It was strange to see a blue reflected light ahead, sharply different from the reddish-yellow of the candle flames, which had been our only source of illumination for a long time, in the darkness of the underground. The light intensified, and it was with a feeling of unspeakable relief, I put out the candle and hid it in my pocket.

A pillar of dim light rose above the square hole at the end of the shaft. I dangled my legs over the opening, then resolutely slipped into it. Now, I stood on the top of a mine's face's upper edge; I turned the other way, and I did the same a second time, and finally found myself on the bottom of the mine face. I helped the foreman down, and both of us, hurrying and stumbling, ran the remaining fifteen meters to meet the increasing brightness of the daylight.

I impatiently parted the dense bush at the entrance, and reveling in the sea of fresh, warm air, blinded by the light to the pain in my eyes, I couldn't restrain my joyous exclamation. I looked at Polenov for fear that the old man would laugh at me, but a happy smile also shone on his face – he was also very pleased to see the beauty of the wide, sunny world.

The high, mid-day sun greeted us with its gentle warmth, and the quiet rustle of the autumn breeze sounded like music to our ears. We'd spent twenty-nine hours in the darkness and in the silence of underground excavations!

"Well, Vasiljicz, let's warm up a little, and rest a bit, before we go to Uranbasz, which was once the Paszkow area – it's nearby. There we'll get a horse because it's too far home for me to walk. Andryushka helped us! Although I don't even know what happened to him after that..."

"Tell me, Kornilycz, how did things end with Andryushka?" I asked, laying out damp cigarettes in the sun.

"There is almost nothing more to tell. We did everything that Andriei asked us to do. The next night we went again with Kostya to the Ordynany excavations. We brought an old sheepskin coat, a barrel, and a larger supply of bread, with us. We also brought a card from Richard.

"I'd gone to see Richard him alone. He read the card, smiled, and went somewhere, while I waited in his office. Then he came back, started whistling, walked around the room, wrote something on the paper and handed it to me. I slipped the paper in my vest and immediately went home. I didn't even say 'thank you' to him. I was still scared because someone could have noticed that I'd gone to Woskresienka.

The next day, we learned everything from Kostya: the manager Afanasyev was almost recovered, and the policemen had arrived. They sat in his office, drank, and schemed how to catch Shavrin.

"Night had barely fallen, when we, like two phantoms in the night, slipped away from our homes! I carried the ax that Andryushka had asked for, and Kostya brought the candles. We lay down in the bushes on the hill opposite the farm and waited until Nadyezda ran up the path next to us. We listened very carefully to be sure that no one had followed her. We lay still listening for a very long time, but no, nothing could be heard! Then together, we all made our way to the Zaowrazny forest. There, I called out my owl hoot again, and Andryushka answered with a low whistle. Then he joined the three of us standing under the birch.

"'It's necessary to do it, Nadyezda,' Andriei said.

"'I will do everything,' she replied.

"'Well, thank you, my dear! Goodbye, and please don't remember me as bad!'

"Nadyezda embraced him, pecked his cheek and quickly left...

"Andriei then led us to the hollow, and on the way, he told us what we were to do. He said that he knew that tomorrow, the manager wanted to personally go around the mines to track him down. The old fox guessed that the fugitive hid somewhere in the underground excavations. So, when everybody goes to search, Kostya and I were to slip away and go to the farm and set fire to the last granary, the outbuilding next to the stable on the hill. And when we set it on fire, we would then have to go fast to Buranowski Hill, watch from there, see what happens next, and then return home without being seen. Then we were to visit Andryushka no sooner than in a few days, because after the fire, everyone will be watching, and they will start to search in the Ordynska Valley. We agreed, said goodbye, and left.

"In the morning, the manager Afanasiev, with the police, helpers, and favorite hounds, went to the management of the Bogojawlenska Mine – where our

Gornyj village is now. And at lunchtime, Kostya and I, made our way to the gardens above the river on the farm, to the back of the stable. Looking around at the granary, we noticed a clover feed trough for the manager's horses. We set fire to the granary and to this trough – and then we ran away fast. We hadn't gone far when we heard a terrible cry and the calls of panic in the air... We ran faster, through Fiedorowski Gorge, until we reached the hills. Then we ran along the road, and exhausted, we reached Buranowski Hill. Our hearts pounded in our chests. It was now up to Andryushka whether he would achieve everything he had planned. Smoke rose high, so huge, and the noise and uproar could be heard from far away...

"We returned to work successfully, on time. Everyone sat in their mine shafts as quietly as a mouse – pretending that we didn't know anything about it... Nothing happening here, just talk about this fire on the farm. 'They say the granary fire is arson, but it's been quickly extinguished...' they said.

"After work, I went home with Kostya. And at home, we were greeted with immediate questions.

"'How do you not know anything about it?'

"'What happened?' I asked.

"'Andryushka appeared in the village and set fire to the granary together with the stack next to it. When everyone ran to the fire, he went with the ax to the manager's house – and how horrible he was!... His eyes burned like a madman's. The women who guarded Nastya fled! Andryushka knew exactly where Nastya was being held, and he broke the door in a flash, grabbed her hand, and they both ran through the orchard and out into the steppe. They were closely followed by the management of the Wierchotorski Mine, and they should have been caught – because how it possible to hide in the steppe? They were almost caught, but they reached the first outlets of the old mine, and then seemed to disappear under the ground. By the time the sent to the office for a foreman, organized candles and lanterns – all traces of Andryushka and Nastya all traces were lost.'

"They searched for a long time; the entire valley was searched because it was clear that when Afanasyev arrived, there would be trouble! However, no sign of them was found. Meanwhile, Afanasyev returned. His face darkened when he was told by the clerk about the fire and Nastya's escape. The manager then gathered a lot of people and rushed around everywhere to search for himself. After the mines, he went to Srodkowa Kargalka. He searched and searched, but he came back with nothing...

"Kostya and I were delighted. Everything had gone according to Andriei's plan. We waited one day – all was quiet. On the second day, we decided to go to Andryushka that night, that was... until they suddenly call us to the office.

"In the office, we found everyone who had ever been friends with Andryushka, and even all his and Nastya's family had been summoned to find out who had helped him and who knew where he was hiding!...

"Nobody knew anything, and Kostya and I remained silent. We were very much under suspicion – they shouted, they threatened us with Siberia, but they didn't catch us out so they could do nothing...

"Still, they kept us in isolation for three days, but to no avail; We insisted we didn't know anything.

"'We know nothing about it,' we kept repeating. 'Ask whoever you want, and they will tell you the same thing: that we worked in the mine and we were at home every evening.' In the end, they let us go.

"We waited another two more nights because we wanted to be sure that they were not watching us. Then we made our way along the well-known route to the Ordynska Basin, straight to the underground chamber of Andryushka. We looked around. No one was there – no stores or clothes; only a barrel, and sheepskin remained. And on the stone lay a letter to Kostya and me: 'Goodbye, friends, Nastya and I will remember you for the rest of our lives; we are going far away, and we probably won't ever see each other again.'

"From then on, no one heard anything about Andryushka or Nastya.

"And despite Afanasyev prowling all over the steppe and sending his spies everywhere, he never achieved anything. About a year and a half later, the serf law came to an end.

"I waited for a letter from Andryushka, but I never received any. Then, much later, I asked Richard if he knew anything about Andriei. He said nothing for a long time, and only after three years, he admitted that he had helped Andriei. It so happened that their inspector at that time was to go to Samara. He hid the fugitives in his carriage – it was such a big chaise, good horses – and at dawn, Andriei and Nastya were far away from our steppe. The inspector drove them to Samara, provided them with money and letters, and he instructed them what to do next. The Volga River transported the fugitives. They went to Astrakhan.

What happened next with both of them – I don't know; I only know that they escaped from our bondage...

***

Kanin sighed, his story complete.

"This is actually all I can say about the adventure that has left indelible marks in my memory. The following year, later than usual, I went back to the mine. In the Gornyj village, I found out that the old foreman Polenov had died at the beginning of the summer. 'He was still waiting for you, but he couldn't wait anymore,' my friends from the village told me.

"Five years later, in Moscow, at the great congress on colorful metals, my attention was drawn to a tall, well-dressed engineer, who severely criticized the organization of mining ventures in one of the great mining regions in Siberia. His wise and bold speech delighted me, and I asked one of the Siberians who it was.

"'That's Shavrin,' said the engineer. 'An excellent employee, from a mining family that goes back generations...'

"I tried to meet with this Shavrin, but somehow I didn't succeed because the next day he went to Siberia."

About The Author

Ivan Efremov (1908 – 1972) was a Russian writer of science fiction, a renowned scientist in paleontology and geology and known as a progressive social thinker for his time. His last name is sometimes spelled Yefremov.

After a brief military career in the Red Army, he was discharged and went to St Petersburg to study, where he completed his education and went onto the Leningrad State University to study paleontology. He led several expeditions, headed a research laboratory, and received awards and degrees during his career, including a doctorate, in biological sciences.

He wrote his first work of fiction in 1944, 'The Land of Foam' and his most recognized science fiction novel 'Andromeda Nebula' was published in 1957.

In the 1960's he became disillusioned with the communist system, with his subsequent books becoming a rarity, and banned. Eventually, he was interrogated by the KGB, his apartment searched, his manuscripts and writings confiscated, and all his works also confiscated and banned from all public libraries and schools in the Soviet Union. He remained under suspicion, surveillance, and censorship for the remainder of his life, and died in 1972.

About The Publisher

Royal Hawaiian Press is a publishing house located in Honolulu Hawaii. It was established in 2005, primarily to promote the works of author and founder, Maria Cowen. Since then, it has expanded to encompass an assortment of other authors from around the world.

Royal Hawaiian Press specializes in providing books in a variety of languages and genres, including translating and publishing existing European-language books into English for the English-speaking market.

To learn more about Royal Hawaiian Press and the books it represents, please visit:

www.royalhawaiianpress.com

To receive an alert when new books are released, subscribe to the Royal Hawaiian Press Mailing List:

http://tiny.cc/rhp